A CROWN OF SNOW AND ICE

THE FOUR KINGDOMS AND BEYOND

THE FOUR KINGDOMS

The Princess Companion: A Retelling of The Princess and the Pea
(Book One)

The Princess Fugitive: A Reimagining of Little Red Riding Hood
(Book Two)

Happily Every Afters: A Reimagining of Snow White and Rose Red
(Novella)

The Princess Pact: A Twist on Rumpelstiltskin (Book Three)

A Midwinter's Wedding: A Retelling of The Frog Prince (Novella)

The Princess Game: A Reimagining of Sleeping Beauty (Book Four)

The Princess Search: A Retelling of The Ugly Duckling (Book Five)

BEYOND THE FOUR KINGDOMS

A Dance of Silver and Shadow: A Retelling of The Twelve Dancing
Princesses (Book One)

A Tale of Beauty and Beast: A Retelling of Beauty and the Beast
(Book Two)

A Crown of Snow and Ice: A Retelling of The Snow Queen (Book Three)

A Dream of Ebony and White: A Retelling of Snow White (Book Four)
Coming in 2018

A Captive of Wing and Feather: A Retelling of The Swan Princess (Book
Five) *Coming in 2019*

A Princess of Wind and Wave: A Retelling of The Little Mermaid (Book
Six) *Coming in 2019*

A CROWN OF SNOW AND ICE

A RETELLING OF THE SNOW QUEEN

MELANIE CELLIER

LUMINANT PUBLICATIONS

For my parents-in-law, Graeme and Denise,
who are endlessly interested and supportive

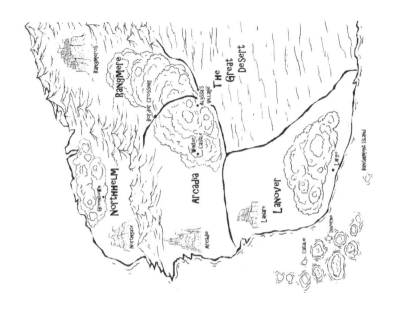

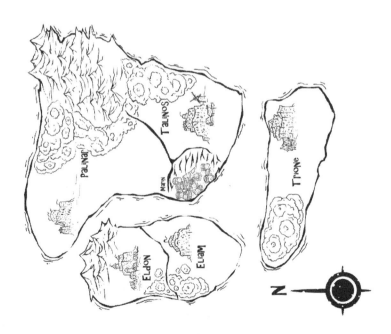

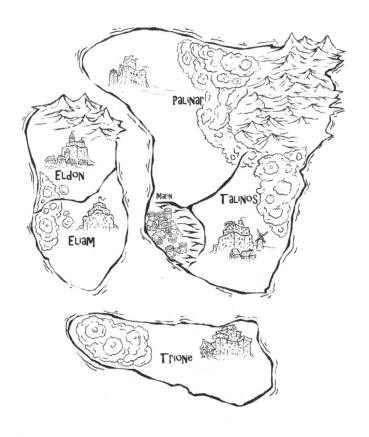

PART I
THE FROZEN KINGDOM

CHAPTER 1

I grumbled under my breath as the carriage bumped over a particularly large hole in the road. Prince Oliver's chestnut stallion flashed past the window, and I directed my ire toward him, although I lowered my voice even further so as not to be overheard by the other passengers.

I would have been riding too, if I was anywhere but Eldon. I hated being cooped up in the carriage, especially with no one but Emmeline and Giselle for company. They weren't exactly scintillating conversationalists.

"We will reach the capital by sundown, Celine," said Giselle, as if in answer to my inaudible grumbles. Her tone suggested she had no complaints to make about several more hours trapped on the uncomfortable seats. I waited for her to go on, but she directed her gaze out the other window, returning to silence.

I sighed and looked out my own window. Perhaps I should have ridden, after all. But a moment's glance at the landscape reinforced my original decision.

Despite asking everyone I could find, I hadn't been able to garner much information on Eldon before my departure. The one thing everyone had agreed on, though, was that it was cold.

Really cold. And if there was one thing I hated, it was being cold. Not a problem I usually had in my tropical kingdom of Lanover.

So far in these new lands I had visited Marin, Palinar, and now Eldon, and none possessed the clinging warmth of my home. But Eldon still stood out from the others. Here we were only an hour's drive from the port, and already patches of snow covered the ground. We'd hardly even begun to ascend yet. I hated to think what it would be like once we hit the capital.

Eldon was so mountainous that it had apparently always been on the colder side. Or so the inhabitants of Palinar informed me. Like their own barely inhabited eastern region. But the Eldonian capital, located in the foothills rather than the true mountain ranges, had once been pleasant for a good portion of the year.

And then things had started to change across the kingdoms. I shivered and rubbed my hands together, although the fur rug across my lap was actually keeping them rather toasty so far. On reflection, I thought I would have preferred dealing with wolves and bears and invisible people—as Sophie had done in Palinar— over this icy cold. Why couldn't I have been sensible and gone to visit Gabe in Talinos—or even better, Millie on the warm southern isle of Trione?

"We seem to be making good time," said Emmeline, out of nowhere. Like her sister, the princess's tone suggested she didn't much care one way or the other.

I resisted the urge to glare at her. After all, this was exactly why I had come to this awful place. Something was decidedly not right about Princesses Emmeline and Giselle. The same something that wasn't right about their older brother, Prince Oliver. And something wasn't right about their kingdom either. That was the one thing everyone I asked could agree on. Ever since the darkness had spread its way across these lands, Eldon had grown more and more icy. And from what I could see, it wasn't just the weather.

The young Eldonian royals were as cold as their kingdom. I

had never seen either girl display anything I would consider an emotion. With my own eyes, I had witnessed Giselle fall, apparently to her death, in the Princess Tourney the year before. And yet neither her inseparable older sister, nor even Giselle herself, seemed in the least perturbed by the terrifying accident. Decidedly not normal. And I intended to find out why.

When I was drafted into the Princess Tourney, along with my friends Lily and Sophie and all of the local princesses, I had been newly arrived from the Four Kingdoms. I had known no one from these lands, but I had made plenty of friends during the months of the Tourney. Emmeline and Giselle had not been among them.

So it had shocked me when the sisters invited me to visit them after the Tourney ended. What could possibly have motivated them to do so? The whole thing smelled of adventure—and if there was one thing I couldn't resist, it was the prospect of an adventure.

Idiotic. That's what I was, I reflected sadly as I watched the snow build up beside the road. Why couldn't I have found an adventure somewhere with a warm climate?

I had already put off the invitation until after Lily and Sophie's joint wedding, remaining behind in Marin when Emmeline and Giselle returned home after the Tourney. And then my mother, along with one of my brothers and his wife, had sailed over from the Four Kingdoms for the twins' wedding. They couldn't sail home in winter, and my mother insisted I remain in Palinar with them for the duration of their visit.

I think my mother was surprised at my acquiescence. My brother less so. At least once he heard the stories about the climate in Eldon.

But, come spring, I had grown altogether tired of being back under my family's wing and decided it was time to follow through on my promise to visit Eldon. It was spring, after all. How cold could it be?

I shivered again, this time directing the grumbles at myself. I glanced at the girls across from me. How would they react if I made my complaints aloud? So far common courtesy had been holding me back, but my curiosity to see their reaction was growing by the minute. It was horribly tempting to see how far I would have to push to get a response from the detached princesses.

I had actually been a little touched when all three of the younger Eldonian royals had traveled down from the capital to meet my ship at the port. Touched enough that I had even insisted on taking the front seat so that I faced backward, and they were both able to travel forward. But we had now been stuck in the carriage together for some time, and I could no more see a reason for their coming to meet me than for their making the invitation in the first place. They certainly weren't expending any further effort to make me feel welcome. And Prince Oliver had managed no more greeting than a murmured "Princess Celine" and a head nod.

My mother had wondered if the icy kingdom was hoping for a marriage alliance with my distant kingdom of Lanover. But after meeting the Eldonians at the wedding in Palinar, she had been forced to admit that neither the Eldonian delegation, nor Prince Oliver himself, seemed in the least interested in either the Lanoverians or me, their youngest princess.

A pang in my right ankle made me scowl. The broken bone had healed months ago, but it still sometimes ached in the cold. An unpleasant reminder of the ordeal of the Tourney. My mother seemed to think the Tourney should have been adventure enough for her seventh child and couldn't understand what pulled me to visit Eldon. But the Tourney hadn't been my adventure. Not really. At least not after I had broken my ankle in the first trial. The Tourney had been the twins' adventure, and I had been nothing but a burden on the eleven other princesses.

At least my mother knew me well enough not to argue. With

six older siblings, I had long ago determined to find my own path. I had always longed to get out of the shadow of a family full of far too many outstanding royals. My one fear had been that my mother would insist the Duchess of Sessily accompany me to Eldon. The older noble was far too canny for my taste, one of the few who could see through whatever scheme I currently had underway.

But it seemed the duchess was needed back in the Four Kingdoms, so I had received a reprieve. I had been saddled with the usual collection of guards and maids and such, of course, but I didn't mind them—none of them would attempt to manage me.

For the first time ever, I was truly on my own. And I relished every moment of it. At least until a fresh blast of freezing air somehow swept its way through the carriage. Hopeless dreams of Lanover's bright, sandy beaches filled my mind until a sudden lurch sent me tumbling off the seat and on to the two other princesses.

The tangle of girls and rugs took some moments to straighten out, our efforts impeded by the strange new tilt of the now-stationary carriage. Emmeline was the first to free herself, moving over toward the door. But instead of opening it, she shifted back toward us.

"Perhaps it would be best if we stayed in the carriage for now." Her calm voice didn't fool me.

"What's going on?" I finally kicked free of my rug and half crawled over to have a look myself.

"It also might be wiser to keep away from the windows."

I ignored Emmeline, and she made no further move to stop me. The scene that greeted my gaze would have been accompanied by a great deal of noise in any other kingdom. But the coachmen, grooms, and guards all filed along in near silence, dropping their weapons in a pile in front of a masked figure. I pressed myself against the window to get a better view.

We appeared to be surrounded by mounted, armed men. Only

my own two Lanoverian guards looked appropriately horrified, but I could hardly blame them for falling into line. Our party was vastly outnumbered. For a moment I wished I hadn't left the rest of my guards to follow with the baggage, but even their number wouldn't have been enough to tip the balance.

I scooted to the other side of the carriage, hoping to spot an opening in the circle of assailants. But, if anything, there were even more of them on this side, stretching out into some sort of field on the side of the road. Prince Oliver's stallion danced uneasily, and the prince seemed wholly occupied in keeping the animal calm.

I sighed. Clearly I could not expect any heroics from him. For the first time, real fear gripped me. Who would dare attack a royal carriage traveling the well-used road between the port and the capital? And what did they intend to do with us?

I glanced back at Emmeline and Giselle sitting calmly on the carriage seat, despite the awkward new angle. A warmth ignited inside my chest, the pity that surged through me taking me by surprise. What could possibly have made them this way? They seemed more like empty shells than people.

I looked back outside and met Prince Oliver's eyes. He watched me without any sign of fear or perturbation. My pity transformed into something more closely resembling anger, and the spark grew into a burning sensation. If they had no care for themselves, they should at least have some concern for their guest, surely?

If it was up to me to save myself, I didn't know what hope I had against a large company of armed guards. Especially when they were mounted, and I was not. I had a small dagger hidden in each boot, but I couldn't see what good they would do me. Reluctantly, I decided my best hope was to wait and watch for a better opportunity of escape.

But, as I thought it, one of the attackers moved forward to attach a lead rope to Oliver's mount. The prince's calm acquiescence caused the fire inside me to leap into an inferno and, without thought, I thrust out my hands as if I could push the attackers aside from inside the carriage.

A rush of hot air shook the vehicle, nearly toppling us all again. Outside, it looked more like a gale. Those on the ground stumbled, some falling, and the horses screamed and snorted as their riders desperately tried to control them. Some failed, and their mounts took off, scattering in all directions.

A half-second before the unexpected gust, Oliver had looked up, his gaze meeting mine. And I could have sworn that as I thrust out my hands, something sparked between my eyes and his. For the first time, a glimmer of warmth filled his blue eyes, lending animation to his pale face. But a moment later his horse reared, and I lost sight of his expression.

The man holding the chestnut's lead rope lost it as he attempted to control his own mount. When the prince's stallion found his feet again, he charged forward. Again I couldn't be sure in all the commotion, but it looked as if more than random chance directed the horse toward the newly opened gap in the circle surrounding us. The prince appeared to be actively guiding him as he leaped through and disappeared from sight. So there was some life in the prince, after all.

For a wild moment I considered flinging myself out of the carriage and scrambling after him. But on foot I wouldn't make it far, and already the gaps were closing as riders returned with their now calm mounts. One of the returning men focused his gaze on my face as I peered out of the window, and I drew back hurriedly.

Retaking my seat as best I could since it still sat at an angle, I hid my trembling hands in my lap. The idea of escape had momentarily distracted me, but now my thoughts whirled back to the source of the sudden and violent wind. It had not been natural, that much was obvious. The temperature, even in the carriage, still lingered several degrees warmer than it had before.

But that wasn't what scared me. The timing on its own would have been uncanny. But it had been more than that. The moment I had thrust out my hands, I had felt the fire raging inside me rush down my arms and out of my hands to heat the air around me. And now, although the air felt warmed, my insides had returned to their usual cool state.

My stomach roiled, to be sure, but it carried no unusual heat. It made no sense, and I couldn't explain it, but I couldn't help thinking that somehow that hot wind had come from me. When I thrust out my arms to push away our attackers, the air itself had moved to obey me.

CHAPTER 2

*T*he carriage lurched, righted itself, and began to move again before my shock had faded enough for me to look around. Giselle watched me with a slightly puzzled look, while her older sister watched the riders outside our window.

"Oliver seems to be gone," she said.

I nodded. "I think he escaped when..." My voice faded, so I put more force behind it. "When that wind hit."

"How strange," said Emmeline. She glanced at her sister, the two exchanging a look I couldn't read before subsiding into silence.

I turned away to look out the window, not seeing the passing scenery as my thoughts swirled inward again. I wasn't a godmother, of that I was sure. So the only way I could wield magic was through a godmother object. And unless a godmother had enchanted my gloves in secret, I had never owned such an item. Which made what had just happened entirely impossible.

Or was it? I frowned, worrying at my lower lip. Enchanted objects were not the only gifts given by godmothers. One of my older sisters had unnatural beauty and intelligence due to her Christening gifts. The twins had also received a Christening gift from their godmothers, and while I didn't know exactly what use their gift was, I had always suspected there was something strange about my two friends.

After the debacle of my sister's Christening, everyone had thought it best to avoid gifts at my own ceremony, so I had grown up without any direct experience with them. But just because godmothers traditionally seemed to give gifts such as beauty and grace, did that mean they were unable to give gifts of a more...active...nature?

Perhaps it was possible, after all, for them to gift someone with the ability to wield a specific sort of magic. And I had, only recently, had a rather unexpected encounter with my own godmother.

The memory filled my mind: a bright, celebratory scene. It had been Lily and Sophie's wedding, during the feast, and her appearance had taken me by surprise. I knew that the darkness had been lifted from both Marin and Palinar, and that godmothers had been seen in both. But I would have expected to see the twins' own godmother at their wedding, not mine.

She had appeared from nowhere and pulled me into a large potted plant on the edge of the ballroom. Well, not into it, exactly, but close enough. My questions had been greeted with only cryptic mutterings, her one straight-forward utterance being to confirm my intention to travel to Eldon. She had then informed me that she wished to rectify the omission of my Christening and give me a belated gift.

I had been excited about the whole thing, as well as intrigued. And it had made me even more interested in visiting Eldon since her question about the kingdom had been so pointed. But it had never occurred to me that her gift might grant me some sort of actual magical ability. And as the weeks in Palinar passed with no noticeable effect from the gift at all, it had faded from my mind.

Now I struggled to even remember the exact wording of it. After some effort I managed to recall it. *I grant you the gift of fire,* she had said, *to match that which already burns within you. May it light your way no matter how black the darkness.*

I had assumed she meant to give me some sort of extra perception or passionate focus. An added clarity of vision, or something like that. It seemed the type of thing the godmothers would deem important. I hadn't expected it to mean I would be able to conjure hot gales with the power of my mind.

I looked down again at my hands, scrunching my forehead as I concentrated all my will on them. The more I considered it, the more certain I was that the gale must have been connected to me and to my new gift. But with the wording I would have expected fire balls over wind. Perhaps I could…

Nothing happened. I glanced at the carriage's other occupants with embarrassment. Thankfully they couldn't possibly know I had been unsuccessfully attempting to sprout flames from my fingers.

I went back over the earlier events. Now that I thought about it, it had started not with my hands themselves but with the warmth inside my chest. I turned my attention inward but had no more success kindling an internal fire than I had an external one. After the minutes stretched out without success, I slumped back against the seat.

It appeared I couldn't control it, then. Too bad. I would have liked to greet whoever eventually opened the carriage door with fire balls. But apparently my gift—if that's what it was—had more use for rescuing others than myself.

The prince had yet to reappear, so I assumed he truly had escaped. I wished I felt more confident that he was doing something useful with his freedom.

"We're traveling west," said Emmeline, breaking the silence of the carriage.

I started and looked outside again—with some interest, this time. The capital lay north-west from the port. Further west, against the southern border with Eliam, lay large forested plains.

At least we weren't traveling closer to the northern mountains and their inevitable snow.

"Perhaps the robbers' hideout is in the forests, then," said Giselle.

"Robbers? Do you really think they're robbers?" I asked.

"But of course," she said. "They certainly look like thieves."

I frowned. "Except they haven't robbed us. They're abducting us. If their aim was robbery, they could easily have achieved it back on the road."

Giselle blinked at me. "My father, King Leopold, has long pursued a band of robbers who are believed to make their home in the southern forests. I'm sure this must be them. They have simply stolen us rather than our possessions."

Now it was my turn to blink in confusion. Emmeline and Giselle were even further gone than I had thought if they viewed themselves as no more than objects that could be stolen in the same way someone might steal a jeweled necklace.

"But...why?" I asked at last.

"Ransom, I suppose," said Emmeline. "Our father is known to have great reserves of gold and diamond mined from the northern mountains."

"He is?" I hadn't heard such reserves talked of myself.

Giselle shrugged. "They aren't so very large, really. But you know how people are wont to talk."

"I...suppose." Rumors of wealth did tend to become exaggerated over time. But abducting four royals—including a visiting royal from a largely unknown kingdom—seemed a desperate course to take based on a rumor. Could it be the tales of my own kingdom of Lanover's wealth that had tempted them? Perhaps I was the true target. But that still represented a desperate gamble since they could have no way to know if Lanover would respond with overwhelming physical force rather than payment. Based on the current state of things, I suspected Lanover could easily send a flotilla and overwhelm Eldon if it wished to do so.

Of course, by the time they did that, who knows what would have happened to me? I had been relying on my hosts to keep me safe during my visit—a plan that seemed increasingly fool-hardy at this point. I looked over at Emmeline and Giselle. If we were going to get out of this, I suspected it would be up to me. I fisted my hands, disappointed at the frosty feel of my chilly fingertips. I could really do with some fire right now.

"So how are we going to escape?" I asked.

"Escape?" Emmeline frowned out the window. "I don't see any way to escape. Perhaps an opportunity will present itself."

"In my experience," I said briskly, "it's best to make your own opportunities."

"You have a lot of experience in escapes, do you?" asked Giselle.

"You'd be surprised," I said wryly. I focused my eyes on the road outside which seemed to be curving slightly south. I'd managed to trail along for a fair number of adventures with my siblings. Only they always saw me as a child who needed to be protected. I straightened in my seat. It didn't matter if Emmeline and Giselle weren't going to be any help. This was what I'd wanted—no one telling me what to do or keeping me safe. I could hardly complain now that it looked like everything was going to be left up to me.

Unfortunately it was hard to make any plans until we reached some sort of destination, however temporary. And as the hours passed, my tension and anxiety faded into boredom. Eventually I curled up on the seat and napped. If an opening for escape arrived, I didn't want to be so tired I missed it.

~

The quiet murmur of the sisters woke me just before the wheels hit cobblestones. I stretched and peered outside only to realize we were entering the inner courtyard of a small stone castle. I stared between the view and the two princesses.

"We don't know where we are," said Emmeline. "Other than in the forest somewhere."

"I can't believe you managed to sleep," said Giselle.

I shrugged. "I can sleep just about anywhere. It's a handy skill. You should work on it."

My mouth twitched as both sisters stared at me blankly.

"Or don't." I shrugged again.

The light was failing, but I examined the courtyard in the twilight, helped by the odd flaming torch. "I'm surprised your father was never able to track the robbers down if they live in a *castle*."

I turned to the other girls, eyebrows raised, but neither said anything. Sighing, I turned back to analyze the scene outside. Many of the attackers milled around in the enclosed space, but I saw none of our own people. Dread filled me. I had assumed they were behind us, blocked by the attackers who had traveled in a ring around the carriage.

What had happened to them? My maids had stayed behind with my other guards to travel to the palace with the baggage, but we had still had a sizable entourage of Eldonian guards and grooms, not to mention the coachmen.

A tall, older man, his dark hair at odds with the pale coloring of most of the Eldonians, strode into the courtyard. His quick gaze took in the situation, an air of authority clinging to him as he approached a small group standing near the carriage.

"Where is the prince? Did you put him in the carriage with the princesses?"

The other men shifted uncomfortably, glancing at each other.

"Well?"

"He got away, I'm afraid, m'lord."

"What? How?" The man's tone was hard, but his face held more calculation than anger. He certainly wasn't the aggressive—

16

or perhaps blustering—robber leader I had expected. And the other man had called him m'lord. I glanced again at the small castle on the other side of the courtyard.

By the end of the men's stumbled explanations, the newcomer looked thunderstruck. "And you still brought the princesses here?"

The other men eyed each other warily, shrugging.

"Just following the plan, m'lord."

The apparent lord massaged his temples and sighed. "I knew I should have gone myself. For all we know, the prince may have already tracked us to this place. And now it sounds like the godmothers may even be involved."

"The godmothers? Surely not! There hasn't been one here for generations." The protester looked bemused at the suggestion.

"Perhaps a godmother object, then?" The man in charge shook his head. "You've heard the same reports I have. Things are changing in some of the other kingdoms. Newcomers have arrived. There's really no telling what may happen."

"Well, that's for sure," muttered one of the other men under his breath.

"Indeed." The lord's voice sounded icy. "And now there is nothing to be done but proceed." He turned toward the carriage, and I hurriedly drew back, trying to look as calm and proper as the Eldonian princesses.

The dark-haired man pulled open the door and surveyed the three of us before executing a stiff bow. "Your Highnesses. Welcome to my humble home. I apologize for the manner of your arrival."

Emmeline straightened. "We demand to be released at once."

For the first time I was glad to hear the ice in her voice. Unfortunately the man merely spread his arms wide.

"Night is upon us, and Your Highnesses are alone without mounts. I could hardly turn you out at such a moment. It is still cold, though winter has officially passed."

"It's always cold in Eldon, as far as I can tell," I said, not bothering to mask the displeasure in my voice.

He regarded me steadily. "Indeed. But it was not always so."

Something in his tone and his apparent reference to the increasing strangeness of his kingdom made me pause and assess him again. Nothing about this situation was playing out as I had imagined, and my desire to launch fire balls at everyone I could see was diminishing by the second. Curiosity was growing in its place. Did he know something of what was going on in Eldon?

I shook out my skirts and slid along the bench seat toward the door. "Well, I for one will gladly accept your hospitality. I have had enough of this carriage to last a lifetime."

He stepped back, the smallest twitch creasing his mouth, and held out a hand to help me alight. Once my feet were on the ground, I turned back to my companions.

"Well, ladies? A meal awaits us." I spun back around and gave the man my haughtiest look. "At least so I assume. You did speak of welcome, did you not?"

This time the twitch was more pronounced. He bowed again. "Indeed, Princess Celine. A warm meal awaits you. In your room." He gestured, and a circle of guards formed around us. "Allow me to escort you there."

I raised an eyebrow but said nothing. Clearly we were to walk a fine line between prisoner and guest. For now, I would play along. A warm meal and comfortable room—if such they turned out to be—were better than I had expected to encounter at the end of this journey.

But as we walked, I surreptitiously rubbed my palms against my thighs, willing the friction to ignite warmth of some kind. I might be playing along for now, but I would still have preferred to keep the option of fire balls open. Unfortunately, the movement did little to reduce the icy cold creeping through my limbs.

The air temperature warmed somewhat when we entered a large antechamber through double wood doors. Neither the man in charge nor the guards slowed, hurrying us up a red carpeted staircase and down a stone corridor. I expected the three of us to be separated, but when the dark-haired man held open a wooden door, we were all ushered inside.

Once we had filed in, the man smiled, directing his gaze at me. "I will leave guards out here in the corridor, should you require anything not already provided."

I raised an eyebrow. "And if I require a nighttime stroll?"

"I would not recommend such an activity. Anyone unfamiliar with the castle might find it an unsafe place in the darkness." The threat in his words was clear, but I could have sworn his eyes were laughing at me.

"Your concern for our safety is truly touching," I said, my words as dry as I could make them.

"You honor me." His smile broadened before he shut the door in my face.

"Well, then." I turned to assess the situation. "This could be worse." Four beds lined the room, the sheets and covers of fine material, if a little worn. And a small round table in the center of the room held the promised food. My stomach rumbled at the sight of the steaming soup and soft bread rolls. We had been offered nothing while we traveled, and I immediately decided that any further explorations could wait until I had eaten.

When I sat, the other girls followed my lead.

Giselle watched me as I buttered my roll, making no move to eat herself. Did she suspect it was poisoned?

I answered her unspoken question. "I don't think they would poison us. If they wanted us dead they've had plenty of opportunity already. Plus, we'll have to eat eventually, anyway. Personally, I'm going to keep up my strength. And I'd recommend you eat, too. But suit yourself."

Both Emmeline and Giselle regarded me so blankly I must have misread their hesitation. And on second thought, they didn't seem to have the initiative to consider the possibility of poison.

But my words goaded them into action anyway, as if they had been waiting for the prompt.

All further talk ceased as we quickly emptied the trays provided. The food was basic, but well flavored. And, more importantly, it was still hot. Between it and the fires burning on both sides of the room, I actually began to thaw out.

"Well," I said at last, stretching back in my chair, "now that I'm warm and full, I'm ready to start plotting our escape."

CHAPTER 3

"$\mathcal{E}$scape?" Giselle actually sounded surprised. "Surely we should wait for Oliver."

I attempted a diplomatic answer. "Waiting for rescue is certainly one option." I paused and then couldn't resist adding, "Are you sure Oliver is coming, though?"

"Certainly he will come for us," said Emmeline, "we're his sisters."

"Touching," I muttered under my breath without any real heat, "it's good to know I count for something." More loudly, I said, "But will he know where we are?"

Giselle frowned. "I suppose it depends on whether he decided to track our carriage or return immediately to the capital for reinforcements."

I waited for her to continue, but she lapsed back into silence.

"Well," I said, eventually, "I, for one, have no intention of sitting around and hoping for the best."

"But what exactly do you intend to do?" asked Emmeline. "You heard what Lord Treestone said. It sounds to me like you're going to get yourself killed. And that doesn't sound particularly helpful."

I ignored this sad mistrust in my abilities, my attention caught on something else. "Lord Treestone? Don't tell me you two know our captor!"

"But, of course," said Giselle. "We know all the nobles of Eldon. He's a minor lord with a small estate in the southwestern forests."

"I thought you said they were robbers!"

Giselle shrugged. "I didn't know they were answering to him until he appeared. Even nobles can turn to thievery, I suppose."

I rubbed my head, deciding now was not the right moment to address their strange detachment. But how could they not be more incensed to be kidnapped by one of their own nobles? And how had they not thought it worth mentioning?

I shook off the thought and explored our surroundings. Other than the beds and some empty chests and drawers, the room was bare. No surprises there. The windows were tall and narrow— too narrow for any of us to fit through—and there was only one door.

Ignoring Giselle's murmured warning, I opened it and stepped out into the corridor. Two guards immediately moved threateningly toward me. I stopped them with a haughty look.

"We have completed our meal. Please send someone to clear the trays." I retreated back into the room without waiting for a reply.

So just walking out of the castle definitely wasn't going to be an option. Just as this Lord Treestone had intimated. I had been in more dangerous situations in my life, but I had to admit, I couldn't readily see a way out of this one. And the manner of Lord Treestone had raised enough questions in my mind that I wasn't sure I wanted to run straight for the capital, anyway. Not without some further investigation.

But the guards prevented any immediate explorations, and the thought of just climbing obediently into bed chafed too much to be considered. Especially since I was hardly sleepy after my long nap in the carriage.

"Maybe one of you two could have a medical emergency?" I mused aloud. "I could send one of the guards for a doctor and, in the chaos, I might get a chance to slip away."

But one glance at the faces of the Eldonian princesses made me abandon the plan. Neither of them had the dramatic streak necessary to pull off such a deception.

I sighed. It looked like direct was the only way to go. I strode back toward the door and then paused.

"I'm going to see what I can find out. Would either of you like to come?"

Emmeline and Giselle exchanged looks, but neither of them spoke.

"Very well, then. If I manage to escape, I'll send someone back to rescue you."

"I'm really not sure..."

I didn't wait to hear the end of Giselle's sentence, pushing the door open and striding confidently out of the room. I could have sworn one of the guards sighed at the sight of me, and I had to suppress a smile.

"I wish to see Lord Treestone."

The guards exchanged a concerned look. I put my hands on my hips.

"Well? I assume you can't leave your post, so call for someone to escort me to him."

Still nothing.

I gave them my best royal look. "I'm not accustomed to being kept waiting."

After another silent exchange, one of the guards shrugged and called down the corridor. A young boy appeared and was charged with fetching more guards.

The three of us waited in silence for their arrival which took less time than I would have liked. Reinforcements were apparently to be found in close proximity to our room.

The two new guards looked somewhat skeptical when told they needed to take me to Lord Treestone's study, but neither actually protested. I had intended to take the opportunity to learn something of the layout of the castle, but it turned out to be so simple that study was hardly needed.

The small building had two floors, each boasting rows of rooms off a single corridor. Presumably a larger receiving, and possibly dining, hall could be found off the front antechamber. Not many people moved about, but there was enough activity to suggest that the rooms were being used for the purposes I would have supposed given the basic layout. It was certainly nothing like the sprawling single-story palace I had grown up in.

We arrived at a closed wooden door, and one of the guards knocked, disappearing inside for a quiet conversation with the occupant. When he returned, I was gestured into a spacious study decorated in dark wood with black metal accents.

The man from earlier—Lord Treestone, apparently—sat behind a large, neat desk. If he was surprised to see me, he didn't show it.

"Princess Celine. This is an unexpected visit."

He didn't offer me a seat, but I took one anyway. Like everything in the room I had left, the padding on the chair was slightly worn but comfortable. I looked around, noting the rows of books and ledgers, and the general lack of adornment. When my attention returned to the noble in front of me, I found him watching me with a look of interest.

I folded my hands in my lap and waited for him to speak. One of my older sisters had led a network of spies for years, and I had picked up a few tips from her. I would take any opportunity I could to keep this man on edge.

"What can I do for you, Princess Celine?" he said at last.

"Besides the obvious, I suppose you mean?"

A small smile twitched one side of his face. "Certainly let us leave aside anything obvious."

"Very well. I should like to know what has happened to my people. We had rather an entourage, as you must know, and two of the guards were in fact Lanoverian and not Eldonian."

"You show great concern for them."

My gaze turned icy. "I have great concern for all my people. As every royal—and noble—is obligated to do. If you have harmed them, you will find yourself with a stronger enemy than your own monarch." I looked around the room again, still amazed he had brought us to his own home. "Since clearly you have no fear of him."

The man seemed to deflate slightly, running a hand lightly across his face. "Fear...no, indeed. We seem all too short of fear these days."

My eyes narrowed. He sounded disappointed and defeated. Not at all like someone taking advantage of a weak ruler.

Looking back at me, the noble sighed. "I have no wish to find myself or my kingdom at odds with yours. Your people—along with the Eldonians—were left bound but otherwise unharmed. We didn't want them following us, but we have no quarrel with them."

"In that case, you can only hope someone came along quickly enough to prevent them freezing to death."

He shrugged. "It's a well-traveled road."

His unconcern rankled, but relief still filled me. The knowledge that we had not left a pile of dead bodies behind us lifted a cloud from my mind. Assuming he told the truth—and I could think of no reason for him to lie about it—he had once again confounded the expectations I had built of our abductors—the alleged robbers. I decided to change tack, leaning forward slightly and fixing him with an encouraging look.

"I cannot speak for the others, but I, at least, am uninvolved in whatever is happening here in your kingdom. Tell me what it is we should all be afraid of. And what you seek to gain with our abduction. Let us work together. If you mean me no harm, there is no reason for us to be enemies."

He leaned back in his chair, rubbing his chin thoughtfully. "You're not what I expected, Your Highness."

"Neither are you."

Something shadowed his eyes for a moment, and he looked away. I was used to being overlooked and underestimated, but something told me he wasn't as familiar with the role of robber and kidnapper.

"I must think on this situation," he said when he looked back at me. "We will speak more in the morning." Raising his voice, he called for the door to be opened again, and the two guards from earlier reappeared.

As they led me back the way we had come, I looked around for some means of escape, but nothing presented itself. The few people who had still roamed the halls earlier all seemed gone, and only our footfalls could be heard. I saw only one face—a young girl who watched us and who I was sure I saw in two different places during our walk—but she made no response to my smile on either occasion.

All too soon we arrived back at my assigned room. It seemed patience would be required, after all. I sighed. Patience had never been one of my strengths.

~

The next day, despite his words, Lord Treestone failed to send for me. Meals were delivered to our room, but my requests to be taken to see the noble were denied. Emmeline and Giselle's calm only further exacerbated me, their stillness driving me to ceaseless pacing.

The sun outside had begun its descent when a creaking filled the air. My first glance went to the door, but it remained firmly closed. After a wide-eyed scan of the rest of the room, I noticed a small section of the wall creeping slowly open. Emmeline and Giselle both remained unmoved, positioned far from the new opening, leaving me to greet whoever appeared alone. I recovered one of the knives from my boots, unwilling to wait entirely unarmed, but the figure that appeared was small enough for me to drop my defensive stance.

The girl looked contemptuously at the other two princesses and approvingly at my dagger. It took only a second for me to place her as the girl I had seen in the corridors the night before.

"I thought I liked the look of you," she said in a low voice. "And what you said to Uncle, too."

I raised both eyebrows. "Lord Treestone, you mean? Were you listening to our meeting?"

She grinned. "I'm always listening. At least when there's anything int'resting to hear." She paused, glancing again at Emmeline and Giselle. "Come on." She stepped back inside the secret passageway, gesturing for me to follow.

I paused for only a moment, looking at the other two with raised eyebrows. Once again, neither made a move to accompany me, so I disappeared into the darkness on my own.

"I'm Cassandra, by the way," said the girl's voice, just before she pulled back the shutter of a small lantern. A narrow passageway appeared around me, the walls rough and unadorned.

"Celine," I said, although it seemed unnecessary if she'd been spying on me since my arrival.

"I know." Cassandra took off at a brisk walk, and I trailed behind.

"I'm surprised they locked us in a room with a secret passageway," I said as we wound our way through the walls. I was kicking myself for not examining the room for just such a possibility. There must be an opening mechanism hidden somewhere inside.

Cassandra looked back at me and grinned. "I don't think anyone else knows they're here. It's a very old castle, and no one seems to want to explore it but me."

"Why did you come for me?"

She stopped abruptly, and I nearly collided with her back. Spinning, she surveyed me with a creased brow before nodding once. Resuming our forward progress, she spoke over her shoulder.

"I like the look of you, even though you're a princess." She wrinkled her nose. "You're certainly nothing like our princesses. When Uncle didn't send for you today, I thought I'd better take matters into my own hands." She shrugged. "He isn't a bad person, you know. He's just cautious. Too cautious."

A small snort escaped me, but she didn't seem the least offended.

"I know kidnapping you all probably doesn't *seem* cautious, but he's getting desperate. He debated forever about doing it, and then you heard what he said when you first arrived. If he'd been there when the prince escaped, he would have called it off. Now that the plan has gone awry, he doesn't know how to proceed."

I refrained from asking how she had overheard that conversation. There weren't any hidden passageways in the middle of a courtyard.

"So, when you asked him to tell you what was going on," she continued, after a brief pause, "of course he wanted to think about it. And he's been thinking about it all day." She ducked into a small alcove. "He's going to think about it so long that the royal guards show up, and how's that going to help anyone?"

I refrained from pointing out that the royal guards would be of some help to me.

The alcove turned out to be almost a small room, and the girl had obviously turned it into a hideaway of sorts, decorated with threadbare rugs and cushions. A small collection of lanterns and several old books stood on a small wooden shelf.

The girl plonked down onto one of the cushions, and I did the same. My travel dress was already in dire need of a wash, so I didn't think a bit more dirt could hurt it at this stage. Still, I felt a passing pang for the gown. I wasn't sure if it would be able to be salvaged after this adventure, and it was one of my favorites—worn to impress during my expected arrival at a foreign court.

"Well, then," I said, once we'd both settled. "So tell me. What's going on?"

CHAPTER 4

assandra opened her mouth, but nothing came out. She frowned. "It's a bit complicated."

"I've started to get that impression."

She grinned wryly. "I suppose the problem is that we don't know what's going on. Which doesn't make a very good answer to your question. My uncle's been trying to find out what's going on for three years now, and we can't get any real answers."

"We? I suppose you're deep in your uncle's confidence." I gave her a dry look, already knowing from her talk of spying this wasn't likely the case.

She grinned back at me, not seeming in the least offended. "I am when I can convince him to include me. As for the rest of the time...well, I have my ways, as I told you."

When I raised an eyebrow, she rolled her eyes.

"You're looking at me like you think I'm young enough to still believe in the Snow Queen or something. I'm a lot older than I look."

I narrowed my eyes. "How old are you?"

"Thirteen."

"Thirteen?" I snapped my mouth shut before I admitted I had thought her no more than ten.

She sighed. "Yes, I know. I'm short. I look young. I've heard it before. Can we move on?"

"Please accept my apologies and the erasure of all future doubt."

By the rueful shake of her head and the twinkle in her eye, I assumed she recognized my dry tone. Thirteen was certainly a lot older than ten, but it wasn't that old. Not really.

But I couldn't help but like her. A lot. And she carried herself with an assurance that made you forget her age. I shook myself. And what did it matter, really? I didn't exactly have other allies leaping out to assist me. I could hardly have turned my nose up at her if she had turned out to be ten.

"The rest of the kingdoms all agree that something strange is going on in Eldon," I said, turning back to the matter at hand. "But I have to admit, I'd hoped you Eldonians might have more of an idea of what exactly it is."

She grimaced. "Well, it's cold now, for one. Really cold."

I rolled my eyes. "That much I'd managed to figure out for myself."

She shrugged. "That's where it all started, anyway. The winters got longer—and colder. Spring and autumn are basically gone now. And we barely even have anything that could count as summer. The south-western part of the kingdom—our woods—are the warmest part. But it even occasionally snows down here now. At least we haven't turned into the ice sheets of the north. Yet."

"And no one knows why?"

She threw up her hands. "Who knows? Someone might. At least, we hope someone does. That's what we're trying to work out. But forget knowing what's going on...we can't seem to find anyone else who cares. Our harvests are barely existent. Trade with the other kingdoms has died. Feeding ourselves gets more and more difficult, and we're relying more and more on stores from earlier, better years."

I worried at my lip. This lined up with what Lily had learned in Marin while we were there. With the exception of Trione, all of these kingdoms had been falling apart when we arrived, and in the case of Eldon, the destruction was coming in the form of ice.

"And it's not just a bad year?" I faltered at her expression. "Or two?"

"Try three. And not even our oldest citizens can remember previous years this bad. Something is going on, and it's not natural."

I glanced unconsciously down at my hands. Snow wasn't the only unnatural thing going on in Eldon. But I didn't think I could blame the godmothers for the kingdom freezing over. They weren't in the business of starving entire populaces. This was more the sort of thing that happened in kingdoms that had turned their back on the godmothers and the High King they served.

"I don't suppose your king has done something really terrible lately?" I asked.

"Umm…Like what?"

"Something bad enough to curse your kingdom?"

She frowned. "Not that we've ever heard of. King Leopold was always a good ruler."

"Was?"

Her expression turned sad. "He's just like all the others now. He doesn't seem to see any threat. Or he doesn't care. My uncle traveled to court last year to seek answers, but no one else seemed worried that we'll all be starving to death in a year or two." She looked at me. "And I don't just mean us down here in the woods. If anything, we're the *least* affected. It just doesn't make any sense."

"No…" I said slowly, "it doesn't." But it did line up with everything I'd seen of Emmeline, Giselle, and Oliver. I could suddenly see how Lord Treestone had grown desperate enough to take drastic measures. Although…

"How does abducting us help with any of this?"

"Uncle thought perhaps the royals do know what's going on, and they're just not telling us. Or the king and queen and the crown prince, at least. Only the king and queen haven't left the palace in months. So he thought if he could just get the prince to his castle, and make him listen, he could convince him to tell us. Or, if not, that surely the king and queen care enough about their children to be roused to action. Uncle thought he could ransom them in a way. Guarantee their safe return in exchange for an investigation into what's going on."

"So…what? It's just bad timing that I got caught up in it?"

Cassandra looked a little guilty. "I believe Uncle thought that the threat of Lanover's reaction might move King Leopold and Queen Camille, even if nothing else did."

I rocked back, a little shocked. How far gone must the royal family be if Lord Treestone wasn't sure they would react to the abduction of all three of their children?

Cassandra examined me unhappily. "I realize it wasn't the best plan. Unfortunately, it was the only one we could come up with."

I frowned, and her unhappy look deepened.

"Is Lanover going to attack us now?"

I started. "What? Oh. No. At least not after I write to tell them I'm unharmed. That's assuming my people have even sent a message about my abduction yet."

I stood up and paced the small space. "I came here to find out what's going on, but it's obvious whatever is happening is coming from the north, so I can't do much good down here." I fixed her with my sternest look. "Which means I'm going to need your uncle to release me. And the others, as well, since I can hardly turn up at the palace without them."

Cassandra grimaced. "Uncle thinks we can't risk just releasing you now that we've abducted you."

"Well, then you'll need to help me escape."

Cassandra's lack of surprise told me she'd already known this was where we would end up.

"How much trouble will you get in if your uncle finds out you helped me?"

She shrugged. "He won't find out."

"All right, then." I looked down the passage in both directions. "Which way is out?"

Cassandra snorted. "Aren't you forgetting something?"

I sighed. "Oh, of course." I couldn't deny that the need to bring the other princesses along would complicate things somewhat. Their motivation seemed to have diminished even in the months since we had all participated in the Princess Tourney together. They had at least been of occasional help then.

For a brief moment I thought longingly of just leaving them behind. But I knew I couldn't really do it—not unless I had no other choice.

"I suppose we'd better go back for them, then."

"I can't just let you out right now anyway," said Cassandra. "My uncle was right about one thing, at least. You wouldn't get far in the cold and on foot."

"What exactly do you suggest then?" I asked, not quite keeping the acid tone out of my voice.

"We'll also need to free your carriage, horses, and coachman. And do it quietly enough that you can get far enough away before anyone realizes you're gone."

"Oh, just that, hey?" I smiled at her matter-of-fact manner.

"As I said, it will need some planning."

As much as I wanted immediate action, I could see she was right.

So together we made a plan.

~

Emmeline and Giselle were sitting at the little table when I re-emerged from the secret passage. Had they even moved while I'd been gone? Cassandra also popped out to show me the trick to opening the concealed door from inside the room—just in case—but she disappeared quickly to carry out her more complicated role.

"We're escaping," I announced to the sisters.

It was a good thing I wasn't expecting any dramatic reaction since I certainly didn't get one. At least they didn't put up any protest. Our plan had purposely kept their roles to a minimum, but I still explained them carefully. Again, neither protested, so I could only hope they didn't put up any fuss when the time came.

After that, we had merely to wait until our evening meal was served. Sitting down calmly to eat took some exercise of willpower on my behalf, but I managed it in the end, summoning a maid to clear away the dishes as imperiously as I had done the night before.

When I finally heard the creak of the passageway opening, I was more than ready for action. Cassandra poked her head around and waved us in, disappearing without bothering to check that we were actually coming. I ushered Emmeline and Giselle ahead of me, giving a last scan of the room to make sure we hadn't left anything behind.

Nobody spoke as we followed Cassandra through the walls of the castle. I slipped past the other girls and sidled up to the youngster to give her a questioning look. She smiled reassuringly, so I could only assume everything had so far gone to plan.

It felt like we'd been walking far longer than possible given the small size of the castle before she stopped, holding up a hand to halt us as well. Nothing about this stretch of wall looked different to me, but she felt around for something I couldn't see, and several large stones shifted. I gazed at the opening—much smaller than a normal doorway—and then down at my dress. With a sigh, I got down onto my hands and knees. If the dress wasn't already ruined, it would be now.

Icy air hit me as I squeezed through the space and out into the night. I moved away from the opening to allow the others to follow but stayed low to the ground. When Emmeline appeared, she opened her mouth as if to speak, and I quickly put my finger to my lips. We had emerged behind the stables, but we were still inside the courtyard of the castle.

Thankfully she merely shook her head and moved to join me without speaking. Once all four of us had gathered, Cassandra touched another hidden mechanism, and the opening disappeared. I shook my head. I couldn't imagine the hours it must have taken her to find all these doors and openings.

Clambering to her feet, but bending low, Cassandra led us around the back of the stables, keeping to the shadows. This time I waited to bring up the rear, rubbing my arms and wishing again I could conjure magical warmth at will. I had forgotten just how cold it was outside.

As we crept from shadow to shadow, every sense tense and alert, I thought I saw something move against the closest wall. I blinked and looked again, but this time could see nothing. It had been a mere shadow, but I could have sworn I saw the flicker of movement. I bit my lip but had no choice except to keep moving and hope it had been nothing but my imagination.

On second thought, I removed one of the daggers from my boot. Better prepared than not.

My hesitation had put me behind the others, so I had to hurry to catch up. By the time I reached them, the other two princesses were clambering into our carriage. It stood in the deep shadows between the far side of the stable and the wall. Cassandra had managed even better than I had dared hope.

A tall figure stepped forward, and I jumped, stifling an exclamation as the form of one of our coachmen appeared. We had originally left the port with two coachmen, so I could only assume one had been left behind by our abductors. They must have thought one enough to drive us here, and the fewer people to imprison the better.

The man in front of me nodded before disappearing after Cassandra. I followed, wondering if he had been the shadow I saw earlier. But that one had been behind us...

A carriage could be hidden silently, but horses were another matter. Our only choice had been to bring them out at the last minute. After some debate, we had decided that we would sacrifice the extra speed of four horses in the interest of keeping this step as quick and simple as possible.

I had been taught how to care for and saddle my own horse, but I'd never attached one to a carriage before, so I was only able to follow simple directions whispered by the coachman. He worked quickly and efficiently, but still it felt as if it took forever for everything to be ready. At every moment I expected a shout of discovery, and every sound seemed to ring through the night air.

We would never have gotten away with any of it in a larger castle, the type of place with guards posted at regular intervals around the wall. But Lord Treestone's small domain had only the simplest of walls and two guards posted at the gate. And Cassandra had assured me they were occupied watching for a rescue attempt from outside. Over and over I reminded myself that no one was paying attention to what was happening in the shadows of the courtyard.

Finally the horses were in place, and the coachman stood ready for the next part of the plan.

I turned to say farewell to Cassandra, who would have to disappear at this point or risk having her involvement discovered, and was surprised with a tight hug around my waist. She hadn't struck me as the sentimental type, an impression confirmed when I looked down into her face. She looked positively fierce.

"Don't let me down, Celine," she whispered. "Find out what's trying to kill us all. And then you kill it, instead."

I nodded. "I will." *If I can,* I added silently in my head, unsure how I had managed to inspire such faith in her, but glad she had trusted me enough to help us.

As she slipped away, my smile disappeared. The next part was the hardest. With a grim nod to the coachman, I led him forward through the shadows. I had returned my dagger to my boot while helping with the horses, but I gripped it in my hand again now. The coachman held a short wooden club—from Cassandra or the carriage I didn't know. We didn't want to kill anyone if we could possibly avoid it. I still believed Lord Treestone that our own people were safe, and even that he didn't intend us any immediate harm. But that didn't mean harm wouldn't come to us—and possibly a great many other people—if we remained as captives. I just hoped the harm didn't start now.

Stepping forward into the light, I called softly to the guards. They both swung around, their expressions shifting to surprise and then suspicion.

"What are you doing here?" asked one, at the same moment as the second asked, "Who are you?"

But their questions had given me the chance to close the remaining distance between us, and my dagger flashed out from where I had hidden it in my skirts. The guard in front of me didn't even have time to draw his sword before my hilt found his head. As he crumpled to the ground, his companion dropped beside him, thanks to the ministrations of the coachman.

Well, not too great a harm, at any rate.

I stooped to check their pulses. Both beat steadily.

I picked the smaller one and lifted his head and torso off the ground, gripping him beneath his arms. The coachman took the other, and we dragged them back toward the shadows next to the gate. Cassandra had promised we would find gags and rope there. With any luck, we would be well gone before any alarm could be raised.

I had nearly reached the darkness when a gasp of surprise split the night. I looked up and into the eyes of a third guard, frozen mid-stride halfway across the courtyard.

CHAPTER 5

I froze as well, and for an endless-seeming second we both stood there in silence, our eyes locked. My back was still bowed from the weight of the unconscious guard, and I noticed the new guard's hands were also occupied—with cups and a flagon. What terrible timing for refreshments to arrive!

The man was too far for me to have any hope of reaching him before he called an alarm. Only his shock had prevented him doing so already. Plus I had nothing but my daggers against his sword, and this time I wouldn't have the element of surprise.

I remained in place as I tried desperately to produce an unnatural warmth inside me that I might be able to send across the impossible distance between us. But the cold air had leached into every part of me. My gift—if that's what it had been— remained far from reach.

While I watched, still motionless, the guard shook off his paralysis and opened his mouth to call for reinforcements. I closed my eyes. We were so close!

When I opened them a second later, I barely registered a blur racing across the courtyard. For a brief moment I imagined my mind was playing tricks on me, conjuring up the shadow I had seen earlier.

But this time the dark figure didn't disappear. The guard swung to face him, his cry lost as the newcomer's fist connected with his middle, violently expelling the air from his lungs. A moment later a second blow to the head felled him. The cups and flagon hit the ground with a thud and rolled against his motionless body.

The shadow stooped to lift the man, dragging him across the courtyard toward me. I shook off my own surprise and resumed pulling at my load. But it was slow going, and when the coachman appeared to assist me, I let him take the guard, preferring to feel the solid hilt of a dagger in my hand once again.

It looked as if the shadow was on our side, but I didn't intend to let down my guard until I knew who he was. Or she. Although their build and gait gave me the strong impression of a male. Still, my sister had taught me not to trust to appearances.

As soon as the coachman had deposited the second of the gate guards in the shadows, he disappeared. Reluctantly I knelt, feeling around for the promised rope. My hand fell on it quickly, tucked up against the wall, and I set to work, starting with the gags. The coachman would be back with the carriage at any moment, and I didn't want any more delays.

The shadow had reached me now with the third man, and I was grateful Cassandra had left an abundance of supplies. I shifted to keep my front toward the newcomer as he followed my lead, binding the man he had knocked down. At least that must mean the man was still alive.

We worked in silence, the shadow not looking up once to meet my constant wary glances. Only once we had finished did he stand and offer a hand to help me to my feet.

I ignored it.

His eyes, the only part of his face I could see given the dark material wrapped around his head, flashed to the dagger nestled back into my palm. When they returned to my face, I could have sworn they looked quizzical. But any words were interrupted by the sound of carriage wheels against cobblestones.

"Quick!" I gasped, realizing my mistake. I'd been distracted by our unknown assistant and forgotten my next task. "We need to get the gates open."

Together we wrestled with them, pushing them wide enough for the carriage to pass through. The coachman led the horses through at a slow walk, shushing them with quiet murmurs. As soon as the back of the carriage had passed through, he swung up onto the front box, gripping the reins.

I began to tug the gates back closed. We wouldn't be able to latch them, but at least we could keep from drawing immediate attention to the situation by leaving them open. But the shadow gestured for me to get into the carriage. I hesitated for a moment, but he began pulling at the gates himself, so I rushed over and threw myself into the carriage.

"Go!" I hissed at the coachman, leaning out of the window to peer up at him. He twisted and glanced back at me, his eyes flicking toward our unknown accomplice. But when I glared at him, he shrugged once and straightened, the carriage lurching and beginning to move.

I knelt on the seat and peered out of the tiny back window. The arrival of that third guard had put me on edge, and I didn't want to waste a second putting distance between us and any pursuit. Certainly not for the sake of someone who wore a mask and had yet to identify himself.

The gates had closed enough now to cut off the dim glow from inside the castle walls, and it was hard to make out much with only the moonlight. But I did see the second gate close into position, and then a moment later I made out a dark figure sprinting after us.

We had only just begun to gather any speed, and reluctantly I stuck my head back out of the carriage to call quietly for the coachman to slow for a moment. The shadow had helped us, after all.

As our momentum fell away, the figure reached us, and I swung the door open. The shadow gripped the frame, still running to keep pace with us, and swung himself in.

I was still half-crouched in the doorway, so he collided with me, and we both fell back against the seat.

"Oof." I struggled to push him off as the door swung wide again, banging against the outside of the carriage as we regained the speed we had momentarily lost. For a moment the carriage seemed full of flailing limbs, and then I got my hands firmly against his chest and pushed him away. A small part of my mind noted that it was definitely a 'him' as I scrambled forward, leaning precariously out of the open door to pull it closed.

Strong hands gripped my waist, steadying me as I hung half out of the moving vehicle. As soon as I had slammed the door closed, I wrenched myself out of his grip, throwing myself onto one of the seats. He paused briefly and then sat across from me.

I took a deep breath and looked over at Emmeline and Giselle. I had nearly forgotten about them in all the chaos and could only be glad they had flattened themselves against the far side of the carriage, out of our way.

But neither of them were looking at me, both of their gazes fixed on the man wrapped head-to-toe in black who sat across from me instead. I could hardly blame them.

I opened my mouth to demand an explanation, along with his identity, but Giselle spoke before I could. And she had transferred her gaze to me.

"I told you he would rescue us."

"Thanks for your faith, little sis," said a familiar voice, as he unwound the strip of material from his head. "Although here I was thinking my disguise was rather good."

The fair hair and handsome face of Prince Oliver appeared. He wore a wry smile—an expression I had never seen on his usually impassive face before. And the blue eyes that swept from his sisters to me retained the animation I had thought I glimpsed in them in the moment before his escape.

I sat back. Prince Oliver. I should have guessed. But then I hadn't expected anything so daring, or...well...active from him. And I rather resented Giselle's comment about our rescue.

Crossing my arms over my chest, I raised an eyebrow at him. "You don't look like a thirteen-year-old girl to me."

"Excuse me?" He looked confused, but I hadn't really been aiming my comment at him.

I looked over at the other two princesses. "We were rescued by a thirteen-year-old girl, remember?"

Oliver looked intrigued, although he also shook his head at me. "I could have sworn you were in need of some rescuing when I intervened. My mistake." A small grin twitched across his face, and I relented.

"I will allow you credit for a partial rescue," I said in my most gracious voice, accompanying it with a regal nod.

He snorted. "Very generous." Then the grin returned. "Although you did seem to do rather well with those gate guards. I thought you must be mad when you called to them."

I shrugged. "Don't worry, I'm used to being underestimated. Why do you think my tactic was so successful?" I glanced at him consideringly. "So you were already there watching us at that point? In that case, I'm guessing it was you I saw in the shadows by the wall when we first came outside."

I thought I caught a gleam of admiration in his eyes. "You saw me then? When you paused, I wondered. I'd come over the wall as soon as it got dark, but I hadn't worked out a way into the castle yet when you all appeared. And then I thought I should watch and see what was happening. I didn't want to upset any carefully laid plan."

"A good idea as things turned out," I said, a little begrudgingly. It seemed Prince Oliver wasn't the only one among us who had done some underestimating. I had never expected such sense and initiative from him, but he had well and truly proved me wrong.

"I look forward to arriving home," said Emmeline. "Cassandra seems to have supplied the carriage with blankets, and even warming pans, but a hot bath would not go astray."

I shivered as her words reminded me of the cold. A blanket appeared in front of me, held out by Oliver, and I took it gratefully, wrapping myself in it.

"I wouldn't say no to a hot bath myself," I said. "But I want to hear your story first, Oliver."

"I have nothing exciting to tell, I assure you." He lounged back against the seat. "After I managed to escape the attack, I thought it best to follow the abductors before returning to the palace for reinforcements. I didn't want the trail to go cold. When I realized where you had been taken, I decided it should be safe enough to conduct a scouting trip before returning. The place wasn't exactly teeming with guards. And then I found you all."

His story was simple enough, but a shadow in his eyes suggested he was holding something back. I opened my mouth to ask what he was hiding, but his eyes flicked to his sisters. A crease appeared on his forehead as he watched the way they sat calmly on the seats, Emmeline watching the dark forest move past the window.

I shut my mouth again but determined I would find a chance to talk to the mysterious prince in private. Soon.

"And now it's your turn," he said, returning his attention to me. "I want to hear about this thirteen-year-old."

I told the story as succinctly as I could. Oliver seemed as unconcerned with the news that our entourage was likely alive and relatively unharmed as his sisters had been, and my rapidly rising opinion of him dropped sharply. He seemed a little more interested in Lord Treestone and in his niece's desperate assertions that something was very wrong in Eldon.

But he said nothing more than, "Hmmm…", making no effort

to discuss it with me. When his eyes again flicked over to his sisters, I refrained from pushing the matter. At least he didn't seem intent on punishing Lord Treestone for the abduction. Despite being one of the main victims, I empathized with the noble's desperation and had no desire to see him stripped of his land and titles, or executed, or something. Now that we were free, it was actually somewhat reassuring to me to know that at least one other person in this kingdom had an interest in finding out the truth of what was going on. And that person had access to at least some resources—even if he'd misused them in this instance.

The exchange of stories had distracted me, but I now found myself straining to hear any sound of pursuit. But I could hear nothing beyond the sound of our own progress through the forest. We just needed to get far enough away before the new shift arrived at dawn for the change of guards. I checked the sky for any signs of lightening, but everything looked black outside the windows.

Giselle was the first to fall asleep, tipping slowly sideways until she rested on the shoulder of her brother beside her. When Emmeline began to nod off, I resigned myself to the same fate. And, sure enough, I soon had the weight of her head pressing against me. I remained upright, too alert to sleep, as did Oliver across from me. We refrained from talking in deference to the sleepers, but the prince watched me, off and on, as the night stretched out.

I tried to read the messages in his eyes, but his contradictions foiled me. I could have sworn he regarded me as curiously as I regarded him. But he had never shown much interest in me before. And I kept remembering the disregard he'd shown for the fate of his own people, left bound on the cold road. And even his lack of interest in the crimes of Lord Treestone—against his own sisters, too. Was I fooling myself to imagine that something had changed in this cold prince?

A whisper of warmth stirred inside me and crept down my arms to warm my fingertips. And was it even greater foolishness to think that the change could have had anything to do with me?

The puzzle of Prince Oliver occupied my mind until we reached the royal palace of Eldon. And then I could think of nothing else.

CHAPTER 6

I'd seen plenty of royal palaces before—I had grown up in one, after all. But I had never seen anything like this one. At first glance it seemed to be made entirely of towers, rising in sleek shards of differing heights. It nestled against gray rock at the base of a mountain, crafted from a sleek marble that shone almost blue-green in the rising sun. I had never seen that exact color of rock before, and for a heart-stopping moment, I wondered if the entire building was carved from ice.

"Welcome to Eldon," said Oliver, his voice a quiet rumble.

I looked across to find his eyes fixed on me. I snapped my mouth shut.

"It's incredible."

His smile looked a little twisted as he turned his head to regard his home. "One of a kind—or so they say."

"Well, I've never seen anything like it."

Emmeline stirred and pulled herself upright, mumbling sleepily, and I immediately scooted over to peer out the window. Where was the city? I had expected to reach the capital before I saw the palace. But I could see no city wall, other than the wall of the palace itself, crafted from the same stone as the building.

Something on the mountain behind the palace sparked, reflecting a ray of sunlight. I blinked and then blinked again.

Instead of spreading out around the palace, like in other capitals, the buildings all sheltered behind it, climbing up the face of the mountain. As I looked closer I made out steep roads, and in some places even steps, carving various paths up the slope.

Oliver was still watching me. "It's a bigger city than it looks. Most of what you can see are the fronts of buildings, with the bulk of the rooms carved back into the mountain."

I shook my head and repeated myself. "It's incredible."

A slow smile spread across his face, and for the first time his expression looked truly warm. "I'm glad you like it."

The coachman slowed as we approached the gate but didn't actually come to a stop. To my surprise, the gate was open with a small trickle of early morning activity. I had expected the palace to be on lock down after the attack on our party. Instead we were waved through without the coachman even needing to identify his passengers.

I glanced at Oliver, my brows lowered, and caught a look of faint concern on his face. Emmeline and Giselle, on the other hand, showed no response to the manner of our arrival. Both were still waking up and had begun to murmur about hot baths.

I examined the stone as we passed through the palace walls. The impression of ice hardly abated with closer inspection—it was truly an incredible material. The courtyard was one of the largest I had ever seen. I supposed any carriages or wagons which couldn't make it up the steep mountain roads would have to be unloaded here, their burdens transferred into smaller loads.

Oliver jumped out first, turning to offer each of us a hand. I ignored his offered help, jumping down on my own and turning to take it all in. A small stir rippled out around us among the various grooms, guards, and palace messengers who were outside at this early hour. But the response was nothing to the commotion I would have normally anticipated. Except I was fast learning to expect nothing normal in this strange kingdom.

The other three had already begun to mount the steps to the front doors, so I hurried after them. The grand entrance had been carved with a series of intricate scenes, but the doors were swinging open before I had time to take any of them in. The servants in the entrance hall paused to bow and curtsy but seemed otherwise unaffected by our sudden arrival.

I did notice one scurry off up a broad staircase carpeted in deep red velvet. And, sure enough, a small flood of newcomers soon began to fill the large space. By far the loudest of these new arrivals were my own people. The guards looked grim but relieved, and two of my maids even had tears on their cheeks as they exclaimed and swirled around me.

I could barely make my own questions about their safety heard and ended up doing a head count just to reassure myself they were all there. Thankfully my maids and guards were all accounted for, including the two who had accompanied the initial group and been left bound on the road. One of the maids heard me over the hubbub and assured me that the second party with the baggage had found them before anyone suffered any serious harm.

A quick conversation with the captain of the guard reassured him of my safety, and he promised to obey my directive to send a new message hard on the heels of his previous one to let my family know I was unharmed and safely arrived at the palace. He apologized for failing to protect me on the road, and for failing to find me subsequently, but I brushed his words aside.

He shifted uneasily, though, clearly unwilling to let it drop.

"I must confess to grave concerns, Your Highness," he said, dropping his voice low, and glancing at the Eldonians around us. "I'm no longer confident I can assure your safety here. The attack and your disappearance did not—"

I cut him off, my voice equally low. "Let me guess, no one

seemed sufficiently concerned about our abduction, and your attempts to organize some sort of search and rescue attempt met with little enthusiasm?"

His lips flattened into a grim line, and he gave a reluctant nod.

I shrugged. "I understand your concerns, Captain, but I came here to find out what is wrong with this kingdom, and I don't intend to turn tail now. I'll write a full accounting of the situation to my family at the earliest opportunity absolving you of all responsibility if anything further should occur."

He grimaced but made no further protest. With no other Lanoverian royal to turn to, he couldn't gainsay my orders.

My maids informed me that I had been assigned a large suite and that my luggage had already been delivered to it. They were clearly determined to carry me off immediately for a hot bath and some sleep, and my own enthusiasm for that plan was strong. But first I wanted to speak to Oliver.

When I turned to find him, however, I saw that King Leopold and Queen Camille had arrived. I had seen them from afar at the royal wedding in Palinar, but we hadn't been formally introduced. They smiled and embraced their children, but I read no undue anxiety or relief on their faces. When Oliver looked up and caught my eye, he broke away from the others to gesture me over. When I stepped close enough, he introduced me.

"Mother, Father, this is Princess Celine of Lanover."

I gritted my teeth and thrust the state of my dress and my overall appearance firmly from my mind as I gave a curtsy, hitting the exact depth required from a younger princess to a reigning monarch. I was used to looking my best on such occasions, but I would salvage what I could from the situation.

When I rose back up, I found them both smiling somewhat vacantly at me.

"Welcome Princess Celine," said King Leopold. "We are honored by your visit."

"And sorry for the unpleasantness around your arrival." Queen Camille's soft words carried no depth of emotion.

"But I see it has all worked out in the end," said the king, "as I felt sure it would."

Emmeline nodded and declared her intention to retire, Giselle trailing behind her. I waited for the king or queen to go on, but silence fell. Should I speak in defense of Lord Treestone? I looked over at Oliver for some sort of clue. Nothing had been said of their intentions from here. King Leopold followed the direction of my gaze.

"My son has informed me of the circumstances, and I am glad that no one was harmed. Clearly no true ill-will was meant." He nodded his head once and clapped his son on the back. "Tonight we shall have a banquet to welcome our new guest." He gave a half-bow in my direction, while I just blinked at him stupidly.

Surely that couldn't be it? I looked at Oliver again, and he gave me a slight shrug, his eyes clouded. I bit my lip. I hadn't wanted any great harm to befall Lord Treestone or his people, and had even considered speaking in their defense, so I could hardly complain now...

Still, this went beyond even what I had expected.

My maids swarmed me, and I could no longer resist following them in the direction of a bath and fresh clothing. And the sight of the large and comfortable bed in my beautiful room drove other thoughts from my mind. As soon as I was clean, I sank into the soft mattress and let the icy blue velvet of the room and the warm, flickering fire fade from view as I sank into unconsciousness.

~

I woke in the afternoon to a quiet room. The fire still burned, driving back the cold that had plagued me in this kingdom so far, and I spent an enjoyable half hour looking through my gowns which had already been unpacked into an expansive wardrobe. After my dismal appearance that morning—I had unfortunately caught sight of myself in a mirror before my bath—I wanted to take extra care on my presentation for the evening banquet.

I ran my hand along the various materials and sighed with pleasure. I didn't love gowns or materials with quite the passion of my sister-in-law Evie—a talented ex-seamstress—but I loved the effect they could produce. I had learned that from my unnaturally beautiful sister Celeste—the master spy. Looks were simply another tool in the arsenal of a princess. And if wielded well, they could be effective indeed. As a royal, the way you dressed sent a message—and I had always loved making a strong impression.

I grinned to myself as I remembered the fights I used to have with my mother over some of my more daring ensembles. She had never understood the burden of being the youngest. The Lanoverian princesses were famed for their beauty, but I had to work to make mine stand out among so many sisters. At least once I hit eighteen she stopped trying to interfere in my clothing choices.

In the end, I settled on a deep-red, long-sleeved evening gown that exposed my shoulders and tapered down into a point part way down my back. Daring, but not too daring. And the rich color showed off my golden skin and dark hair and eyes. I laid it out on the bed so my maids would know what I had chosen. I could trust them to choose accessories to match.

I smiled. I was sure to stand out among all these pasty-skinned, pale northerners. Unbidden, the warm blue of Oliver's eyes flashed through my mind. How would he react to my appearance? We would be a striking couple standing side-by-side —his fair hair the perfect foil to my dark looks.

But thought of the prince drove my mind into more serious topics. I still needed to find the chance to talk to him privately. I had questions that wouldn't wait.

I slipped into a simpler gown that I could fasten without assistance and crossed to the door. Pausing, I reminded myself that unlike in Lord Treestone's castle, I wasn't a prisoner here. There was no reason for me to feel guilty about going exploring.

The corridors didn't have the same cozy warmth as my room, but they were still warmer than they had any right to be based on the appearance of the palace. I wandered through what turned out to be something of a labyrinth, full of staircases and long, echoing corridors. The furniture I saw was all dark wood, with simple elegant lines, and the occasional touch of velvet kept the overall impression from one of icy inaccessibility. To my surprise, I found that I liked it. It took the best of this icy climate and made it beautiful and somehow welcoming.

As I explored, I lost track a little of my original goal. After so many hours on a ship, carriage, or locked in a room, I was enjoying the sense of freedom. And the décor fascinated me. It seemed far richer and deeper than the people themselves, none of whom had given me so much as a curious look.

A concentration of the blue velvet I had seen elsewhere made me pause, my attention drawn to an elegant alcove. It contained a large portrait of a young woman wearing a gown that appeared to match the velvet hung around her picture. Had she been the one originally responsible for the soft touch in the palace?

The style of her dress told me she had likely lived some time ago, and the crown on her brow suggested she must have had the authority to redecorate in her day. I examined her face for a long minute. The artist had done a good job with her expression, capturing a strange mix of sweetness and determination. Was it an accurate reflection of how she had looked in life?

But what made me even more curious than her face was the small pedestal resting in the alcove alongside the portrait. An empty glass dome stood on top of it, holding nothing but empty air. Clearly it had been designed to display something. But what?

And why was it no longer there? It gave the whole alcove an unfinished look I hadn't seen anywhere else in the palace.

A passing footman startled me from my reverie, my mind suddenly flashing to the time. How much had passed while I lost myself in the palace? I stopped him and asked for directions. His assumption that I wished to return to my rooms to dress for the banquet confirmed my fears about the late hour, so I didn't demur. I would have to find a chance to talk to Oliver at the meal.

As I followed behind the well-dressed servant, I watched the other people we passed curiously, looking for any who showed signs of greater animation than the others. Only one man caught my eye.

His nondescript clothes made it hard to guess his profession, but he had stepped back against the wall to clear our path. Some sort of servant, then. Unlike the others, however, he watched me with a gleam in his eyes I found hard to decipher. It sent a small shiver down my back even as I frowned, something tugging at my memory. It was almost as if the man were familiar. I was good with people and faces, but I couldn't place this one. And I could think of no reason I would recognize an Eldonian palace servant. Unless he had accompanied his monarchs to the wedding?

We reached my suite shortly after, and I tucked the thought away for later examination. Most likely it meant nothing. But my spy-sister Celeste had taught me never to ignore my instincts. And that the smallest details sometimes turn out to be the most important.

CHAPTER 7

*B*ack in my room, my attention was swept up into preparations for the upcoming welcome event. I had lost even more time than I realized, and my maids pounced on me as soon as I appeared. Before long, they had my hair elaborately arranged, and my gown and jewelry in place. I surveyed myself in my full-length mirror with a satisfied smile. I twisted to see the glowing skin of my upper bare back. If I wanted to make an impression—and I did—I was confident of my success. Again, a certain face dropped into my thoughts, but I pushed it away. Prince Oliver was an intriguing mystery, to be sure, but it was the Eldonian court as a whole that I wished to sweep off its feet.

When I entered the receiving hall where the dinner guests gathered, a herald announced my arrival. All talk hushed, and everyone turned to regard me. I paused, allowing everyone to look their fill, and then swept into the room. Heading straight for the king and queen, I dropped into the curtsy I would have liked to give that morning.

Everything went perfectly, and it should have been a triumphant moment. But the expressions around me hadn't shifted much from their previous polite disinterest. The king and queen both smiled a distant welcome, and my gaze moved to the prince standing at his father's side. He looked frozen, but not in the way he used to do when I first met him in Marin, and later Palinar. More like he had been immobilized by shock. And there was no mistaking the gleam of admiration in his eyes.

I hid a satisfied smile. That was the sort of response I had been trying to achieve, and for some reason receiving it from him was enough.

He finally seemed to shake himself free of his stupefaction, moving toward me. But they must have been waiting on my arrival because the herald stepped forward again to announce the meal. The noise of voices and movement drowned out any attempt to talk, so I had to settle for taking Prince Oliver's arm and allowing him to lead me into the banquet hall behind his parents.

The royal table sat on a small dais, and I had been given the place of honor beside the king. Oliver sat on my other side, but our proximity to King Leopold made any private conversation impossible. Instead, a general discussion of the various places of interest I might like to visit occupied us all. Although even that conversation often dropped into silence and required prodding from me to regain momentum.

I expressed my admiration and amazement at their capital city, and Oliver promised to take me on a tour the next day. Apparently I could be carried about on a special chair, but I assured him I was fit enough to make the journey on my own two feet, despite the steep inclines.

The topic of our recent abduction came up only briefly, and again King Leopold showed no great interest in our abductor.

"You don't intend to enact any punishment on Lord Tree-stone?" I asked, my curiosity growing too much for me.

"Punishment?" The king raised both his eyebrows at me. "That hardly seems necessary when everything has turned out just fine."

"The poor man is immured in the far south, away from the heart of our beautiful domain," said Queen Camille. "Surely that is punishment enough."

If she was making a joke, her expression didn't show it. But I could hardly think she was serious.

Really? For treason? For abducting your own children? I closed my mouth on all the questions I wanted to ask. Hopefully I could get some answers from Oliver later. Except my confidence in that possibility had diminished somewhat as I watched him during the meal. The spark of concern and confusion that I had seen in him during our carriage ride—and even on our arrival at the palace—seemed to have disappeared. He nodded agreeably with his parents' words, and I could detect no sign of deeper thought in his eyes.

Only when his gaze rested on me did I see that hint of warmth that had so animated his face for the brief period between the attack on our traveling party and our return to the capital. I hated to see him sinking back into frozen unconcern, and my frustration at this whole place was growing into a raging torrent inside me.

And yet, despite my feelings—and certainly without my control—every time his eyes rested on me with that glint of lingering fire, I felt an answering trail of warmth shoot from my chest down into my hands. Toward the end of the meal, he leaned in, after a particularly brilliant smile from me, to whisper something into my ear, and I felt his warm breath against my skin. Without warning, a puff of heated air swept around my hands, rattling the cutlery and crockery on the table in front of me.

I gasped and jumped, and Oliver gave me a strange look, glancing between the table and my face. I gulped and plastered the smile back in place, but his frown remained. Thankfully the king had been occupied in a quiet conversation with the queen and appeared not to have noticed.

Whatever this new power was, I needed to get it under

control. And fast. I had thought desperation—or perhaps fear, or even anger—drew it out, but I felt none of those emotions now.

We talked of nothing of consequence for the rest of the meal, but the admiration in Oliver's eyes had been joined by a lurking question. And though I still knew I needed to find a chance to talk to him, I now feared the questions wouldn't all be coming from me. And I wasn't ready to give this strange prince, who seemed to alternate between heat and ice, any answers of my own.

When the main courses had all been cleared away, desserts were brought out, accompanied by a long line of ice sculptures. The carved shapes were easily the most intricate and beautiful I had ever seen, and the king gave me permission to leave the dais and wander among the other tables to admire them.

Oliver accompanied me, introducing me to other diners seemingly at random. But their faces were all so bland and empty that I found myself struggling to keep the introductions straight —not a usual problem for me.

"We hold an annual ice carving competition every winter," he told me when I stopped to admire a particularly beautiful one. "That was carved by this year's winner. I wish you had been here to see it."

I murmured polite agreement—and I would have liked to see the competition. But not at the expense of being here in the dead of winter. I shivered. The banquet hall itself was well heated, but I still found myself wishing for the bright flames of the fire in my chambers. Even in the warm palace, the cold seemed to find a way to creep icy fingers deep into my bones.

Oliver placed a light hand on the small of my back to lead me around another table, and his thumb brushed against my bare skin. A shot of fire burned through me, pushing out the earlier ice, and I barely refrained from jerking away. He looked back at me, something stirring in his eyes, and I forced a quick smile, pointing at another sculpture and taking the chance to put some distance between us.

But though we didn't touch again, I could feel a coiling warmth brewing inside me for the rest of the evening. It filled me with a barely repressed excitement—a feeling bordering close on fear. My godmother had gifted me with something extraordinary, and I would learn its secrets and force it to obey me. I was determined.

When the evening finally ended, I said my goodnights with as much attention as I could muster and had turned toward my suite when Oliver's voice spoke behind me.

"Do you know the way back on your own?"

I turned to him, realizing in my distraction that I hadn't even considered how to get there. I thought I could probably find it. Maybe. I cast him a considering look.

"I'm not sure that I do, to be honest." I smiled at him, looking up through my lashes. "I don't suppose you would be willing to show me?"

"More than willing," he said gallantly and offered me his arm.

I ignored it and fell into step beside him. I said nothing until we had left the others behind and found ourselves alone in yet another long corridor.

My smile fell away as I turned to him, still careful not to so much as brush against him. I didn't want to accidentally set him on fire or something.

"What is going on Oliver? Lord Treestone attacked you. He abducted both your sisters, along with me—a royal guest under your protection—and your father intends to do nothing about it? Not even a show of punishment?"

He looked at me with the faintest hint of curiosity. "Are you offended Celine? I got the strong impression you were somewhat sympathetic to the renegade lord."

I huffed in frustration, throwing up my hands. "No, I'm not offended! I'm frustrated. And confused. What is going on here?

Because whatever it is, Lord Treestone is right—it's certainly not natural."

Oliver laughed softly. "Such heat, Your Highness! You'll exhaust yourself."

I stared at him in disbelief. Had I imagined the change I'd seen in him? The hesitation and curiosity when he told his story in the carriage?

But even as we stood there, our steps having faltered at some point during our exchange, I saw a light in his eyes as they roamed over my expression. I knew that anger brought color to my cheeks and a sparkle to my eye, and apparently he had noticed. My eyes narrowed. He had never noticed or admired me in Marin or Palinar when we had occasionally crossed paths. Something had definitely changed.

Without thought, I leaned forward and placed both my hands flat against his chest.

"Oliver, this is madness! Wake up!" And as I said the words, I pushed with all my mental might, willing him to snap out of whatever fog seemed to hold him captive. But it wasn't my thoughts which rushed down my arms and out of my hands into his chest—it was the warmth that had been building throughout the evening and roiling inside me.

For a moment he lit up almost as bright as daylight, a golden glow outlining his tall form. And then it was gone, and he was staggering back. For a step I moved with him, without thinking, and then I realized my hands were still pressed all too intimately against his muscular chest, and I stepped back myself.

We stood in silence, staring at each other, Oliver sucking in deep, gasping breaths.

"I...What...What happened?" he managed to choke out.

"I don't know." I bit my lip. "I don't know."

"What did you do to me?" He watched me with wide eyes.

I shrugged helplessly. "I really don't know." I took a deep

61

breath. "But I do know something very strange has been happening in Eldon." I watched him closely. "Do you see that?"

He blinked and rubbed a shaking hand across his face. "Yes… Yes…" His voice faltered, and he inhaled slowly, before dropping his hand and fixing me with a look that made me stumble back another step.

I had thought I saw warmth in his eyes during the attack on our traveling party, and again at Lord Treestone's castle. But it was nothing to the way they lit his face now. The bright sapphire seemed like a flaming fire that transformed his pale face, and even his cheeks held more color now, too. If I had thought him coldly handsome before, it was nothing to how he looked now, his face alight with passion and strength.

He raised a hand to the side of his head as if it hurt him. "I remember…I remember meeting you in Marin, at the Princess Tourney. And again at the wedding in Palinar."

He paused, and I nodded silently.

"But…" He shook his head. "I feel as if I hadn't really seen you. You're…" He flushed and looked away from me.

As he broke our eye contact, I took a deep breath and steadied myself. There could not be the faintest question now that something had been wrong with him before. This was not the same prince who I had met before. He wasn't even the same one who had helped rescue us from the castle—although he was closer to that one.

He shook himself and stood taller, looking back toward me again. "All those memories, from before…they're still there, but it's like trying to remember something from a dream. It's all hazy, and the details seem fuzzy." He frowned. "My memories after the attack are stronger, although they start to fade again once we returned to the palace."

I nodded. "You seemed different, then. More…active? To be honest, I hadn't been expecting you to come rescue us."

He sucked in a sudden breath, his hands balling into fists. "No one was coming to rescue you! And if I had not…" He turned to survey the empty corridor before spinning back to face me. "That so-called lord deserves to be whipped, and if my father does not intend to act…"

"No." I shook my head quickly, stepping toward him although not quite far enough to bridge the gap between us. "Lord Treestone did not intend to harm us. I'm sure of that. He is worried for your kingdom—and can you really fault him for that?"

I watched him with raised eyebrows, and he slowly relaxed. At last he sighed.

"No, I suppose I cannot. Perhaps I should be glad that someone at least still seems to care about *something*. I cannot describe to you how it felt…as if nothing was worth the effort. As if nothing really mattered. At least how it felt until…" He looked over at me, and I quickly looked away. "Until you came here."

Silence stretched between us.

"How did you do it, Celine? *What* did you do?"

I shrugged. "I don't know." It was the truth. Of sorts. But I wasn't ready to share my secrets with this new prince who stood before me. His transformation seemed complete this time, and I hoped it would last. But he had changed too many times in the last few days for me to feel certain of anything.

"You were showing me to my rooms," I said at last, gesturing down the corridor.

Reluctantly he nodded and resumed walking. I kept pace with him, sneaking sideways glances at this new Oliver. He seemed lost in thought, and I could hardly blame him. It must be a lot to take in.

When we reached my door, he took my hand. I flinched but didn't pull away, and nothing happened. No heat, no fire, no golden glow. I drew a shaky breath and focused on his face.

"I will leave you for now, but we will talk again."

A threat or a promise? It felt a little like both. I forced a smile.

A promise I could handle, and I had never backed down from a threat before.

"You promised to show me the city tomorrow, remember? I'm sure there will be plenty of opportunity for talking then."

He looked like he wanted to say more, but eventually he merely nodded, bowing over my hand. For a moment I thought he would kiss it, but his lips didn't quite reach my skin.

As I closed the door behind me, I shook away a foolish feeling of disappointment. Until I learned to control this fire inside me, I was better off keeping a distance from this prince whose eyes seemed to burn as strongly as my new and unknown power.

CHAPTER 8

*T*he next morning I dressed in a practical dress and my most comfortable boots. I had been working on my physical fitness ever since I got swept up in my older sister's spy network at the age of fourteen, but those mountain roads looked steep. I didn't want to disgrace myself.

I had slept badly. Once alone in my room, I tried to call on my new powers, but all my efforts to expel light or heat or wind from my hands ended in failure. And then my dreams had been haunted by the many different faces of the unexpected Prince Oliver. By the time I awoke, I was entirely uncertain which prince would greet me today.

But when we met in the entrance hall at mid-morning, one glance was enough to tell me that none of his new fire had dimmed. His eyes were bright and the aura of strength which I had seen for the first time only the night before remained.

Something in his eyes flashed at the sight of me, and he smiled, coming forward to greet me warmly.

"I'm glad to see I didn't frighten you off last night." He bowed over my hand.

I raised an eyebrow. "I'm not so easily scared, I assure you, Your Highness."

"Oliver, please," he said. "I remember enough to know that's what you were calling me before, Celine."

I shook my head at his bold use of my own name and conceded the point. I didn't want to admit to him that I felt as if I were dealing with an entirely new person.

He led me out of the palace and around behind it. The palace wall only encircled the front and sides of the building, blending almost seamlessly into the mountain itself which guarded the rear of the palace. A steep road, wider than I had been expecting, zigzagged up the mountain, starting from the very back of the palace. A number of people traveled it, some pulling small carts, others leading slightly bigger carts pulled by goats. When I gazed upward, I even saw a lady being carried on an elaborate chair mounted on two long poles. The poles rested on the shoulders of four strong men, dressed as footmen in a livery I didn't recognize.

Oliver followed my gaze. "It's not too late if you would like me to fetch a chair for you."

I grinned. "I'm no more feeble than I am easily scared. Oliver," I added for good measure.

He laughed. "I suspected as much. In that case, let us be off."

I needed every bit of my conditioning to keep from puffing as we wound our way up the mountainside using a maze of roads and stairs carved into the rock face. I could only be glad so many months had passed since my broken ankle, and that I had lost no time in regaining my shape once it healed. Oliver certainly showed no discomfort despite the steep inclines.

We passed every type of business from blacksmiths and grocers to tanners. Several roads were lined with shopfronts, replacing the more traditional market squares. They looked like normal buildings from the front, except they were so close to the mountain face it didn't seem there could possibly be room inside to move, let alone store any goods. But I soon saw that it was just as Oliver had told me when we arrived. The shops stretched back into the mountain itself, looking remarkably like an ordinary building from the inside except for the solid stone walls and lack of windows.

As we got higher, we found a number of noble residences, some of them using the same stone as the palace to decorate their facades. I supposed they could afford to position themselves higher up the mountain if they had servants to carry them up and down in chairs.

"Isn't all of this snowed in during the winter?" I asked, as we wound through a less affluent section of the city where the building fronts crowded close together and contained little orna-mentation. Some were no more than wooden doors and shutters over what looked like cave openings.

"This is one of the smallest mountains and is right at the foothills of our main range," Oliver explained.

It didn't look like a small mountain to me, but I hoped my face didn't show my incredulity. Mists mostly obscured the far distance, but they had parted once to show me a glimpse of higher peaks behind.

"We get snow, of course," he continued, "but not normally so much that it cannot be cleared from the roads. And with most of the buildings inside the mountain itself, even in the case of a heavy snowfall or avalanche, the people are out of harm's way."

"But wouldn't they be trapped inside?"

"We have lived here for many generations now," said Oliver. "All of the buildings connect to at least one tunnel. When the weather is truly bad, the palace can be cut off for several days, but the inhabitants of the city simply use the internal roads."

The idea fascinated me, but I also hated the thought of going days without seeing the sun. Something of my distaste must have shown on my face because Oliver grinned.

"Yes, most people prefer to use the open roads if the weather possibly allows. Especially the nobles, since some of them keep horses up here, and the horses hate the tunnels."

"It's an incredible place," I said. "I never imagined anything like it."

Oliver looked around, pride in his gaze as he surveyed his city. "You can't imagine my surprise as a child the first time I visited a flat city. I didn't know what to make of it and kept asking my mother what happened when it snowed too much to go outside."

He laughed. "I couldn't quite understand it when she told me that in some places it never snows at all."

I shivered involuntarily. "My home kingdom of Lanover is one of those. In the south it's impossibly humid and hot all year round. We have jungles and deserts instead of snow."

A faraway look entered Oliver's eyes. "I would like to see it someday."

"My family would welcome you for a visit anytime, I'm sure." I smiled at him even as I tried to work out why the image of Oliver in my home unsettled me so much.

Perhaps it was because I was already feeling unsettled, or maybe it was some other instinct, but something made me turn around and scan the road around us. I felt the invisible presence of eyes on my back.

And, sure enough, I got a quick glimpse of a man watching me, before he turned and started up a steep stairway branching off the road. I frowned. It had only been a moment, but I was sure it had been the same man from the palace the day before. He wore identical nondescript clothing, and his eyes had held the same curiosity.

My skin prickled. Of course, it wasn't ridiculous to think that a palace servant might have an errand in the city. Or that, in an entire day of wandering, we might cross paths with such a person. But still…something about him irritated me. Where had I seen him before?

"Would you like to see the tunnels?" Oliver asked, unaware of my inner perturbation.

I pulled my attention back to him. "I would love to."

He led me back a little way, and into a brightly lit tavern. The owner called a cheery greeting, apparently unsurprised to see the crown prince in her establishment. Oliver waved back but didn't stop to talk, leading me past the tables and chairs and into a back room.

He opened a perfectly ordinary looking door, revealing a large stone passage. It was nothing like the bright stone corridors of the palace. This one was rough-hewn, the walls made of the gray stone of the mountain. No natural light reached back here, all illumination coming from a series of lanterns hung at regular intervals.

"Everyone who works or resides in the city pays taxes to contribute toward maintaining the tunnels and the lanterns," said Oliver when he saw my speculative gaze resting on the lights. "There's a whole team of people whose sole job is to tend to them."

I nodded and shivered as I imagined what it would be like if the lanterns were allowed to go out. At least dug back into the mountain, the air had a more consistent temperature. It was cold, but not freezing, and there was no wind to pierce through your clothes and into your bones.

Oliver strode confidently down the tunnel, and I followed, watching the people around me with interest. The passage was wide enough to allow the carts I had seen outside to pass through, although the traffic here seemed lighter. Most people must be taking advantage of the opportunity to escape outside.

The further we walked, the more lost I became.

"Do you have a problem with people getting lost back here?" I asked.

The look Oliver gave me was all too knowing, and I raised my chin defiantly. I wasn't nervous for *myself*.

We walked past an opening, and he stopped to point out a series of letters and numbers etched into the wall beside it. "These are like a map of sorts. Or directions. Children learn how to interpret them as soon as they learn to read."

Now that he had pointed them out, I saw that they were everywhere. Every turn, every opening, every branch of the passage had a code against it. And I could see how necessary they must be. The longer we stayed down here, the more everything began to look the same, and I lost any sense of distance or even direction. I could tell that we were slowly moving downward, though, so I assumed Oliver was leading us back toward the palace.

"Do the tunnels extend all the way into the palace?"

Oliver quickly shook his head. "Apparently when the city was first built there was some talk of it, but it was deemed too dangerous. The royals at the time didn't want direct access from the city to the palace."

I narrowed my eyes when I saw a slight twitch across his face. "Very sensible. Of course, it would also be sensible to have a bolt-hole of sorts. A small passage known only to the royal family, perhaps. Not one used for general traffic."

Aha. This time the twitch was slightly more pronounced. I smiled to myself, but when I caught him watching me suspiciously, it grew into something closer to a smirk. He said nothing to confirm my certainty, but he did give me a rueful smile and a slight shake of his head before turning the conversation.

When we passed the next turning, he paused, his eyes flickering to the marked directions.

"I could have sworn..." he muttered to himself before shrugging and turning to lead me down the marked passage.

"Sworn what?" I asked, a feeling of foreboding sweeping over me.

"We're close enough to the palace now, that I thought I remembered the way. But don't worry, the markings were clear."

He smiled reassuringly at me. "That's why we have them. No one has to rely on their memory. It's easy for it to play tricks on you down here."

We were still moving downward, so I tried to relax and trust in his words. But still the feeling of unease remained, and I noticed that this passage seemed deserted.

And I hadn't seen any openings to other tunnels. I stopped.

"Are you sure? With everything going on—"

I never finished the sentence.

A loud rumbling sounded, and a rush of air blew past us, blowing out some of the lanterns. The distant noise of other traffic cut off, and dust billowed around us.

Oliver took off running back in the direction we had come, and I followed close on his heels. We didn't have to run far before we hit darkness. He didn't stop, hurtling forward. I followed, heedless of where I was going, until I collided with his back.

He seemed to be braced against something since he held steady, keeping us both from falling. I splayed my hands across his back—heedless of both propriety and my unpredictable powers—and worked my way over his shoulders and then down his outstretched arm.

Until I felt what he was feeling. A solid wall of stone made up of boulders of various shapes and sizes. He hadn't mentioned anything about cave ins during our travels, and I had seen no sign of any elsewhere.

"I'm guessing this passage isn't the way to the palace," I said.

CHAPTER 9

*O*liver sighed. "No, I don't think it is."

I kept a tight rein on myself, refusing to give in to panic. We would find a way out of here. Or someone would come looking for us.

I bit my lip. Actually, on second thought, perhaps best not to rely on that possibility.

I realized with a start that I was pressed up against Oliver, one hand on the fallen rock, but the other still grasping his shoulder. I stepped back quickly, an unaccustomed flush stealing up my cheeks. At least he couldn't see it in the dark.

"Do you think…" I cleared my throat and tried again. "Do you think we should go and fetch a lantern at least?"

Oliver didn't say anything, but he started to move, returning the way we had come from the sound of it. We trekked in silence, the darkness lightening as we approached the first lit lantern. He detached it from the wall, and we turned to walk back the same path.

It looked exactly as we had expected. The tunnel, narrower than many we had traveled, was completely blocked by the fallen stones. It was actually a wonder we hadn't tripped over any of the loose ones as we had run this way in the dark.

"Well, I can't see us digging through that," said Oliver matter-of-factly.

Reluctantly I had to agree with him, and a small spark of fear lodged in my gut. I pushed it down.

"I suppose we'll have to see what we can find in the other direction, then," I said.

He nodded, and once again we traipsed back along the now well-worn path in the other direction. As we walked I tried to think of options. I couldn't see any way we could move those rocks on our own. So we had to hope this passage actually led somewhere.

Of course, if it did, it might not be somewhere we were too eager to go. Someone had changed the markings to direct us down here, after all...

"I'm so sorry, Celine." Oliver's words jerked me from my imaginings.

"For what?" I looked at him blankly.

"For leading us down here. I should have known better." He grimaced. "I did know better. I should have trusted myself."

I shrugged. "Don't be silly. Why would you suspect that someone had changed the tunnel markings?"

"You're very calm."

"Would you prefer me to go into hysterics? I could probably manage it if you liked."

He shook his head quickly. "Please—no hysterics."

I tapped my chin thoughtfully. "I've never actually tried it, but I think I could do excellent hysterics. I have just the right flair for the dramatic." I grinned. "Or so my family have always assured me."

He glanced sideways at me. "I suppose if we disappear into the tunnels and never return, your family might send their army against Eldon. I can't imagine what would happen to my kingdom if they do, given its current state."

"Look who's being dramatic now." I kept my voice light despite my sense of disquiet. I didn't want my kingdom getting involved with this strange place. Not until I'd worked out what was going on and could be sure the strange enchantment—whatever it was—wouldn't spread.

We had walked for some distance before we discovered that my fears were unfounded. Well, one of my fears anyway. This hadn't been a ploy to force us somewhere we didn't want to be. The tunnel ended in a wall of solid rock.

Which, of course, meant something far worse. Someone didn't want us to escape these tunnels alive.

"I was afraid of this," said Oliver grimly. "There are dead end branches everywhere, although they're all marked as such, of course. And they usually have fewer lanterns. Just enough to keep them from becoming dark pockets perfect for crime." He crossed over to the wall to examine the lanterns there. "It looks like some of these have only been newly fixed. All part of the ploy, no doubt."

I sighed. "And I don't suppose you have any idea who would want to assassinate us?"

He shrugged helplessly. "No more idea than who is behind enchanting and destroying my kingdom."

"Well." I smiled. "When you put it that way, at least we can console ourselves that we likely don't have any new enemies. And what's a little assassination attempt against the enchantment and destruction of an entire kingdom?"

"I'm very reassured," he said dryly.

Without talking about it, we both turned to walk back to the cave in. It seemed a slightly less hopeless situation than this solid rock wall.

Just as we reached it, Oliver tripped over one of the small rocks that had rolled forward from the cave in and dropped the lantern. With the smash of breaking glass, it went out, plunging us back into darkness.

I jumped, and the earlier spark of fear that had taken up residence inside me flared. Only it rushed all the way out of me, jumping from my fingertips as small tongues of flame.

I gasped, staring at my now illuminated hand for a brief second before they disappeared. Darkness and near silence returned—broken only by my panting breaths. I pressed my fingertips against my palms, but they felt cool now, and I could feel no burns.

"Celine," Oliver whispered. "What was that?"

"Umm…I don't know?"

"Uh uh, you're not getting out of it that easily this time. *What was that?*"

I grimaced, but he couldn't see me in the dark. "Can we at least fetch another lantern?"

"Do we need one? Maybe you could just light the way for us." His voice sounded hard, and I couldn't tell if he was angry or just intrigued.

I concentrated on my fingertips, but just like all the other times I had tried to do it consciously, nothing happened.

I sighed. "We definitely need a lantern."

For a moment neither of us moved, and then I heard the crunch of Oliver's boots against glass. "Stay here. I'll get one and come back."

I listened to the sound of his retreating footsteps, and then watched for a distant glow. It appeared quickly and grew rapidly as he jogged back toward me. When he stopped in front of me, I could see that his expression was one of interest overlaid with a deep wariness.

"All right, you've got your light. Now tell me what that was. Was it the same as what you did to me last night?"

I shrugged helplessly. "No. Yes. Maybe?"

He gave me an unimpressed look, and I couldn't help a short laugh.

"In all honesty, I truly don't have much more of an idea than you. This is all very new to me." I quickly outlined my family's experience with Christening gifts, and my encounter with my godmother at the twins' wedding.

"I didn't know what she meant at the time by *the gift of fire*. It was all very cryptic. I still don't understand it exactly."

"It seemed pretty literal to me." Oliver's voice sounded a little awed, and it made me uncomfortable.

"It's been months since then, and this is the first flame I've seen," I snapped before taking a deep breath and immediately feeling sorry for my tone. "Sorry. It's just...I've never done that before. Flames out of my fingers is totally new for me."

"Well, what have you done? Wait. That hot wind when we were attacked! That was you?"

Reluctantly I nodded. "That was the first time I suspected my godmother may not have been talking about some figurative light of perception, or something."

"Hmmm..." He set the lantern carefully on the ground so he could pace back and forth in the tunnel. "That was a strong wind. Maybe even strong enough to dislodge some of these rocks."

He looked and me hopefully, and I winced.

"Maybe. Unfortunately I haven't managed to do anything on purpose yet. It doesn't seem to like coming to my rescue." I glared at my hands as if they were the cause of the problem.

Oliver paused in front of me. "So what does trigger it?"

I shrugged. "I haven't been able to figure that out." I looked at his expression. "Not for want of trying!" I snapped again, and he held up his hands placatingly.

"Maybe we can work it out together." He gestured for me to sit, only to stop when he saw the smashed glass beneath our feet. Instead he led me over to the wall, and we sat side-by-side with our backs against it.

I leaned my head against the cool rock, closed my eyes and tried to think.

"It seems to be connected somehow with a sort of…warm feeling that just appears inside me." I opened my eyes and waved vaguely toward my middle. "And sometimes that warmth just seems to shoot out of my hands. Only I don't seem to be able to control when it comes, or when it flames outward, either."

Oliver's legs were propped up in front of him, his arms resting on his knees, his hands dangling as he gazed unseeing at the far side of the tunnel. Eventually he turned his head to look at me.

"Let's go through it. What exactly was happening each time you got this warm feeling?"

I frowned as I tried to remember. "Well, as I said, the first time was when we were attacked. Only it wasn't as soon as we were attacked."

"It's strange for me to remember the attack," said Oliver. "The first part is hazy, and then suddenly it's like the memories clear. But not as clear as my memories of this morning. The change came at the same time as the wind. When one of the men was attaching a lead rope to my horse…"

His words trailed off as he focused on my face. I could read the question in his eyes, and I hesitated to admit what my true feelings had been in that moment.

Except then I realized how he might interpret my hesitation, and annoyance filled me. It hadn't been any great concern for him that had occupied my mind in that moment…

"I was watching from the carriage," I said.

"I remember, I saw you just before my horse reared."

"I was angry with you." I said the words in a rush. "Angry that you were so passive…so calmly accepting of their control. I wanted you to fight them, to push them away. Only you didn't. So I thrust out my own hands—in frustration more than anything—and then…"

"Oh…" He paused before recovering. "Perhaps anger is the key then. Were you feeling angry just before, with the flames?"

"Well…" I tried to think it through. "I mean I'm generally angry with whoever stuck us in here, I suppose. But in that specific moment I was more startled than anything. You'd just dropped the lantern, and it made such a smash."

"If it was merely being startled, I would have expected that gale to strike as soon as we were attacked, though," said Oliver, obviously having as little success puzzling it through as I had previously.

I thought about his words. "The warmth didn't start until after the attack, though," I said slowly. "And that bit seems to be consistent. The warmth comes first."

"All right, so you were already feeling the warmth when I dropped the lantern. When did that start?"

I tried to pinpoint it in my memory. "I think it was when we first brought the lantern and saw the cave in. It was just a small spark at that point. And I think…I think it came with a feeling of fear." I didn't like to admit to being afraid, but we would never get to the bottom of this if I wasn't honest.

"Well, surely you were afraid when we were attacked. Maybe fear is the key?"

I had already considered that possibility. But it didn't fit with every instance when my new powers had manifested. I kept my head bowed, my eyes on my lap to hide the faint flush when I remembered the breeze which had rocked my table setting during the banquet. It certainly hadn't been fear motivating me then. But I wasn't about to mention it. Oliver didn't seem to remember that occasion, and I had no desire to analyze my feelings in that instance with any depth. Certainly not with him, anyway.

I focused my thoughts back on the attack by Lord Treestone's men.

"You know…" I said slowly, "…the warmth didn't start when I

felt the first stirrings of fear. First I felt fear, and then I looked at your sisters, and I felt...well, pity." I glanced at him sideways, but he didn't look offended, so I went on. "There just seemed to be something so clearly wrong with them that they had no reaction to a situation like that. And I felt this unexpected surge of intense pity accompanied by a warmth." I nodded, the memory clearing in my mind. "Only then it became more like anger that none of you seemed concerned about me, either. And then when you did nothing while they tried to lead you away, it all sort of over-whelmed me."

"Pity, anger, fear...Maybe it's not about the specific emotion. Maybe it's just about strong emotion."

I considered his suggestion. "It did seem like the warmth grew as my emotions became fiercer." I thought through the other instances. I still wasn't willing to examine the examples in the banquet hall too closely, but the warmth that had begun growing then had only fully surged out afterward, in the hallway. And that part came easily to mind.

"I was certainly feeling frustrated and angry when I commanded you to wake up last night. I was so desperate for you to come out of whatever enchantment seemed to keep you in thrall. It was infuriating that you seemed to come out of it briefly only to fall back under again."

He looked at me, really looked at me.

"Have I thanked you for that yet?" he asked, his voice soft. "That wind you sent through me on that first day dislodged it a little, but the fog came back again when we returned to the palace. I'm sure I would be back to my fully detached state again by now if you hadn't freed me."

I flushed a little. "I really don't think I can claim credit." I held my hands up in front of me and wiggled my fingers. "I don't seem to be in control of what they do."

"Maybe not, but I can't believe it was coincidence that you touched me and commanded me to wake up, and I did. I think you might have more control than you realize. Or your emotions do, anyway."

He stood up suddenly and reached down to pull me up as well. "Come on, then. Let's give it a try."

I stood up and joined him facing the fallen stones, but I couldn't help glancing at him dubiously. "Try what exactly?"

"Whether strong emotion might bring out another gale force wind." And with no further warning, he pulled me against him, one hand around my waist, and the other around my neck, and kissed me firmly on the mouth.

CHAPTER 10

$\mathcal{H}$is arms around me were strong, and his lips warm, and if I thought his thumb on my back the night before ignited a fire, it was nothing to the inferno that immediately sprang to life inside me. I wasn't entirely sure what emotions were fueling it, but it was stronger than any I had previously felt.

And I didn't intend to waste it.

Ripping myself from his grasp, I turned and thrust both hands toward the pile of rocks, imagining them as giant battering rams that could sweep the rocks away. A hot wind burst from my palms, whipping around me and nearly sending Oliver to the ground, although I remained steady, my skirts merely twining around my legs.

The gale hit the stones with terrible force, and they exploded outward away from us. A second loud rumbling, like the one that had accompanied the initial cave in, rang around us, settling slowly into the gentle patter of stones.

Dust filled the air, and I waved my hands in front of my face and coughed. As it settled, I drew a deep gasping breath. Rocks still lay scattered all around, but a clear path now showed, leading through to a further stretch of tunnel, and undoubtedly the main passage beyond.

I drew a second breath before spinning around and slapping Oliver hard across the cheek. He made no move to defend himself, merely grinning down at me.

"Sorry about that. Or, well…" He gestured at the cleared stones. "Maybe not so sorry?"

I glared at him. "What did you think you were doing?"

In truth I was too grateful it had worked to be really angry. But my dignity required I at least make a show of it.

"Well, I figured you were already feeling as much fear as you could, given the circumstances. And it didn't seem to be enough." He leaned in slightly and lowered his voice. "And I remembered that little breeze at the banquet."

I bit my lip. So he *had* remembered that, after all. Thankfully he said nothing more about it, merely straightening, his eyes still laughing down at me.

"I figured it was worth a try. And that it couldn't really lose. If I had it wrong, then anger and shock might do the trick just as well."

He looked at me expectantly, as if waiting for me to tell him which emotion had fueled the burst of power, but I merely turned and stalked off. As I picked my way over the rocks, he scrambled to collect the lantern and follow.

Nothing would have made me reward him with an exposition on my feelings, but the truth was that I didn't know which emotion it had been myself. Well, other than shock. That one had certainly been there.

When we made it to the intersection with the original tunnel, Oliver stopped to examine the markings on the one we had just exited.

"They did a good job of changing them."

"Nothing about this was the work of a moment," I said grimly. "But then we're dealing with someone with the power to enchant an entire kingdom. I guess we shouldn't be surprised."

His shoulders slumped a little. "No, I suppose not." He looked over at me. "I say we get back to the palace before anything else disastrous happens."

"No arguments from me." I eyed him. "Assuming you can remember the way, of course."

"I'm leading us straight to an exit tunnel," he assured me. "We can go the rest of the way outside."

I tried not to let the relief show on my face. I had had more than enough of these tunnels for one day. Or one lifetime, more like.

We only walked a short distance before Oliver stopped at a large wooden door and pulled it open. I followed him into a large store full of pottery. He nodded a polite greeting to the storekeeper but led me straight outside.

I drew in a deep breath of fresh air and held my face up to the remaining rays of the sun. It looked like we had lost most of the day in there, and my stomach rumbled as if just noticing the passage of time.

"Come on," said Oliver. "Let's get back. I don't want to miss dinner as well."

In the light of day I could see that dust and dirt covered us both. And somewhere along the way I seemed to have ripped my skirt. I sighed. Another one ruined. At this rate I'd have no wardrobe left soon.

I was becoming familiar enough with the detachment of the locals that I wasn't in the least surprised when we wandered into the entrance hall in such a bedraggled state and received no response from anyone. Oliver, however, was still new to it all. At least from this side of it, anyway. He looked around and actually shivered a little as he watched the blank and uninterested face of a passing servant.

"It's almost creepy," he said.

"Welcome to my world." I shook my head. "Just wait until you get the same reaction to being abducted."

He sucked in a breath. "Poor Emmeline and Giselle. They're not like that normally, I swear. Well…" He chuckled, looking every inch the older brother—a look I knew all too well. "Emmeline is a little like that. Far too sensible and serious for her age. But Giselle…" He shook his head. "I wish you could properly meet her."

"And I shall once we work out how to defeat this thing—whatever it is." I tried to inject more confidence into my voice than I really felt.

Oliver met my gaze, and then his eyes fell to my hands. "You know I actually think we might have a chance. Now that we have you on our side." His warm smile reminded me forcibly of the feel of his lips against mine, and I clamped down without thought on a flicker of warmth in my middle. To my surprise it went out instantly.

A slow smile spread across my face. Maybe I was actually getting the hang of this thing. I remembered the power that had brushed aside a cave in. Maybe he was right. Maybe we did have a chance.

~

The next day I was eager to try out my powers again, but I had no idea how—or where—to start. And when Emmeline and Giselle turned up to my rooms to invite me to spend the day with them, I couldn't think of a reason to refuse.

As the day crawled by in their uninteresting company, I wished I had been quicker with an excuse. I kept thinking of what Oliver had said about them. How different this would be if they were their true selves. I tried to see hints of it in their words or actions, but the honest truth was that I could barely distinguish between them.

Emmeline, at seventeen, was quite a bit taller than her fifteen-year-old sister. And although their fair coloring was identical, their features were different enough. And yet their manner made them almost into twins.

They gave me a never-ending tour of the palace, the highlight of which was a delicious midday meal, served in a small but elegant dining room. I had hoped Oliver would join us—so I could have some real conversation if nothing else—but I saw no sign of him all day.

I hoped I would be able to escape in the afternoon, but it seemed that we had seen only half the palace before lunch. I sighed and trailed after them again. At least life as a princess had given me some experience with surviving boring days full of unavoidable responsibilities. Even as the youngest of seven, I had been required to attend a myriad of official functions. And the number of them had only increased as more and more of my older siblings had married and moved out of Lanover.

I thought a little wistfully of the years I spent running through my own palace with the two sisters directly above me—Cordelia and Celeste. We had been good friends before they both married and moved to Northhelm. I examined Emmeline and Giselle from the back. Did they have the potential to be equally good friends? Once they were freed, of course.

The thought brought another puzzle to my mind. That first gale I had produced had shaken something loose in Oliver, even if it hadn't completely freed him. But no one else seemed to have been affected by it. Why?

I pondered the question, not listening to Emmeline's drone as she conducted the tour, until I looked around and realized we were in a display room of some kind. I turned my attention back to her words in time to hear this was where the Eldonian royal family both stored and displayed their most valued treasures.

I wandered around the room with interest, examining several crowns, and an intricate golden scepter. Two of the small pedestals held ordinary-looking objects, protected under glass domes. One was a simple slipper, and another a wooden flagon, interesting only for the simple carvings that decorated it.

The pedestals and domes reminded me instantly of the empty one I had seen next to the portrait on my first day. Seeing the same display case here only confirmed my impression that the dome was meant to hold something.

At my questioning look, Emmeline explained that they were ancient godmother artifacts. "Their enchantment is long gone," she said. "But they hold great value to us still as relics of the past."

Was there an object missing from the pedestal in the corridor then? I was about to ask Emmeline about it, when another thought flashed through my mind, distracting me. Something Sophie had told me before her wedding. I looked around the room, scanning the walls.

"Where is your royal mirror? I would love to see it."

A soft sigh sounded from Giselle, and I focused my attention on her. She met my eyes, and her own reflected sadness. The sign of an emotion—any emotion—made me cross closer to her, curious.

"As would I," she said. "But it was lost many years ago. When I was just a small child."

"Lost? How can such an object be lost?"

Sophie had explained to me that all of these kingdoms possessed an enchanted mirror. It had been gifted to each of the monarchs by the godmothers too many years ago to count and had been passed down from generation to generation. It allowed each royal family to see and hear events happening far from them. They could either watch over their own people or use it to communicate with the royal mirrors in other kingdoms.

I knew the Palinaran royal mirror had been limited in its functions by the curse, and I had suspected the same of the Eldonian one—or the king would have used it to find his children. But I hadn't expected to hear he didn't have it at all. Sophie had described it as a large, wall-mounted mirror, and it didn't seem like the kind of thing that was prone to being lost.

Giselle seemed confused—trying to remember what had happened, or perhaps trying to remember why she cared. I moved even closer, fascinated by the signs of struggle within her. She looked up at me, her gaze so lost and confused that I couldn't help the surge of compassion that filled me.

"Celine…" Her voice was soft. "I can't…" She shook her head and tried again. "I can't…"

I closed the remaining distance between us and placed a gentle hand on her shoulder. "Try Giselle! Try to remember." I wanted so desperately to really meet her—this friend who might be.

And though the feelings were gentler this time, they were no less strong. A surge ran up my arm and through my hand into her shoulder. She reeled, almost falling, as a bright illumination lit her from within. For a moment she looked as if she would take flight, her whole body rising from the ground, but then the light was gone, and she gasped and crumpled in on herself.

I caught her beneath one arm, steadying her as she gazed wide-eyed at me and then around the room. Her gaze lingered on her sister, examining a painting on the far side of the room and apparently oblivious to what had just happened, before turning back to me.

"Celine!" She stopped to take several more gasping breaths before righting herself and moving away from me. "Celine! What just happened?"

As much as the whole thing had taken me by surprise, I was at least slightly more prepared than I had been with Oliver.

"It's a long story. But the short version is that you've been under some sort of enchantment. Maybe. We think. And that the godmothers seem to have given me some sort of power to break it. Sometimes."

She raised an eyebrow. "Sounds like you've got it all figured out then." Her sardonic tone took me so much by surprise that I laughed out loud.

"It's nice to meet you, Giselle. I have the feeling that I really haven't met you before."

"Really? I seem to remember something about a Princess Tourney. It's all strangely hazy, though." She turned to me with wide eyes. "Did I fall down a very deep hole?"

I grimaced. "Yes. But that is definitely a story for another day."

Her eyes narrowed. "You said *we* earlier. Who else have you freed?"

I nodded. She was sharp. "Only Oliver, I'm afraid."

She looked back at her sister. "Can you free Emmeline as well? You could do it right now!"

I could tell by her tone that the devotion I had previously observed between the sisters wasn't false—despite Oliver describing them as so different from one another.

"I don't know. To be honest, I don't really have these powers completely under control."

Giselle frowned. "You could try at least."

I shrugged. "I suppose so."

Giselle immediately began to drag me toward her sister. "What do you need to do?"

"Um, touch her. I think. Like how I had my hand on your shoulder."

"All right. Try it." She gave me a final shove forward, and I approached Emmeline.

The other princess turned calmly to face me. "This painting shows my great-grandparents."

I glanced at it quickly, then placed my hand on her arm. I tried to muster up some warmth or emotion. But the only feeling I could manage was awkwardness. Still, Giselle's face silently pleaded with me to try harder, so I stood there a moment longer, trying to spark something to life inside me, even if only pity.

The pity seemed to work, a little, and a soft tingle grew in my chest. I focused on it and then on my hand.

"Wake up, Emmeline," I said firmly.

Nothing happened. I tried again.

"Wake up!"

She looked at me quizzically. "I'm already awake, Celine. Did I look like I had fallen asleep?"

"Um…" I backed away, shrugging helplessly at Giselle.

Thankfully Emmeline shrugged the whole thing off without need for further explanation—turning instead to continue her tour as if nothing had happened.

Giselle watched her with wide eyes.

"That's what it's like," I whispered to her under my breath. "That's what everyone is like under the enchantment."

She swallowed and shook her head, her eyes growing even wider. "You and I have a lot to talk about."

$\mathcal{I}$ didn't see Oliver until the next day, but obviously Giselle had found him sometime after she and I had parted. He strode up to me, his face split by a broad smile, and actually lifted me off my feet, spinning me around.

He swung me through the air easily, his arms firm and strong. Warmth filled me, but I kept it carefully contained inside. I didn't want any more unexpected outbursts of any kind.

When he put me back on my feet, I couldn't help grinning back at him. "I take it you've seen your sister."

"You did it! You freed Giselle." He regarded me curiously. "Does that mean you're learning to control it?"

My smile turned rueful. "To be honest, I didn't actually intend to free Giselle. Not ahead of time, anyway. It was a spur-of-the-moment sort of thing. And it didn't work at all when I tried it on Emmeline."

His face fell. "Yes, Giselle told me about that."

I thought of the warmth his presence seemed to spark and the progress I had made on containing it, but I decided against mentioning those. He didn't need to know everything about my powers.

"I've been thinking," he said. "Clearly the godmothers have given you these powers and sent you here to help us free ourselves. So we need you to learn to control them."

I glared at him. "I'm trying!"

"Well, I was thinking I could help. I know a place where we could go—somewhere private and secluded, where you won't be able to damage anything if you suddenly start a fire or a tornado or something."

I raised both eyebrows. "And you're going to help me. In this private, secluded spot." I shook my head. "I don't think so."

He stared at me for a second and then burst out laughing. "Not like that. I swear. Not that I would be unwilling, of course." He grinned at me wickedly. "But it isn't the most practical means to control it."

I put my hands on my hips. "I forgave you because we were literally going to die otherwise," I said. "But if you ever try something like that again, I'll just turn all those 'powerful emotions' against *you* instead of a pile of rocks."

He held up both hands. "I promise Princess Celine that I will never kiss you again." He leaned in, dropping his voice to a whisper. "Unless you ask me to, of course."

I rolled my eyes. "Sometimes I think I liked you better when you were a walking ice block."

He just continued to grin, unrepentant, and I shook my head.

"All right, then. Let's give this practice thing a try. If you're certain there's nothing I can damage, then I guess it can't do any harm."

I made him wait while I ran up and changed my dress, though. I'd already ruined two in Eldon, and I was wearing one of my favorites. When I came back down in my plainest dress—a fine wool gown with intricate embroidery—his eyes laughed at me.

"Yes," I said, before he could say anything. "This is my most practical dress. I *am* a princess, remember?"

He grinned. "I didn't say anything."

"Your eyes did," I muttered as I stalked past him and out of the huge front doors. He had said I wouldn't be able to damage anything which meant there was no way we were staying in the palace.

He caught up within a few steps and directed me up into the mountain city. To my unspoken relief, he made no move to take me back into the tunnels. Instead he led me upward by the most direct route before selecting a small side road. We quickly branched off even the smaller road, taking a steep—and apparently unending—staircase.

I was puffing slightly—and trying to hide it—by the time he led me sideways off the stair and onto something that looked more like a goat track than a road. I eyed him suspiciously, and he shrugged.

"Secluded, remember?"

We followed the track for some time while I tried not to think of the drop off to my left. We weren't exactly walking along a cliff edge, but it was close enough. The path wound around a large outcropping of rock and then turned sharply. I stopped and blinked.

Oliver spread his arms wide. "Welcome to my favorite place in the world."

I walked forward slowly and spun around so I could take it in. I could see why. Tucked back here, hidden by that outcropping, was a large mountain meadow. The flat space spread well back from the edge of the mountain, ringed by several tall evergreen trees. Soft grass covered the ground, and I even saw a few bright wildflowers—the first I had seen in this not-quite-spring. A burbling sound drew me toward the far side of the meadow where I found a small stream, the mountain water clear and icy cold, but not actually frozen.

"It's beautiful," I said softly.

"And perfect for what we need."

I eyed Oliver uncertainly. "Up until I accidentally burn it down."

He seemed undaunted. "This meadow has survived worse than you—I promise."

I looked around at the beauty uneasily and then shrugged. I wasn't likely to find a better spot, and I did need to learn to control my powers.

I turned back to Oliver. "So what now?"

He rubbed the back of his neck, his eyes thoughtful. "I've been thinking about that. Emotions are key, but it doesn't seem to matter which ones. So I guess it's up to you. What emotion do you think you can most effectively conjure at will?"

"Uhh…" I stared at him blankly.

He narrowed his eyes at me consideringly. "Anger, maybe?"

"Hey!" I put my hands on my hips. "Are you saying I'm an angry person?"

He kept his face straight, but I noticed his lips twitching. "Anger is a strong emotion, that's all."

I walked around in a circle, needing the activity while my mind raced. Could I make myself angry? This beautiful haven didn't promote anger. My gaze turned upward, to where I could see the higher slopes of the mountain. Snow lay heavy there just as it did in pockets throughout the Eldonian capital. And yet it was well into spring. It should have melted by now, turning that little stream into a strong current.

I glanced back at Oliver, his expression curious as he watched me silently. The fire in his blue eyes still burned, making his face alive and bright with color. So different from how he had been before. Whatever this enchantment was, it did the worst thing possible—stripping people's true selves.

I shivered at the thought and felt something stir within me. It was anger, yes, but also fear. I couldn't imagine anything worse than losing myself.

Burning heat erupted from my chest and surged down my

arms. It took me by surprise, but I clenched my hands into fists just in time, holding it inside. Nothing happened, and elation filled me. I'd done it! I'd called it, and I'd controlled it.

The warmth inside me turned ferocious, and for the first time I felt an uncomfortable burning sensation. I looked around frantically and spotted a large boulder on one edge of the meadow. Striding toward it, I held both fists out in front of me before unfurling my fingers. Pointing them at the stone, I flung all the heat down my arms and through my hands.

Enormous tongues of flame burst from my fingertips. Unlike in the tunnels, they didn't cling to me, instead flying through the air and engulfing the boulder.

"Whoa!" Oliver's startled exclamation barely made it through the roar of the unnatural fire. For a moment it swirled around the stone, singeing the grass beside it, and then it winked out as quickly as it had appeared.

I stood, panting, my hands falling slowly back to my sides.

"Well, that seemed to work. What did you do?" Oliver's voice approached me from behind, but I shook my head and gestured for him to stay back. I needed space to think, and I didn't want to end up hurting him by accident.

I walked toward the boulder and touched it. I could feel searing heat, but when I pulled my fingers away they remained unburned. Interesting. But that fire inside had felt as if it would burn me when I tried to keep it in.

I closed my eyes and conjured the same emotions, focusing this time on the fear that I might suffer the same fate as the Eldonians. The warmth inside, which had disappeared when it transferred through my fingertips, returned—faster this time and stronger.

I gripped my hands into fists again, once more holding it inside. But this time I worked, not on containing it, but on calming it. I reminded myself that I was strong. That I could fight. That I wouldn't let anyone strip my true self away.

Instead of burning stronger and hotter, it began to fade, growing weaker until it was a mere warmth curling around my belly. I opened my eyes and glanced around. A tall group of trees stood some distance from me. I looked at them contemplatively.

Could I use this gentle warmth, or did I need to burn myself to be effective? Whipping my hands up from my sides, I thrust my flat palms toward the trees. At the same moment, I willed the gentle warmth back into a raging inferno.

It didn't quite obey me, but it did leap into greater life, and a hot wind rushed from my hands to shake the ancient trunks. It wasn't exactly a gale, but it had been more than a breeze.

I turned to Oliver with a triumphant smile on my lips.

He gazed at me blankly. "Well. That was fast."

"What can I say? You're an excellent teacher."

He looked at me skeptically, still in shock apparently, and I spun around, the giddy smile still on my lips. I barely restrained myself from pumping the air with my fists. I did it. Now just let this enchantment come for me. It didn't know who it was dealing with.

"So it looks like fingertips are flames and palms are hot air?" Oliver seemed to have recovered from his shock. He squinted his eyes as he glanced around the meadow, as if considering which bit he would most willingly sacrifice. "I wonder how big you could get the flames?"

I rolled my eyes. "Typical male. I'm more interested in how controlled I can get it."

"Yes, I suppose that might be more useful." He looked a little deflated, and I barely refrained from rolling my eyes again. All three of my brothers—even the calm, sensible ones—would have been the same. If it had been up to them, the whole meadow would have been gone in some kind of flash forest fire.

"In that case," said Oliver. "Can you do the little flames on your fingers thing? Like you did in the tunnel? It didn't seem to burn you…" He waited for my nod of agreement. "So, I wonder how long you could keep it up for."

I frowned and bit my lip. Sustained power. That wasn't something I had managed yet. I wanted to be allowed to bask in my success for a moment longer, but curiosity soon overwhelmed me. Could I do it?

I pushed up both sleeves. Neither the wind nor the fire seemed to harm me, but the wind had whipped my skirts around in the past, and I didn't want to end up with a burning dress.

Holding my hands extended in front of me, I kept them initially balled into fists. I thought back to waking Giselle in the display room. I suspected that I needed a more gentle emotion for a smaller, sustained use of my power.

Unfortunately, gentle wasn't really my thing.

My mind flitted over Emmeline and the others I had met at the palace and then traveled back to the woods. I recalled Cassandra's tight grip around my waist, and the lurking desperation at the back of her eyes. She exuded confidence, but she was still only thirteen.

Compassion and sadness gripped me, along with a determination not to let her down. This time the sensation inside me was more like hot coals than a live flame. I directed it down my arms as I slowly unfurled my fingers, aiming them all upward in bent claws.

A flicker of light on one finger was followed by another, and then all ten burst suddenly into flame. I stumbled back, and they instantly went out.

"Try again," said Oliver, his voice encouraging, but I barely heard him. My focus had returned inward.

The coals were still there, banked, not extinguished, and I quickly brought them back to stronger heat. This time, when the flames appeared, I held steady, ready for it. The tongues flickered a little and then settled, burning brightly.

I looked up at Oliver and found him inching closer to me, clearly fascinated.

"It really doesn't hurt you at all?"

I shook my head.

"Does it even feel hot?"

I considered my answer. "Yes—and no. I can feel that the heat is there, but it isn't unpleasant like it normally would be. It doesn't burn me."

Before I could stop him, he reached out a hand and stuck his fingers into the flames sprouting from my closest hand. I gasped and jumped backward, the fire going out at the same moment as he exclaimed and stuck his fingers into his mouth.

"Ouch! That burned."

"Of course it burned! Idiot! It's fire."

"Well, it wasn't burning you. I was curious."

"Of course you were," I muttered, holding out my hands in a demand that he show me his fingers.

Reluctantly he pulled them out of his mouth and laid them in my open palms. I examined them, conscious of the strength in his hands and the calluses that told me he spent a lot of time training with various weapons. At least they didn't look seriously burned.

"Do not try that again," I told him firmly, releasing his hands abruptly when I felt a coil of now familiar warmth in my chest.

"I won't." He grinned at me, unrepentant. "I've learned my lesson, I promise."

I narrowed my eyes at him but then turned away, my mind already elsewhere. The warmth I now felt burned quietly, under control—or so it seemed. How long could I keep it burning there without letting it out? And how much attention did I need to give it to keep it from extinguishing?

Glancing speculatively back at Oliver, I picked up my skirts and fled across the grass. "Catch me if you can," I called back over my shoulder. If this was going to be a true test, I needed to be distracted by something else while I tried to keep it burning.

After a surprised pause, Oliver took off after me. His longer stride meant he was soon closing the distance, so I aimed for some trees, weaving in and out of their trunks. With a sudden spurt, I twisted out of his sight behind a particularly dense group of trunks and ducked off to the side, crouching behind a large boulder.

I tried to still my breathing, pressing a hand against my chest. Yes, the warmth still burned, but faintly. It was going out. I coaxed it back to life, careful not to allow it to grow too strong.

The effort distracted me, so that I startled and shrieked when Oliver jumped around the boulder. Briefly the coals inside burst into open flames, but I clamped down on them hard, ducking under his arm and taking off running again.

With a playful growl he raced close behind me, and I threw myself forward, going as fast as I possibly could. It felt good to stretch my legs and run without purpose after all the worrying.

Still, he was catching me when my foot caught on a small stone hidden in the grass, and I tipped forward. Oliver lunged after me, trying to catch me, but instead we both went down, rolling over before landing flat in the grass.

It took a moment for me to catch my breath, and then I was laughing. My uncontrollable giggles went on and on, as my over-burdened emotions finally found an outlet.

Oliver's deeper chuckle sounded in my ear, and then I suddenly realized that we had fallen almost on top of each other, my skirts tangled in his legs. His chuckles softened, and he pushed himself up on one elbow, looking down into my eyes. I thought he would speak, but instead he swayed down toward me, until our faces felt far too close. He paused there, his eyes asking me a question. But he didn't speak, the moment drawing out between us so taut as to be almost painful.

I realized he was staying true to his earlier word—the question needed to come from me, not him. But I found I had no breath—and no idea what I wanted to say. I had never seen the blue fire in his eyes burn so strongly, and suddenly the coals that had been simmering inside me all this time leaped in response. The unleashed inferno felt as if it would melt my insides like wax.

Gasping, I rolled away from him and thrust my hands blindly out to my side. My hands were neither flat, nor pointed, and the wind that leaped from my hands and rushed across the meadow carried actual tongues of flames with it. It hit the trees on the far side with enough force to bend them sideways, the fire dancing around them, but thankfully not actually catching alight.

I breathed a sigh of relief just as a piercing scream echoed across the open space.

CHAPTER 12

*B*oth Oliver and I scrambled to our feet and took off running in the direction of the sound. Dread filled my stomach. If someone had been over there, they would have received the brunt of both my wind and fire.

A short figure stumbled out of the cover of the trees, and my relieved brain noted that she didn't appear to have any burns. A moment later I realized I recognized her.

Giselle.

Oliver reached her first, gripping her by the shoulders and inspecting her for injury. When he started berating her, I breathed a sigh of relief. He wouldn't be doing that if she was hurt.

"What did you think you were doing?" he demanded. His voice sounded stern, but she looked entirely undaunted.

"I was spying on you, of course. What do you think I was doing?"

Even I raised an eyebrow, impressed at her pluck. I could see why Oliver had said he wished I could meet her. She reminded me of my younger self.

"You could have been injured—badly!" Oliver now sounded

more resigned than angry.

Giselle ignored him completely, her attention turned to me. "You told me you had power to release people from the enchantment. Not that you could shoot fire from your hands."

I shrugged. "I'm still working on that part. That's why we're out here."

"Well, it looked pretty impressive. I want to see it closer up."

I looked over at Oliver, and he shrugged helplessly.

"All right," I said. "But no more hiding. I don't want to singe your hair off."

"No, indeed." She patted her pale blond locks.

I eyed them. "Although it might be worth it, just to see if it would get a reaction from Emmeline."

She gasped and clutched at her hair. "You wouldn't!"

"Relax, sis," said Oliver. "She's teasing you."

Giselle glared at me before moving a few feet away. "Well, come on then. Let's see these impressive powers." She crossed her arms over her chest.

The fear from when I heard her scream remained close enough to the surface that I easily whipped my internal heat to a raging bonfire. When it began to grow uncomfortable, I swung my hands in front of me, clapping them together, and pointing all of my fingers toward a rock at the base of the trees.

A column of fire roared from my clenched fingers, a rush of air moving with it, and slammed into the stone. The rock exploded from the pressure, spraying shards of stone in all directions. We all flinched, raising our arms to protect our faces.

When the fire had died out and the rock fragments had all hit the ground, I slowly lowered my arms.

"Did I mention I'm still working on it?"

"Wow." Giselle's eyes glowed. "That. Was. Amazing."

She would have happily kept me out there doing tricks for hours, but after a glance at the sky—and another one at his sister —Oliver declared it time to return to the palace. Giselle looked disappointed but didn't protest—so not entirely like me at her age, after all.

Together we trekked back in near silence. What had happened in that meadow wasn't something any of us felt like discussing where someone else might overhear us. Even if we were surrounded by people who seemed unmoved by anything.

We had made it most of the way back when we passed a particularly deep drift of snow pushed between two building fronts. I shivered at the sight, but a moment's reflection made me realize I didn't actually feel cold. Instead a pleasant warmth had settled inside me, too low to be particularly noticeable until I actively thought about it.

So my experiment with the running had been a success. I had managed to kindle an internal fire that could last through distractions. But when I remembered how the memory had ended, I frowned. It made me feel both safer and warmer—a not insignificant side-effect—to have the heat always burning. But I would have to be more careful of unexpected flare ups. I didn't want to end up blasting a hole through the palace wall or setting someone on fire just because I was startled.

Days passed and became weeks. At first the inactivity suited me fine. I returned many more times to the meadow with Oliver to further refine my skills. Giselle always accompanied us, not bothering to ask permission, just appearing at some point during our walk through the city. Oliver tried to send her back the first time, but she merely shrugged and silently continued toward the meadow, drawing ahead of us.

Eventually he had sighed, and we had accepted her presence. She often turned up whenever we were together after that, and I grew used to it. I even told myself it was a good thing that I was rarely alone with Oliver now. I didn't want to lose control again.

Oliver had done his best to launch an investigation into the cave in, but none of us were surprised to discover that no one remembered seeing or hearing anything suspicious. And since we were all in agreement that it would be best not to advertise my new powers, he couldn't even be too specific with anyone about exactly what had happened. Not when we had no explanation for our escape.

But it wasn't worth letting word about my gift spread. With an unknown enemy wreaking havoc on the kingdom, it felt good to have one advantage they knew nothing about.

As weeks passed, however, the three of us grew more and more concerned. Instead of warming up as we approached closer to summer, the air was growing colder and the snowfalls more frequent. Snowdrifts began to appear in the meadow, and eventually the day came when we couldn't make it across the path to reach it at all.

Any idea that this unseasonal change might cause concern to the locals had long since faded. The three of us drew closer together—an island in the midst of a sea of cold and passive faces. Even regular conversation seemed an effort for most of them now. And attempts to express our concern were met only with blank expressions and shrugs.

While Oliver did his best to keep the administration of the kingdom functioning in the face of his parents' increasing disinterest, Giselle and I had taken to roaming the palace, searching for something—anything—that might help us. I preferred lobbing fireballs to spending hours on musty old record books, but we spent part of every day in the library. We could find no account of any previous encroachment of winter to rival this one, however.

We also poked through every bit of the palace, unwilling to overlook anything that might help us understand what was happening to Eldon. I often found myself back in the room of treasures—as I had mentally dubbed it—wishing one of the objects displayed there still held power.

Sometimes I also found myself lingering in front of the old portrait in the corridor, wondering what object was missing from beside it. Giselle told me that display had always stood empty, so I knew it was a foolish thought. But still I found myself there.

So when we ended up in the long portrait gallery one afternoon, I easily recognized the same woman in another painting displayed among the many past royals. Once again she wore a similar blue velvet to the material that decorated the palace, but she looked older in this portrait. Still determined but a little more careworn.

Giselle noticed my interest and came to stand beside me.

"It's the same woman," I said. "Who was she, do you know?"

"She's one of the previous queens." Giselle paused. "My great-great-grandmother? Or maybe it's just one great. I get confused about the order of them all."

"Why is her portrait out in the corridor? Was she special?"

Giselle scrunched up her face, thinking. "Depends what you consider special, I suppose. She lived back before our kingdoms turned away from the High King and the old laws. Before the godmothers turned away from us in turn. She had a godmother, I believe, although she was only a servant originally. And she and the crown prince fell in love and were married. It was all terribly romantic, I suppose." Giselle didn't seem particularly impressed.

"She sounds like Lily and Sophie's mother. She was a servant —sort of—before she married the prince."

"Maybe it's because she was a servant that she found the palace cold and unpleasant," said Giselle. "At least, that's what I remember mother telling me. She apparently redecorated the whole thing." She gave a wry smile. "I guess when you're responsible for decoration you get to put your portrait wherever you want."

"I wonder what was supposed to stand beside it."

Giselle shrugged. "You should ask Oliver, maybe he knows. As crown prince he spent much more time than Emmeline and me learning all about the family history and the previous kings and queens."

From her scrunched nose, I deduced that she didn't envy him the role. I let the conversation drop, although my curiosity about the servant-girl-turned-queen had only increased.

Moving down the line of portraits, I stopped in front of a particularly grand and imposing one. It portrayed a tall king, standing alone, his hand upon the hilt of his sword and his brow stern as he gazed into the distance.

"Another one of your ancestors, I suppose. He looks..." I trailed off as I tried to think of a non-offensive description.

"Conceited?" Giselle appeared beside me. "Don't worry, I won't be offended. I've never liked the look of him myself."

From his stance and expression it surprised me somewhat that he hadn't had himself painted on a victorious battlefield or on his throne, at least. But as my eyes roamed over the background of the picture, they landed on an unusual object.

Excitement filled me, warmth swirling around my insides which I quickly suppressed. The last thing I wanted was fire erupting in this room of all places.

"Giselle, what's that? Behind him?"

Mounted on the wall behind the figure, the painter had included a large mirror. The elaborate frame appeared to be covered in gilt, and it seemed a strange thing to include in a portrait. Unless...

Giselle sighed. "That's the Eldonian royal mirror."

I nodded. "You told me it was lost. Just before I freed you. What did you mean by lost? How do you lose a mirror?" I couldn't quite keep the excitement from my voice.

"Well, I suppose lost is a bit of a euphemism." She looked pained. "The truth is that it was stolen."

"Stolen?" Some of my eagerness drained away, replaced with confusion. "How does something like that get stolen out of a palace?"

She just shrugged. "It was before my time. All I know is that someone managed to take it. It was gone before I ever got the chance to see it." She sounded genuinely sad, and I remembered the echo of the emotion pushing through the fog of her enchantment when we had talked about it previously.

I tried not to sound impatient or critical when I asked, "I assume your family has tried to recover it?"

"Of course." She sounded a little sharp despite my efforts. "Many times, in fact. The thief was tracked up the mountain. Only then a blizzard hit. The tracks were lost after that." She sighed. "No one can survive up the mountains in winter. The thief froze to death long ago and the mirror is stashed in whatever hidey hole or cave he found before he died. My grandfather announced a reward for anyone who could find it, and every summer at least one expedition goes looking. But the mountains are vast, and the thief could have fled to any corner of them before he succumbed." She sighed again. "Such a waste."

I groaned, the remaining elation seeping out of me. A waste indeed. Because if we could have found the lost mirror, we could have used it to find the source of the enchantment. Find it and stop it.

"It would be a useful thing to have now," Giselle whispered, her mind obviously in the same place as mine.

"Maybe we could—"

"In this weather? That would be crazy." Giselle didn't even let me finish the thought.

Reluctantly I conceded the point, and we moved out of the room. But I couldn't get the thought of the royal mirror from my mind. It was out there somewhere, and if only we had it, we could finally make some progress on defeating this curse.

CHAPTER 13

$\mathcal{W}$ hen I raised the question of the mirror later with Oliver, he was no more hopeful than Giselle.

"If none of the expeditions could find it in the summer, we would have no chance at all of finding it now."

The pain on his face made me back away from the conversation. I could see how frustrated and desperate he was becoming, and the last thing I wanted to do was remind him of all the ways we weren't making any progress. But still, the thought of the mirror haunted me.

Oliver wasn't the only one becoming more desperate as the days passed. The three of us wound tighter and tighter, in direct opposition to the rest of the palace's inhabitants. I had thought Emmeline, at least, might show some response to Giselle abandoning her to spend her time with us, but she seemed completely unaffected.

"It's horrible," burst out Giselle one day from where she lay sprawled across one of the sofas in the sitting room of my suite. "It's like a stranger is wearing Emmeline's face."

Oliver, who stood by the fire, one leg propped against the grate and his arm resting along the mantel, didn't look up, but I saw his expression tighten. I could feel his frustration at his impotence and had to restrain the instinct to go over and place a comforting hand on his arm. Despite my gift, I hadn't managed to free anyone else. Why would he want comfort from me?

"I'm sorry," I said, focusing instead on Giselle. "I've tried."

And I had. As I gained more control of my powers, I had tried several more times to wake Emmeline without success.

Giselle sighed. "It's not your fault. Without you, Oliver and I would be just as bad."

I blew out a frustrated breath. "I just wish I knew why it worked then and not now."

Oliver did look up this time. "I've been thinking about that. Whatever enchantment holds them in thrall is obviously getting stronger. I think you got to us just in time." He looked back down at the fire. "And you didn't have as much control back then. I think it only worked instinctively. And probably only on people…"

He trailed away, but when he glanced up, both Giselle and I were watching him curiously, so he was forced to continue.

"I was just thinking how Giselle is much more like you in personality than Emmeline. Perhaps you sensed that somehow… some connection. Some small lingering part of her true self that called to you, and you instinctively responded."

It seemed as good a theory as any, but I noticed he said nothing of himself. *Can you deny it, though?* asked a small voice inside me. *That you've felt a connection to this prince ever since you got a glimpse of his true self?*

I shook the thought aside. I had more important things to worry about than fanciful connections.

"But what can we do then? If it's too late for me to reach any of them…"

Giselle sat up. "Don't say that! It's not too late."

Oliver glanced between us. "We can only hope it's not. At this point, I suspect we'll need to defeat it at the source."

I stood up and began to pace the room. "Yes, but what is the source? None of us have any idea, remember?"

He ran an angry hand through his hair and shot me a look that made me instantly regret my words. Of course he remembered. I doubt he thought of much else. And it was eating him up inside. He thought that as heir he should know his own kingdom better.

I reached the window and spun around to pace back again. They had both given up on the mirror as hopeless, but I'd been thinking about it. And it's not like we had any other ideas.

"What if the thief didn't die up the mountain?"

"The thief?" Oliver raised an eyebrow, and Giselle's face looked no less confused. I rushed to explain myself.

"The thief who stole the mirror. What if he evaded his pursuers and somehow came back down the mountain somewhere else? It would explain why no one could ever find it."

Giselle looked skeptical. "The size of the mountain and the weather would also explain it."

"Right. But what if it wasn't up the mountain? What if we could find it?"

Oliver's mouth twisted, but he didn't immediately protest. No doubt he was desperate enough to consider any option at this point, however crazy.

"Perhaps…perhaps we could go on a royal tour," I said.

The other two stared at me, so I kept going. "My father sent my oldest brother on a royal tour of the kingdom when I was fifteen. There were rumors of trouble at the time. We visited all the different regions and, sure enough, we chased the trouble out into the open. Maybe we could announce we're going on a tour, and go searching for the mirror. If we could find it…"

"We could finally find out what's going on." Oliver sounded half-hopeful, half-despairing.

But Giselle was already shaking her head. "It might have worked a year ago, but I can't imagine trying to rouse anyone at the palace to be involved or even to help organize such a thing. Not now. They're barely maintaining even our most simple routine."

Watching her face, I realized the depth of her fear. She worried that one day they would all stop caring enough to do anything at all. That they would just sit down and die. And I couldn't say I blamed her for her concern.

Oliver groaned. "Then we go ourselves. Just the three of us." But his eyes flickered to Giselle as he said it, and I knew he would leave her home if he possibly could.

"Don't look at me like that," she said quickly. "I am *not* staying here on my own."

He looked at me instead, but I shook my head. "Don't look to me for support. There's no way *I'd* want to stay here on my own. And I remember what it was like to be fifteen too."

Giselle threw me a grateful look and Oliver a frustrated one. I just shrugged. "Well, I do. I'm not that old, you know."

Oliver's gaze caught on my face. "No. No, indeed…"

Giselle cleared her throat loudly, and he looked away quickly, his face flushed from his proximity to the fire. Silence fell between us, eventually broken by Oliver.

"I don't like it. It's a desperate plan, and in all likelihood we'd be chasing a fool's errand. But we can't just sit here and do nothing."

"Well, that's decided then," said Giselle, although she hadn't actually given her opinion on the plan either way. She climbed off the sofa. "I'll start collecting supplies."

She disappeared from the room, and Oliver went to follow her. "I'll pick us mounts. The hardiest I can find since it looks like we should expect conditions more like winter than late spring."

I stood as well, although I wasn't sure what help I could be beyond packing my own bags. Oliver paused as he crossed in front of me, and I waited for him to suggest what I might do, but he said nothing.

Instead he raised a hand and laid it gently against my cheek. I stilled, only the slightest tremble running through me as the ever-present warmth in my chest stirred and grew.

"I'm being selfish." His words were a bare whisper. "Too selfish. It's unforgivable."

"What do you mean?" My voice was hardly louder than his.

"There is no reason for you to face this danger with us. Leave now, while there's still time."

"No." I would have shaken my head except that his hand still burned against my cheek. "I was sent here remember. By the godmothers. To free you all."

"But perhaps it's too late for Eldon." The weight in his eyes made me want to cry. And his next words were so quiet I could barely catch them. "You are too alive, Celine. Too full of fire. I couldn't bear it if you were snuffed out."

A bone deep shiver shook me as he voiced my own deepest fears. At my movement, he dropped his fingers as if burned. But I leaned forward and placed my hand against his chest—just where I had placed it when I released him from the enchantment.

"No," I said, more forcefully this time. "I'm not leaving you. And nobody is snuffing me out. Or you either. I will keep us both alight for as long as I need to."

A deep sigh ran through him. "It's wrong of me to feel so relieved—and yet...I do." He swayed toward me, and I read something in his eyes that both exhilarated and frightened me. I never ran from a challenge, and yet I could not ask what his eyes begged me to ask. Because everything was up to me. I was the keeper of the fire, and what he didn't know was that I had to work far harder to stop it burning us both alive than I did at keeping us from freezing.

When I didn't move or speak, he pulled away, his eyes shadowed. "You are wise beyond your years, Celine." He strode to the door and then paused, looking back at me. "We leave in the morning."

When the door closed behind him, I swayed, nearly falling before I collapsed into the chair behind me. I wrestled with myself for several long moments before I could return my raging insides to their usual quiet warmth. I longed to run and throw myself into the snow that was even now building outside the palace.

"If we're leaving tomorrow, I'll have my opportunity soon enough," I muttered to myself. "I should enjoy being dry while I have the chance."

My door opened, although no knock had sounded, and a small head poked inside, looking around until her gaze caught on me. She instantly disappeared, and I heard her calling down the corridor.

"This is the one, Alexander. I've found her."

I was still blinking in surprise when Cassandra reappeared, wandering in with a friendly smile on her face. She surveyed the room. "Nice suite."

"What are you doing here?"

"Greetings to you too." She grinned at me, although the expression didn't last long, and I could see the concern hiding behind it.

A tall young man I didn't recognize came through the door, closing it carefully behind him. Without thinking, I dropped into a defensive stance, my dagger appearing in my hand. I had no intention of being taken prisoner again—however well meaning Lord Treestone might be.

"Impressive," said the newcomer, a hooded smile on his face. "Princesses don't usually have those sorts of reflexes."

"Maybe not in these kingdoms." I kept my eyes on him.

Cassandra rolled her eyes at both of us. "Have a lot of experience with princesses, do you, Alexander?"

I expected him to be offended, but he merely grinned and shrugged. When neither of them made any move toward me, I sighed and relaxed.

"Let me try again. What in the kingdoms are you doing here, Cassandra? And who's he?"

She climbed onto the sofa recently vacated by Giselle and gestured for the man to sit also. He hesitated but followed her lead, a wry expression on his face. I wondered if he'd ever taken orders from a thirteen-year-old girl before. On the other hand, he was obviously traveling with Cassandra, so…

"This is Alexander. He insisted on accompanying me." She scowled.

"These are dangerous times," he said, unmoved by her obvious displeasure. "And it's what your uncle would have wanted me to do."

I raised an eyebrow at that, and Cassandra looked a little sheepish. "He caught me sneaking out. I must be losing my touch."

I shook my head, trying to follow. "Why were you sneaking out?"

"I was coming to see you, of course. I didn't expect it to be so easy, though." She glanced across at Alexander and shivered. "We just walked straight in and have been wandering the palace ever since looking for you. Not even one person has so much as questioned us. It's going to make things even easier than Uncle hoped." For some reason, she didn't look entirely pleased about that.

Unease stirred inside me.

"Make what exactly even easier?"

"Our coup."

CHAPTER 14

I jumped. "Cassandra!"

She shrugged. "It wasn't my idea. I just tagged along."

"What do you mean tagged along?" My unease deepened.

"Uncle is camped a day's ride from the capital. With all the men he could gather from the southern forests." She glanced across at Alexander. "And with a large contingent of troops from Eliam."

"Eliam?" I frowned. If the southern kingdom had gotten involved, then this was far worse than I'd feared. I followed her gaze to Alexander. "You're from Eliam, I suppose?"

He shifted uncomfortably. "King George has been in contact with Lord Treestone for some time. This blight is spreading south, and we have no reason to suppose that a border will stop it. If King Leopold lacks either the means or the will to try to contain and defeat it, then we must see someone on the throne who will at least try to act."

I looked over at Cassandra accusingly, but she raised both hands defensively. "Don't look at me. Uncle doesn't *want* to be king." She looked out my window and shivered. "Who would want to live up here in the frozen north? But we can't sit by and see everyone die. Not without at least trying to defeat it. Whatever it is."

She looked at me hopefully. "I don't suppose you've worked out…"

I shook my head, and she slumped. "Uncle's still nervous about you. On account of the whole abduction thing. But I knew you would have at least been trying to find out what's going on. So I thought I'd better slip away and see you before Uncle does anything irreversible."

I stood up and resumed my earlier pacing, my mind racing, but coming up with no helpful answers.

"We've been trying. Believe me, we've been trying. But it's just getting worse. And there hasn't been so much as a hint of the cause." I threw my hands up but dropped them again when I caught sight of Cassandra's face. "What?"

"You said *we*. Did you just mean you and your people?"

"No," I rushed over and sat on the sofa beside her. I had to at least try to stop this, for Oliver's sake. "Oliver—Prince Oliver, the crown prince—has been freed from the curse and is working with me to try to undo it. You must tell your uncle that we are trying. In fact…in fact we have a plan. We leave tomorrow." It was true—sort of. I just hoped she didn't ask what our plan was.

"Well…" She leaned back and glanced across at Alexander. "That does change things. Uncle may see things differently if he knows the crown prince is working on the problem."

"Please tell him. You have to convince him to stop this coup. It won't help anything. This kingdom is already under attack—it won't help for it to be divided as well."

Cassandra looked thoughtful. "I'm fairly certain with this news that I can convince him to wait while you try to work it out. But I can't promise for how long. And I want a promise from you in return."

I narrowed my eyes. "What sort of promise?"

"If you and the prince can't find and defeat this quickly enough, or if you come back unsuccessful, you'll help us with the coup. You'll ensure the prince doesn't interfere."

I drew in a breath. Could I make such a promise?

"If he tries to stop us, he's the first one who'll get hurt."

"But he's the rightful heir. If he's trying to solve this, shouldn't your uncle be supporting him?"

She winced. "In an ideal world, yes. Of course. But if he's already tried and been unsuccessful…" She bit her lip. "How drastically is he willing to act? Would he depose his own father? It's not just my uncle, remember. The Elamese are afraid as well, and there's always the chance—however remote—that it's the royal family that's the problem." She gave me a look. "It's happened before."

Now it was my turn to wince. I didn't believe the royal family had brought this on their kingdom, but could I blame the southerners for clutching at unlikely solutions? We were doing the same thing, after all. And as for deposing his father and seizing the throne—I couldn't imagine Oliver agreeing to such a betrayal.

I sighed. She was right, of course. Oliver would get himself killed.

"Done. It's a deal." The words were out of my mouth before I had thought them through. I grimaced. I would just have to make sure we found and destroyed whoever was behind this enchantment before it came to any coups.

Cassandra looked pleased, but I drew my brows together as I remembered she was little older than a child. "Can you really guarantee he'll wait? That he'll hold to our deal? You're not exactly here as an official emissary from the sound of it."

She eyed me with a hint of amusement. "You can say it. I won't be offended. I'm only a child."

I shrugged apologetically, but she merely looked across at Alexander. "That's why I let him come."

Alexander shook his head and chuckled. "I should have

known your protests were all a ruse." He looked over at me. "But she's right. I'm not the commander of our troops, but King George asked me to come personally. The commander will listen to me, and Lord Treestone will listen to the commander. We can give you time. For a while, at least."

I nodded gratefully. For a moment I was distracted by his mention of his king. "If you know King George, do you also know Princess Blanche? Snow, I mean. Has she recovered from the Princess Tourney?"

A guarded look crossed his face, and he sat back. "The princess is well enough, I believe."

His manner didn't exactly invite further conversation, but curiosity drove me on. "I heard...I heard that King George wasn't in the best of health...?"

"His mind remains strong," said Alexander, iron in his voice.

"Oh. Certainly. I didn't mean..." I let the thought trail away and abandoned any further attempt to question him about Eliam. I was glad, at least, to hear that the king remained alive. Snow had been terrified he would die while she was away at the Tourney, but he had obviously managed to hold on longer than expected.

I had more questions about the intended coup, but Cassandra and Alexander seemed to feel they had already told me enough. Perhaps, even with our deal, they didn't entirely trust me. And I couldn't altogether blame them.

～

I paced my room for nearly an hour before I decided to go find Oliver. In the end, I realized that this wasn't my kingdom, and it wasn't my secret to keep. If there was a coup coming, I had to warn the prince, at least.

I wandered the hallways for some time after I realized that I didn't actually know where to find his rooms. Fewer and fewer servants seemed to be in the corridors these days, but I did eventually find one who I managed to rouse enough to get directions. When I reached the right door, I knocked and then walked into his sitting room.

He emerged from his bedroom, a half-full bag in his hands and a questioning expression on his face. When he saw me, his face changed to something I couldn't read. He looked uneasily at the door I had closed behind me.

"You shouldn't be in here."

I rolled my eyes. "I don't really think now is the time to worry about proprieties. And weren't you just in my room an hour ago?"

He shifted uncomfortably. "Giselle was there, too."

I raised an eyebrow. "Not the whole time."

He flushed and looked away, and I remembered why I had come and let him off the hook.

"Never mind. I have something to tell you. Something important. And you're not going to like it."

He frowned and put down his bag, gesturing for me to take a seat. "It's hard to imagine anything else could have gone wrong at this point."

I grimaced, and he sucked in a breath, dropping down to sit beside me.

"Just tell me."

"Lord Treestone has allied himself with Eliam and has an army camped a day's ride from the capital. They're planning a coup."

"What!?" He leaped to his feet and strode angrily around the room. "How could they think of treason at such a time!"

"How could they not?" I asked, my voice soft. "When we're clutching at straws ourselves. After what happened in Palinar, can you really be surprised they're at least considering the possibility that your family is to blame?"

"We didn't turn against our kingdom! We didn't bring this on Eldon!"

"No, of course not. You must know I believe that. But the Elamese, on the other hand…I think they're willing to try anything."

He stopped and looked at me with lowered brows. After a moment his eyes narrowed.

"How do you know this? And what aren't you telling me?"

I bit my lip. He had learned to read me better than I had anticipated. Reluctantly I told him about Cassandra and Alexander's visit. "So, they've agreed to give us some time."

His hard gaze didn't leave mine. "Have they now? And at what cost?"

He was far too sharp. I stood, bringing my height a little closer to his, and took a deep breath. "If we don't succeed—or if it takes too long—then I've agreed that I'll help them. Specifically that I'll keep you from interfering." Just saying the words made me feel like a traitor, although I had no actual loyalty or ties to Eldon.

He sucked in a breath, such a wounded look in his eyes that I felt as if I'd been struck. I closed my eyes for a moment and reminded myself I was doing it for him. Even if he couldn't see it right now.

"I'd like to see you try!" It was his anger speaking, but it still hurt.

I forced myself to meet his eyes and hoped he could see how sorry I was in mine. "I don't know why they placed so much trust in me…but you…you, at least, know that I can." I held up my hands in front of me, and he actually flinched.

I dropped them again, coldness seeping through me for the first time in weeks. How had I gotten myself into this situation?

"There's still hope," I said, trying to fill my voice with an optimism I didn't feel. "We can find Giselle and leave tonight. We can still find a way to defeat this and prevent the coup."

When he met my eyes again I saw a hopelessness there that hurt more than everything else.

"Do you really believe that, Celine? Do you?"

I tried to think of something I could say that would be both true and encouraging. My mind drew a blank. I licked my lips and looked away.

"See." His harsh voice barely registered as something else caught my attention. I held up a hand to silence him, my eyes on his already drawn curtains.

"You might as well come out, Giselle. I don't know why you're even bothering to hide at this point." It felt like months had passed since that first time she spied on us. I thought we had moved past that. But there was no one else in the palace with the initiative to bother hiding in the crown prince's suite.

My breath caught. Unless Cassandra hadn't really returned to her uncle after all...

I strode forward and violently pulled the curtain back from the small window recess. I wasn't feeling very generous toward the southern girl in that moment.

But it wasn't a thirteen-year-old who hid there. I froze, trying to understand what I was seeing. Oliver pushed past me and pulled the man out by his collar, dumping him in front of the fire.

"Who are you? And what are you doing hiding in my room?" He seemed glad to have found another outlet for his anger.

The man cowered back a bit, holding up his hands placatingly. "I didn't mean any harm. I swear it. I was just working up the courage to speak to Your Highness when I heard the princess approaching. I panicked and hid. A mistake, I realize...but I truly meant no harm."

He was almost babbling now, but I wasn't really listening to his words. It sounded like a fairly unlikely story, but was it really any more unlikely than his presence at all? No servant had behaved in anything like such a manner for a long time now.

But none of that was what held my attention. I recognized

him. Or rather, I didn't recognize him. It was the same man I had seen twice before. Once in the palace, and once in the city before we went into the tunnels. The one who I was sure I had seen before. In the excitement of the cave in and then learning to control my powers I had forgotten all about him.

I could see Celeste's disappointed face chastising me in my mind. Despite all her teaching, I had let the small detail escape me. And his appearance now suggested it wasn't such a small detail after all.

"Where have I seen you before?" I finally blurted out, cutting him off.

Both he and Oliver stared at me.

"Seen...seen me, Your Highness? Perhaps in the corridors, I work—"

"No." I cut him off again. "I mean, yes, I did see you in the corridors. But I've also seen you before I came to Eldon. I'm sure of it."

He thought for a moment and then his brow cleared. "Marin, I suppose it must have been. You have an excellent memory for faces, Your Highness, for I'm sure we never spoke." He gave me a half bow. "I would have remembered if we had."

I frowned. "So you were there at the Princess Tourney, then?"

He nodded. "I was one of the servants in the Eldonian delegation. But my position is not significant enough to give me opportunity to talk to foreign royalty..."

"Never mind that," said Oliver. He paused. "What's your name, by the way?"

"Sterling." He didn't specify first or last, and Oliver didn't bother to inquire.

"What I really want to know is why you're not..." He waved his arms vaguely.

"A mindless automaton?" I supplied helpfully.

"Yes, that," he said without looking at me.

I bit my lip and looked at his back. How long did he intend to stay angry with me?

"Oh, right," said Sterling. "Well, that's why I decided to come to speak to you, Prince Oliver. I know it's not my place to approach the crown prince, but I just couldn't take it anymore. Everyone is acting..." An uncomfortable silence fell.

"Bewitched?" I didn't know why the two men seemed to have so much trouble spelling out the true situation.

"I did wonder about an enchantment..." Sterling looked thoughtful, and his eyes flicked to me. Did he suspect me or my kingdom of being involved somehow in the enchantment? Was that why he had hesitated to approach us before?

"Of course it's an enchantment. What else could it be?" Oliver was getting impatient, but I could also hear a barely suppressed note of excitement in his voice. "What we want to know is why it isn't affecting you."

I understood how he felt. This was the first hint we had found of someone inside the capital being able to resist the enchantment without my help.

"I don't really know." He saw our unimpressed expressions and rushed to continue. "Not for sure, anyway. But I have a guess. I come from an extremely remote mountain village. Not many of us ever even leave the village. But I wanted to see more of the world."

He glanced at me. "That's why I asked to be included in the delegation to Marin."

"How remote?" Oliver sounded skeptical. "The mountains are too treacherous in winter for anyone to live up there permanently."

Sterling nodded. "That's what made me wonder..." He looked between us both. "You see our village has a secret. One I've been sworn to keep. But in the circumstances..."

"Spit it out, man," said Oliver.

Sterling wrung his hands together. "You have to understand that our village isn't like other villages. The people who live there don't like the city. They want to live away from all the complications of that life, surrounded only by nature. We like to have our own space. It's the way we've been raised. The way of our ancestors."

"That's all very well," said Oliver. "But *how?*"

"Well, according to the elders, several generations ago, one of my own ancestors came to the aid of a poor orphan girl. A poor, but deserving, girl."

I could see where this was going. "Let me guess. This oh-so-deserving girl had a godmother?" My mind instantly flew to the blue velvet queen.

Sterling nodded. "The royal family at the time were under some sort of enchantment, apparently, and the godmother gave her a magic object. One that kept her safe from all enchantments. She freed the prince and married him. At her wedding, she asked her godmother as a wedding gift to shift the enchantment on the object just slightly. To make it so that it would protect against snow and ice rather than enchantment. And then the girl gave this object to the ancestor of mine who had helped her. She knew what they wanted, and once they had it, they retreated into the mountains and founded our village."

He shrugged. "We've lived there ever since, safe from the mountain snow. Every now and then a newcomer will arrive, someone driven up the mountain by necessity or desire. But few leave."

When I gave him a disbelieving look, he shrugged. "Oh, we have a small number who venture out to trade on occasion, and sometimes someone like me wants to leave. But we don't talk about where we've come from, and the traders at least always return. Otherwise we keep to ourselves. "

My mind buzzed between thoughts, going almost too fast for me to pin any of them down. "And you grew up under the constant protection of this object. And now you think that perhaps..."

He shrugged. "It's only a theory, Your Highness. But this enchantment does seem to be based around snow and ice...even the people..." He stopped and shivered.

"And perhaps some of the original magic on the object lingered," said Oliver, his eyes alight. "Perhaps it combined with the second enchantment, the one to ward off snow and ice..."

He looked at me, our earlier disagreement forgotten in the excitement of the moment. As one we turned back to Sterling.

"Take us to your village," Oliver commanded.

PART II
THE MOUNTAINS

CHAPTER 15

O liver was ready to charge straight out of the palace and up the mountain, but our intended guide wasn't quite so amenable—even in the face of a royal order. I couldn't help but have some sympathy with his situation. It was quite obvious what we wanted—the godmother object that had protected his village for generations. The one they most likely couldn't survive without.

While Oliver argued with the man, I watched them. Of course I knew that there was something else on Oliver's mind. Something we couldn't discuss in front of Sterling. Something that only fueled his determination. And I wasn't immune to Oliver's excitement. This was the first real hope we had encountered. But still...

Earlier I had forgotten about the man despite Celeste's warning to pay attention to the details. I had let myself be distracted by the overwhelming nature of my new gift. But I didn't want to compound the mistake by ignoring the second part of that advice. To never ignore my instincts. The only problem with that was I wasn't entirely sure what my instincts were telling me.

Something about this man had stood out to me from the beginning. But there was a good chance it was the absence of the enchantment that had caught my attention. That and a faint memory of seeing him in Marin. And yet still I hesitated.

Eventually Oliver managed to convince the man that leading us to his village was both the right thing to do given the fast approaching destruction of our kingdom and his duty given an order from the crown prince. There would only be two of us coming, he had reminded Sterling to seal the deal. Two against an entire village. We would have to convince his people before we would have any chance of leaving with the object.

But he flashed a glance toward me when he said it, and I knew he was thinking of our secret advantage. My powers. I just hoped I wouldn't end up having to use them against an innocent village full of people. Surely the villagers would realize they couldn't stand by and allow their entire kingdom to be destroyed.

Once he had finally agreed, Sterling proved his immediate usefulness by beginning to list all the supplies we would need for a trip into the mountains. He was talking mostly to himself, making plans half under his breath. Some of the items I would never have thought of, and some I'd never even heard of. I didn't have much experience with snow. Or mountains.

He left the room soon after with promises to gather the necessary supplies and meet us in the entry hall at first light. Oliver had wanted to leave immediately, but Sterling hadn't been willing to consider it.

"The mountains are treacherous in the dark," he said, and I had readily believed him.

As soon as he was gone, Oliver retrieved his abandoned bag and began to stride around the room, examining items and muttering to himself. I didn't move.

"Oliver," I said. He looked up, his mind clearly elsewhere. "Are you sure about this?"

He frowned. "What do you mean? Surely you must see the

significance of what he said! People do live up the mountain. And they get occasional newcomers—newcomers who stay." He gave me a weighted look.

I nodded. Between the mirror and this potential new object, it had been hard to know what was truly exciting him.

"You told that girl we had a plan," he continued, "and now we do. We go up to this village, we find the mirror, we convince them to let us borrow the object to free the palace from the enchantment, and then we use the mirror to find out who's responsible for this. Find out and then stop them. It really couldn't be more fortuitous timing."

"Well, exactly."

He stared at me in confusion.

I bit my lip. "Do you really trust Sterling?"

He straightened, a look of concern crossing his face. "Do you think he was lying? That he's planning to slip away overnight?"

"Actually, I hadn't even thought of that." I considered it. "No, I think he sounded genuinely committed to this trek. And really, where would he go? Back to his village? In that case, we can just follow him. I don't think there are going to be a lot of other tracks heading up the mountain."

Oliver relaxed. "You're right. And I don't think his village wants the destruction of the kingdom. They do trade with us after all. And we only need to borrow this object..."

He hoped. But I didn't voice that thought aloud.

With his mind apparently put at rest, Oliver turned back to his bag. I cleared my throat.

"That isn't actually what I meant."

He looked up again and waited for me to go on, but I could read the impatience at the back of his eyes. He was already consumed with this new hope and his need to save his kingdom.

"I just meant that we don't really know anything about him. Except for what he just told us himself. After we found him hiding in your room and spying on us." I raised an eyebrow, but Oliver just shrugged.

"He explained that."

I gave him a skeptical look but let that point go. "What does he do here at the palace? I don't think he actually said…"

Oliver shrugged. "I have no idea. Normally I'd direct you to talk to the steward, but given the current state of the steward…"

"Well, do you at least remember him from Marin? Was he really part of that delegation?"

Oliver squinted off into the distance. After a long moment, he grimaced at me and shrugged again. "Sorry, Celine, I can't remember."

I opened my mouth, but he must have read the frustration in my eyes, because he cut me off. "It's hard to explain, but while I can remember things that happened while I was under the enchantment, they aren't really clear. It's like I'm remembering through a haze or a fog. Or like it was all a particularly lucid dream. There's just no way I could remember details like the face of a random servant."

I pursed my lips and began my customary pacing. "Of course whether or not he was in Marin doesn't really have any bearing on anything. I just wish we had a way to prove at least one thing he's told us is true. I just have a…strange feeling about him."

Oliver gave me a look, so I rushed to defend myself. "I don't just recognize him from Marin—or wherever. I saw him that day we did the tour of the city. He was watching us. And I'm sure you remember what happened on that occasion."

Oliver frowned. "You mean you saw him just before we took that wrong turn off? He was there in the tunnels with us?"

"Well, no," I said reluctantly. "It was earlier—outside."

Oliver growled impatiently. "Do you know how many people saw us in the city? How many palace servants run errands up there? And given he's not affected by the enchantment, it's hardly surprising that he might have some curiosity about a visiting foreign princess. You know—enough to stop and look if he happened to cross paths with us."

He gave me a pointed look, and I sighed, running a hand across my face. Everything he said was true, of course. I just wished I didn't feel so uneasy about the whole thing.

His face softened as he watched me, and he crossed over to stand in front of me. He ran his hand up and down my arm, his gaze locked on my face.

"I appreciate your concern, Celine, I really do. But my kingdom is dying, and I've just learned that if I can't save it—and soon—it's going to be ripped apart even further. We were about to go off on a quest hoping to find a clue that might lead us to the mirror. Talk about a hopeless endeavor! And now here we actually have a potential option. The best I've ever heard for what might have happened to the thief. I always thought it strange that someone smart enough to steal the mirror in the first place was foolish enough to flee up the mountain."

I must have still looked unconvinced because he pushed on.

"Maybe everything won't work out as perfectly as I outlined earlier. But at least this way we have a double chance. If this object isn't going to be any help, we still have a chance of finding the mirror. And if the mirror isn't in the village, then perhaps this object will serve us instead. I'll be cautious. I don't have to actually trust this Sterling. But I do have to take this chance. I have to."

I frowned. There was no denying this plan seemed to hold more hope than wandering aimlessly around the kingdom. My thoughts circled back to the blue velvet queen.

"Do you know that portrait in the southern corridor on the second floor? The one surrounded by velvet with the empty pedestal next to it?"

Oliver blinked a couple of times, trying to keep pace with my change of direction. "Queen Estelle, you mean?"

131

I shrugged. "I didn't actually ask Giselle her name. But probably. Has it always been empty? The pedestal, I mean."

Oliver looked at me curiously. "Are you thinking she might have been the orphan girl from Sterling's story? It would fit well enough."

"It just occurred to me that if it was her, maybe she had the empty pedestal placed there to honor the object that she had given away. The one that helped her free the royal family."

Oliver nodded, already turning back to his bag. "That could well be. And it would support Sterling's story."

"Yes, I suppose so." I still didn't feel easy about it, but I could come up with no further reason to oppose the expedition. And after my earlier betrayal, I wanted to support Oliver now. I certainly couldn't leave him to go up the mountain alone. Which meant I needed to pack my own bag.

I crossed swiftly to the door, but paused before exiting, my hand on the door knob. "You told him there were only going to be two of us. I thought we'd already had that conversation."

He looked a little guilty. "That was when we were just going on a tour of the kingdom. A trip up into the high ranges in this weather will be far more dangerous."

I raised an eyebrow. "Good luck with that one." I pushed the door open. "Don't expect any help from me." I could imagine just how that would have gone down with me at age fifteen.

~

Giselle turned out to be a lot less vocal in her protests than I would have been, but it was hard to resist the look of appeal she threw at me.

I held up both hands and backed away. "Uh uh. I am not getting involved. This one is between the two of you."

Giselle looked disgusted, but I held firm. I thought she might ignore me after that, in a huff, but instead she sought me out later when Oliver had gone with Sterling to look over the supplies he had gathered.

She got straight to the point. "I don't like this situation."

I sighed, not wanting to start the conversation again, but she quickly shook her head.

"I don't mean that. I mean this Sterling fellow. And the whole story. It's mighty convenient. Oh, and the coup. I don't like that part either."

I winced sympathetically. Oliver had tried to use the coup as an excuse for why she needed to stay behind. He wasn't keeping her safe, he had claimed. If there was an army camped only a day away, then we needed someone who could still think to stay.

But she saw through that argument as easily as my fifteen-year-old self would have.

"Yes," she had said to him. "Because I'm going to be super effective at holding off an entire army on my own. Or perhaps you think I'm going to rouse the guard to acts of heroism? When I can't even get my own sister—who also happens to be my best friend—to have a conversation with me anymore."

She was right, of course. And I could understand why the knowledge of the impending coup would only make her more uncomfortable about being abandoned here. Which is why I didn't try to repeat Oliver's arguments in his absence.

"Well, if we fail and the army comes, just stay out of the way," I said, instead. "Or better yet, find Cassandra and Alexander. I'm sure they'll protect you once they realize you aren't under the enchantment and you don't intend to put up a fight."

"Thank you, Celine, all my worries are now eased."

I sighed. "You know as well as I do that there are no good options from here. I don't trust Sterling either. But Oliver is determined to go ahead with this. And to be honest, I can't blame him. What else are we supposed to do?"

"You could convince him this is a bad idea," said Giselle, her eyes fixed earnestly on me. "I know you could."

"You overestimate me." I shifted uncomfortably. I wasn't going to ask why she thought I would have more influence over her brother than she did. "I already tried."

Giselle sighed and slumped back. "Not hard enough, clearly," she muttered.

I narrowed my eyes but decided to let the comment go. We were all on edge. Silence enveloped us until she suddenly looked up, her eyes fierce.

"Then you need to protect him. Promise me you'll keep him safe! You're our secret weapon if this Sterling does turn out to be untrustworthy."

"Of course, I will, Giselle. You know I will."

She nodded once, firmly, and seemed satisfied with that.

The remaining hours of the day were consumed with packing and various preparations. Every time I saw Giselle she had Emmeline beside her, so we didn't speak again of our expedition. But her eyes seemed to burn into mine, reminding me of my promise. Even the presence of her sister seemed calculated to remind me of what was at stake.

But I didn't need her reminders. Even as I worked, I constantly turned my attention inward, even if only for a few seconds. The simmering warmth inside reassured me every time. Once, when I found myself alone in a corridor, I even briefly ignited my fingertips, my gaze captivated by the merrily burning flames. I held it for a full count of one hundred before clasping my hands into fists to extinguish them.

I wasn't helpless. Whatever was coming for us, we had a power it couldn't even imagine. Whatever happened, I would get us out of it. I was sure of it. Because I had always been determined. But now I was also powerful.

CHAPTER 16

I knew I needed a good sleep—so naturally I tossed and turned restlessly all night. And still the dawn came all too soon. We gathered silently in the entrance hall, and I could see the relief on Oliver's face when Sterling appeared as promised.

I had half expected Giselle to be absent in a silent protest, but she was there to wave us off, Emmeline accompanying her. Emmeline seemed even more subdued than usual, not showing the least interest in our obvious departure. Oliver looked guilty, his eyes constantly flicking between his sisters, but neither he nor Giselle actually spoke about her abandonment.

Sterling had allocated out the supplies, and it was obvious I had received the lightest pack. I made no complaint, however. I might have been working on my fitness, but I didn't feel entirely equipped for a dangerous hike up a steep and icy mountain range.

None of the other inhabitants of the palace so much as cast us a second glance, and the people in the city were no more interested. Snow now lingered on all the streets and stairways of the mountain, and I actually felt a pang of relief knowing the Elamese army was so close.

At least if something happened to us, Giselle wouldn't end up trapped by snow and left to starve to death.

I shook off the morbid thoughts as we reached the northernmost edge of the city. A trail led upward, but Sterling had warned that it would take us only a small part of the way. His people had tracked a passable route, but they didn't travel it often enough for a true trail to have developed.

I hitched my pack higher and looked down at my clothes in distaste. I had been forced to raid the wardrobe of an unprotesting Emmeline because I didn't have anything even close to suitable for this journey. Giselle hadn't finished growing, so she was too short for me to borrow anything of hers. But, unfortunately, Emmeline was taller than me, despite being younger, and her clothes didn't fit nearly as well as I would have liked. If I'd had more time, I would have had my maids readjust them, but the time available hadn't allowed for it.

And that was if I could have roused them to the effort. I had watched with growing alarm as my own people took on the same disinterested air as the locals. They weren't as far gone—yet—but it seemed my gift had saved more than just Oliver and Giselle. I shivered at the thought of losing myself to the enchantment, but Oliver looked back at me with concern, so I forced a smile.

My thoughts returned to my outfit. It was quite a cunning ensemble, really, and I would have loved to have one that actually fit, sewn especially for me. Particularly if it was designed by my genius sister-in-law Evie. An inner, skin-tight layer provided extra warmth, and every item was water-proof. The fur-lined boots reached almost to my knees, and the long jacket had been designed to look like a dress, although it cut off just above my knees. Still, between the jacket and the boots, only a short stretch of pants was visible.

A clever compromise between modesty and practicality, since

not even the most elegant noble-bred lady could be expected to trek up mountains and through snow in a proper gown. The fur that lined it showed around the hood and along the bottom of the jacket and felt impossibly soft against my cheeks.

Sterling talked as we walked—apparently suffering from no lack of breath—telling me all about the difficulties in finding game so high in the mountains, particularly in the winter. He explained how no part of the animal was wasted and described something of the process of turning animal hides into clothing such as what I wore.

It sounded like a highly unpleasant process to me, but he claimed that his village possessed several experts and that the clothing they created was one of the most prized items their traders brought to the city. I had to admit to some interest in meeting these people and even felt a pang of regret that our visit would of necessity be so short. Perhaps one day, when the kingdom had been restored, I could visit the village again. I could even come with the party returning their object to them, perhaps.

By the time it reached late afternoon, I had sourly abandoned any such plans. If there was one thing I did not intend to do, it was climb up this mountain ever again. My legs ached, and the cold air burned its way down to my lungs with every gulping breath. And yet every time I stopped to look back, it seemed we had come almost no distance at all.

And in case the trail wasn't already difficult enough, we soon encountered snow too deep to be easily waded through. At that point I discovered the use of the strange contraptions someone had attached to the outside of my pack.

A hardwood frame shaped into an oval that tapered at the back supported a latticework of rawhide lacings. Oliver explained it was called a snowshoe and had me sit on a nearby boulder while he showed me how to attach them to my boots.

"Ideally, I would have preferred you to have a chance to practice in them first," he said as he finished his demonstration. "But…"

He shrugged and stood back up, and I wondered why my feet could feel the absence of his hands, despite the many layers between us. I had hoped for at least a smile from him, but it seemed despite his gratitude at my accompanying him, he hadn't entirely forgotten the betrayal of my deal with Cassandra. I could almost read the conflicting emotions in his eyes every time they rested on me.

I soon found I had to adopt an unnatural stride to make the shoes work, and several times I ended up on my backside in the snow before I got the hang of it. Oliver demonstrated the best method, a stride which allowed the inner edges of the two snow-shoes to slide over one another. But it was only through trial and error that I worked out how to correctly roll my feet to make it work.

And even after I thought I had the trick of it, a tight turn between two towering walls of rock sent me straight back onto the snow again. In the end Oliver had to come back for me and help me to execute a strange maneuver which required me to bend my legs at an awkward angle so that one had completely turned while the other still remained straight. He called it a kick turn, explaining it in such a cheerful manner that I muttered dire threats about who exactly I would soon be kicking.

He just laughed, probably because he knew that any actual attempt on my part to kick anyone was more likely to lead to my downfall than theirs. When I made it around what turned out to be a series of difficult turns, I crowed with such triumph that he laughed again.

Sterling, however, merely frowned at me and told me to keep my voice down. "There are predators even up here," he said. "Not to mention the risk of an avalanche."

That effectively rendered me entirely mute for the next hour. And by the time we stopped to make camp for the night, I was far too exhausted to talk. My calves burned more intensely than the magical banked fire in my chest, and I made only feeble attempts to help with the set up before I was thankfully told to sit down and rest.

Sterling had led us to a small, empty cave, protected enough by a rocky overhang to be free of snow. I could only hope his route included such snug shelters for every night of our journey. I didn't much fancy camping out among the snowdrifts.

I detached the cumbersome snowshoes—proud to manage it on my own—and massaged my feet while Sterling piled a collection of small branches ready for a campfire. I had noticed him collecting them as we walked, securing them to the top of his pack with a strap clearly designed for such a use.

When he went out to fill a small pot with snow, ready for melting into water, I pulled off my gloves and called cheerily after him that I would light the fire while he was gone. He didn't respond, but as soon as he was out of sight, I poured all of my exhaustion and irritation into the warm spot inside me. It blazed up more strongly than I had intended, and the trickle of flame I had meant to send at the branches more closely resembled a fire ball.

I spluttered and scrambled backward, cutting off the stream of fire and gratefully watching it subside into a spark that soon became a merrily burning fire. The guilty voice in my head seemed to speak aloud, echoing through the cave.

"You really should be more careful, you know. You'll give yourself away if you keep doing things like that. Or burn one of our packs, or something."

Apparently the slight figure who had entered the cave took my look of surprise as disapproval because she added, "Oh, relax. Sterling recruited Oliver and they're off gathering more wood. He can't hear me."

A slow smile spread across my face, and I actually chortled.

"Oliver is not going to be pleased to see you here."

Giselle shrugged. "And I wasn't pleased he tried to leave me behind. Your point?"

"Oh, nothing at all," I hastened to assure her.

"You say that now," she muttered, "but I don't remember you coming to my defense back at the palace."

"If it had been up to a vote, you would have had my support." I had disapproved of excluding the younger girl, after all. I just hadn't been willing to stick myself into someone else's family only to advocate for a dangerous course.

"So you say now," she muttered, as she busied herself removing her pack and snowshoes. I noticed, somewhat disconsolately, that her pack was bigger than mine, and that she looked all-too-comfortable with the hated snowshoes. It had probably been easy for her to follow us when we had been confined to my slow pace.

By the time the two men returned, we had retrieved the pot of snow Sterling had left outside the cave when he went looking for wood. It wasn't boiling yet, but it had melted into liquid, and we had laid out the ingredients ready for the stew we intended to make.

Funnily enough, it wasn't gratitude that filled Oliver's expression when he came into the cave and got a good look at us.

"GISELLE!!" He choked on his next words, apparently too angry to even speak properly. Sterling merely raised his eyebrows before busying himself as far out of the way as he could get.

"Oh, sit down and relax, Oliver," said Giselle. "What exactly did you expect?"

Oliver turned his incensed gaze to me.

"Don't look at me! I didn't know anything about this. But neither did I like leaving her behind, so you won't hear me lamenting."

He glared at us both and stomped off to the back of the cave.

"Don't worry," said Giselle, dropping a small packet of dried herbs into the water. "He'll get over it quickly."

And, sure enough, by the time he had divested himself of his snow shoes and come back to join us, he seemed reasonably calm.

"I suppose there's no point trying to send you back."

"None at all," said Giselle, still calmly adding ingredients to the pot.

He sighed. "Well, I tried, I suppose." He looked into the fire for a moment and then his suspicious gaze flicked to Sterling and then me.

I just smiled innocently. He clearly suspected I had used unnatural means to light it, but he should have known I wasn't stupid enough to do it in front of Sterling.

He sighed again. "You two girls are going to be the death of me."

"Don't be ridiculous," I said briskly, stripping the bark from a likely looking stick I could use to stir the stew. "From where I'm sitting, we're far more likely to end up saving you."

"Forgive me," he said, his smile returning. "I should know better than to underestimate either of you by now." But I noticed his gaze lingered on me, and I wondered if it meant he had forgiven me.

Secretly I was hoping that having Giselle along meant I wouldn't always be trailing behind, but the next day proved these hopes to be unfounded. I grumbled to myself as the morning wore on. I didn't like being the slowest and weakest, and I had to keep reminding myself that they were relying on my strength in other areas.

By late morning, I didn't have breath or concentration to grumble, even to myself. The trail—such as it was—climbed steeply upward, alternating with occasional sudden drops as we encountered small valleys. The other three easily adjusted their gait for the steeper slope, angling their shoes outward or side-stepping to give them more traction. But I had only just gotten used to walking the other way, and I didn't appreciate being back at a beginner level again.

Eventually it became steep enough that Sterling, who still led the way, began to thrust the tips of his snowshoes into the snow with each step, creating a sort of temporary stairway for those of us behind to utilize. As long as I didn't look behind me, I found climbing up these stairs easier. And I had to admit that at every stage my path had been made significantly easier by having the trail broken ahead of me. The effort of going first began to wear even on Sterling, and by afternoon he was alternating positions with Oliver, and even occasionally Giselle.

When we hit our first descent, I stopped at the top and watched Sterling make his way down. Oliver followed not far behind him, but Giselle stopped beside me, and only her presence enabled me to hold back tears. The two seemed to half-step, half-slide, their exaggerated steps allowing them to basically run down the hill. I wasn't ready to admit it to her, but I wasn't at all sure that I could emulate yet another stride. Not without ending up rolling down the hill as a giant snowball.

Giselle seemed to sense my despair, however.

"Don't worry," she said. "They're just breaking the trail for us." When I looked over at her, she was actually grinning. "This is the fun part."

Sitting down on the very crest of the hill, she gave me one more smile before pushing off. Following the trail packed down by Sterling and Oliver's snowshoes, she slid all the way down on her rear-end. Watching her, I found myself mirroring her smile. Now *that* I was fairly certain I could do.

When I reached the bottom, Oliver held out a hand to help me to my feet, and the clasp of his hand combined with the joy of the break from the unexpected slog. I had to clamp down on a sudden rush of warmth inside me.

Before it could gain momentum, however, Sterling appeared

suddenly at our side, his face grim. I hadn't even realized he had disappeared during our descent.

His eyes kept darting around us, and his voice had dropped low.

"I went scouting a short way ahead. There's a section along here with lots of rocky overhangs. In the past there have even been rockfalls that blocked the way, so I thought it best to have a look."

Oliver frowned. "Is it blocked now?"

Sterling shook his head quickly. "No, but I found something I don't like the look of at all." He paused.

"Well, come on," I said at last, rubbing my arms, despite the warmth burning inside me. "Spit it out!"

"There's a snow leopard den up ahead. And there's nothing a snow leopard loves so much as ambushing its prey from above. Using just the sort of terrain we have coming up."

CHAPTER 17

I gasped, but Oliver and Giselle both merely frowned.

"Snow leopards aren't exactly known for attacking humans, Sterling." Giselle sounded impatient.

Sterling continued to look grim. "Normally, I'd agree with you, Your Highness. But this isn't exactly normal circumstances, now is it?" He gestured around us. "Have you ever seen snow like this in late spring before? At cub time? It's not just us humans affected by this encroaching winter. And it's been three hard years before this."

He hesitated, and I narrowed my eyes at him.

"What is it?" I asked.

"Seeing this one den isn't even what worries me most. I saw another one much too recently. And that one had four cubs not yet old enough to walk."

"Another one? This close?" Now Oliver sounded worried as well.

Sterling nodded. "I think the den I just saw belongs to a male, and it looks fairly new. I'd say his territory is usually higher up. He's likely come down as far as he dares to make a new one. He knows that by coming down here he's encroaching on other leopards' territories. That female's for one, and quite possibly another male's. And if he's been driven to this—who knows what else he may be driven to?"

Giselle bit her lip, and I saw her eyes dart around us in the same pattern as Sterling's gaze kept taking. "What do you suggest?" she asked.

Sterling rubbed his jaw. "It's late afternoon already, and we won't make it all the way through the next section before night-fall. It's dusk and dawn they're usually out hunting, so I say we find a spot to camp now and tackle the next section in the middle of the day."

Oliver frowned, and I knew what he was thinking. More time lost when we were already on an impossible deadline. But his gaze turned to his sister before lingering on me, and when he spoke, his mind seemed to be somewhere else entirely.

"I don't know. You said you just saw this den. I assume the male wasn't actually there."

"Aye." Sterling sounded thoughtful.

"Well," Oliver continued, "if their other patterns have changed, who's to say their hunting hours haven't extended also? It seems he's already out hunting now, in fact. And I haven't seen any convenient caves any time recently where we might camp. I don't like the idea of lingering here for so long or of setting ourselves up in the open."

"You want to hunt him ourselves then, Your Highness?" I couldn't tell from his tone whether Sterling approved or not.

Oliver sighed. "Want to? No. I hate the idea, to be honest. But I hate the idea of ending up food myself even more." Again his eyes flicked to Giselle and then me.

Part of me wanted to tell him we could look after ourselves, but the other part of me was in complete agreement. I had no desire to suddenly find a desperate and hungry snow leopard leaping onto my head. Especially not while I was stuck in these awkward shoes and trying to hide my abilities from one of our party.

"Well, then, I guess we're going hunting." Sterling sounded unenthusiastic but willing, at least. And he began to prepare in a way that suggested he had some idea what he was doing, divesting himself of anything that would get in his way.

"We'll leave our packs with you," said Oliver, striding over to leave them in a sheltered spot between some trees and against a cliff wall.

Giselle opened her mouth, but a stern look from Oliver made her close it again with a resigned look. I wasn't so easily quelled.

"What are we supposed to be? Bait? I'm not sitting around waiting to be picked off by a desperate predator."

Oliver was shaking his head before I'd got close to finishing. "We're not exactly their preferred prey, so I can't see him attacking you in the open snow. Especially not when we're hunting him. I know it's not ideal, but you'd be nothing but dead weight if you came along. At best."

He gave me a meaningful look, and I glared back at him.

A laugh appeared in the back of his eyes. "I'm not impugning your skills, Celine. You've turned out to have a great many hidden talents. And if you tell me that tracking and hunting animals in the snow is one of them, then I'll welcome you along with gratitude. If, on the other hand, you have no experience in that area…"

He waited, watching me with a cocked eyebrow.

"Fine," I said, sitting down in what would be called a huff in anyone less exalted than a princess. "I will sit here and await rescue by the brave and handsome prince." I batted my eyelashes at him as angrily as I could.

"Did you hear that, Giselle?" Oliver grinned. "She thinks I'm brave and handsome."

"Oh, do get on with it," said Giselle, rolling her eyes and plonking herself beside me.

"Ready, princeling?" asked Sterling. It was the least respectful toward Oliver that I'd ever heard him, but I supposed that hunting dangerous animals re-ordered the hierarchy somewhat. There was no denying that out here in the mountains, Sterling was the master.

As soon as they disappeared, I suggested that we start a fire.

"Feeling cold?" Giselle gave me an ironic look.

"Obviously not." I shivered at just the idea of how cold I would be feeling without my internal fire to keep me warm. "But if this takes a while, you'll freeze just sitting here. And I daresay the hunters would appreciate something warm to eat when they get back."

"And it might keep any wild animals away?"

I couldn't tell if she was teasing me or offering the suggestion seriously.

"Well, I know Oliver said we should be safe, but it couldn't hurt, right?"

Leaving our own packs next to Sterling's and Oliver's, we began to gather sticks and kindling. I didn't want to use what Sterling had been gathering for our evening campfire.

It quickly became obvious why he gathered it throughout the day. Finding enough for even a small, short-lived blaze in the immediate vicinity turned out to be difficult. Without noticing, I moved further and further from Giselle and our packs.

Eventually I had gathered nearly enough to make at least a small fire which should be enough to keep Giselle from freezing if nothing else. So I circled back around, hoping she had been equally fortunate. Thankfully it was easy to follow my tracks back in the direction I had come, so I hurried more quickly, my focus on my snowshoes. Moving on the snow with any kind of speed involved a great deal of concentration. Especially when I had my arms full of sticks.

Perhaps that's why I didn't notice anything earlier. A sudden prickling of dread was as much responsible for my sudden pause as the slight sound. Regardless of the reason, I spun around and dropped into a crouch a mere second before a blur of gray leaped at me from a nearby boulder.

Thanks to my quick movement, the creature missed, landing some way further on before spinning to face me. The large cat planted its four feet and hissed. I had imagined a snow leopard as pure white, but in reality, it looked more gray than white, with black spots covering its face and body.

I dropped the wood in my arms and straightened. Somewhat to my surprise, I felt no fear. Giselle's earlier words had reminded me that while I might not be any good for hunting or tracking, I was also far from defenseless. I was heading into the unknown to take down a kingdom-killing enchantment. I could handle one hungry cat.

I didn't even have to think about stoking the fire inside, it roared up to meet me. Thrusting out my hands, palms toward the sky, I ignited a fire ball on each one. For a moment we both stood motionless, facing off. The leopard growled, but its feet shifted, almost uncertainly, and I half expected it to turn and run from the flames.

But I couldn't let it go. It might attack Giselle next, and she didn't have the defenses I did.

As I drew back one arm, however, ready to lob the ball of fire toward the cat, a shout split the air.

"Celine, no! Stop!"

I hesitated, turning toward Giselle's voice in time to see her come stumbling out of the trees. She launched herself toward me, gripping my closest arm with both hands and forcing it down.

My control slipped, and the flame shifted shape, running up my arm toward her. I gasped and extinguished it. The leopard hissed again in response, and I remembered its presence.

"Giselle! What are you doing?"

"You can't do that," she said. "What would we do with the body? How would we explain to Sterling that the leopard exploded in flames? We *are* trying to keep your abilities a secret, aren't we?"

I gave her a blank look, and she lowered her brows.

"Wait—you don't actually trust him, do you? You haven't told him?"

"No, of course not. But..." I looked back at the leopard who seemed to be undecided as to whether it should run now that I had company or attack now that the fire had disappeared.

It shifted its weight forward, a low growl returning, and I swallowed. The fear that had been missing earlier rushed in, almost extinguishing the lingering warmth inside. My eyes flicked from the leopard's bared teeth to the long claws that cut into the snow. I had no sword, no spear, no long weapon of any kind to fend it off.

"Celine!" Giselle cried again, this time in more of a scream than a shout.

The cat had finally made a decision—apparently deeming her the better target. As it leaped toward her, fire sprouted from my fingers without my making a conscious decision to call it. But I hesitated, Giselle's earlier warning ringing in my ears.

Giselle snatched up the longest and sturdiest of the branches I had dropped, whipping it in front of her and bracing it with both hands. The animal smashed into it, thrown off enough to miss its target, although the tip wasn't sharp enough to pierce skin.

It fell hard against the snow, rising only shakily back to its feet. This time it didn't even consider another attack, turning tail and disappearing swiftly into the trees. I followed it with my eyes, my flaming hands still held in front of me.

"Are you sure we shouldn't..."

Giselle had collapsed into the snow, panting. "I don't think she'll be attacking us again in a hurry, do you? Or any humans for that matter."

I nodded, the fire winking out. My mind, which seemed to

have frozen during the attack, began to work again. "She? So that wasn't the one Oliver is tracking?"

"No, it can't have been. She must be the one from the den Sterling saw earlier. The one with the cubs. She did appear to be heading back downhill. I know we weren't expecting her to be out hunting as well, especially out this far, but if other leopards are encroaching on her territory, she's probably getting worried for her cubs. Especially with this weather."

I began to gather the fallen sticks, carefully avoiding looking at Giselle. Shame smothered me, making it hard to breathe. With my powers I had felt strong, but without them I had been utterly useless. What would Oliver say if he knew I had left his young sister to defend herself without even trying to help?

I picked up the last branch except for the one Giselle still gripped. Would she tell him? He was already unhappy with me for my deal with Cassandra—but this time his disgust would be warranted. He couldn't think any more harshly of me than I already thought of myself.

Slowly we returned to the abandoned packs. Giselle walked in silence, and I couldn't blame her. At least she wasn't expressing her disgust aloud.

When we reached the packs, I once again dropped the sticks. I knew I should prepare the fire, but my mind still circled around the encounter with the leopard, a slight shake making my hands rebel against the commands I attempted to give them.

Again Giselle acted without speaking, carefully placing the sticks ready for a fire. When she had finished, she looked up at me expectantly. I stared back at her stupidly for a moment before giving a sudden start and thrusting a spurt of fire at her arrangement.

I had overcompensated, though, and the flames rushed through the sticks, not holding long enough to ignite them. I took a deep breath and tried again, maintaining a more controlled stream this time. When I was sure the sticks had caught, I let my hands drop and sat down.

I knew I couldn't put off my apology to Giselle any longer. But when she threw herself into the snow beside me, her expression made me stop short. Her eyes glowed, her face alive with excitement.

And when she looked up and met my gaze, a grin broke across her face.

"That was amazing!" She smiled into our little fire and then back up at me. "Celine—we fought a snow leopard!"

I smiled back, although the expression felt painful on my face. "We? I'm pretty sure it was all you."

She sat up straighter, seeming to take my words as a compliment to her rather than an indictment of me.

"It was pretty amazing," she murmured again. "Although I think all that fire threw it off. I've never actually seen one up close like that before." She chortled suddenly. "Just wait until Oliver hears!"

I winced, looking down quickly so she wouldn't notice. It seemed foolish to apologize now when she clearly hadn't noticed anything odd. It might even be insulting, since it would imply I hadn't thought her able to handle the situation without me.

Slowly I regained some calm, although the shame still stung whenever my mind wandered back to the attack. To keep ourselves busy, we prepared some hot tea, and when Oliver and Sterling finally returned, they looked grateful for it.

My eyes searched Oliver for any signs of injury, but I could see nothing. He looked tired and sad, but I could also read their success in his eyes.

"He was lurking waiting for prey just where we thought he would be," he said quietly. "Above the next part of our path."

"The way is now clear," said Sterling, and neither of them offered any further details.

Giselle nodded, clearly attempting to look nonchalant. "I

don't think we should be having any trouble from the other one, either."

Oliver frowned at her and then quickly looked to me, his eyes asking for clarification.

I swallowed and forced myself to talk normally. "It seems the mother was also out hunting today. She managed to find us, but we gave her enough of a scare that I don't think she'll be coming back any time soon. She took off downhill."

"What?!" Oliver stood, looked around a little foolishly, and then sat back down.

"You two scared it off?" Sterling's voice held something—although I couldn't tell if it was skepticism or begrudging respect.

Oliver's eyes immediately flew to my hands, and I knew what he was thinking. I shook my head slightly, rushing into an explanation.

"We'd been gathering sticks for the fire, and Giselle wielded one like an expert spearman. The leopard nearly skewered herself on it, and she quickly lost interest after that."

"Two leopards." Oliver shook his head. "What are the chances?"

"What are the chances of any of this?" I gestured wide to indicate the mountain, the snow, and our mismatched little party.

He grimaced, his face acknowledging the truth of my words. But with Sterling present, none of us felt like dissecting the situation any further. Instead we quickly packed up and began the next section. Sterling had assured us that a snug little cave could be found halfway along the rocky section, and at least we would be getting a short break from the snow shoes.

Oliver smiled almost warmly at me as we set off, and it took all of my self-control to smile back. He clearly thought there was more to the story—and he was right. It just wasn't what he was thinking. I hadn't saved Giselle, she had saved me. Twice.

And I had just stood there. Useless without my powers.

CHAPTER 18

The memory of how it had felt to stand helpless before the leopard haunted me. But the mountains also grew steeper and more treacherous, and I had little time to think of other things than keeping my feet and following the path the others broke for me.

Giselle had obviously not filled Oliver in on the true situation with the leopard because he continued to view me more warmly than he had since the deal with Cassandra. And Giselle herself seemed to have forgiven me for not supporting her attendance on the trip. Apparently she viewed us as comrades-in-arms after the run in with the leopard.

But their approval could not rebuild my shaken confidence. I was utterly determined not to prove myself the weak link again. And so I concentrated with utmost focus on my hiking, my technique improving enough that I no longer always trailed far behind the rest.

Undoubtedly we had all noticed the snow growing deeper and the temperature dropping, but no one spoke of it. I could see them all reacting to the cold in various subtle ways, though, and could only be silently grateful for the heat that kept me perpetually warm from the inside out.

I still worried, however, and that third night it took me longer to fall asleep than usual. The steady breaths sounding from around the fire made me think I was the only one lying awake— until Oliver's whisper sounded from the darkness.

"Do you think they're still holding off? Lord Treestone and the Elamese. They know we'll need some time, right?"

I started and bit my lip. It had been constantly at the back of my mind—a pressure that never eased as I tried to move faster up the mountain—but I had no desire to talk to Oliver about the potential coup.

My silence didn't deter him, however.

"Would you really stand against me? If it came to a coup?"

I sighed. "Not against you, never against you. At least, that's not how I think of it."

"What other way is there to think of it?" He sounded bitter.

So the leopard hadn't been enough to win me forgiveness, after all.

"With things as they currently stand," I said, "without our interference, there shouldn't be any bloodshed. A bloodless coup. And possibly only a temporary one. If it comes to one at all."

"And my parents?"

I grimaced, although he couldn't see me in the dark. I didn't want to admit out loud that I didn't know what the coup had planned for them. But surely Lord Treestone and the Elamese didn't mean to execute them? Not until they had actual evidence of what was going on, at least.

The silence lengthened while I hoped a little desperately I was right. I had gone over and over it in my mind, and I still didn't see what else I could have done. We were all trying to save Eldon in our own way.

"They didn't say exactly how long they would wait, but I've been thinking about that. I think they were protected from the enchantment before because they were so far south. But my own people have been slowly freezing up, just like your people. It's hard to say how long it will take, but if they wait long enough, they may lose the motivation for a coup."

Oliver's indrawn breath sounded loud in the darkness, and then he gave a quiet bark of humorless laughter.

"I have no idea what to think of that. Should I be hoping that more of my people succumb to this curse in order to save my family? Soon we might not have a kingdom left to rule at all."

I shrugged and then remembered I needed to speak aloud. "I don't know."

Silence fell again, before Oliver's sudden whisper made me startle for a second time.

"No bloodshed. That's why you agreed, isn't it? To protect me. You think I'm going to get myself killed if I oppose them."

"Of course. What other reason could I have?"

He sighed, the sound heavy in the darkness. "How did we end up here?"

I tried to think of an answer and then decided it must be a rhetorical question.

"I'm so sorry, Oliver. About everything."

He shifted slightly, the sound barely audible above the sleeping breaths of the other two.

"You're not the one planning a coup, Celine. And you didn't create this curse. You're just trying to keep us all alive. I might not like it, but I can understand it."

Did that mean he'd forgiven me? He didn't say any more, and after another stretch of silence, his breaths joined those of the others. I would just have to wait and hope so.

As we headed out the next morning, even I could feel the temperature dropping. I tried to remember if it had warmed at least slightly after the previous sunrises. It didn't help my confidence that Sterling kept glancing at the sky in concern.

"What's wrong?" I finally demanded, looking from Sterling to Oliver and then finally Giselle. "Am I missing something?"

"This weather…" The unease was clear in Oliver's voice.

"It's not looking good," Sterling agreed. "Maybe we should find somewhere to hole up for a day or two."

I was already shaking my head as Oliver spoke.

"And risk getting snowed in? We don't have enough wood for that. We wouldn't be able to keep a fire burning."

He seemed to be carefully not looking in my direction, and I wasn't sure whether he was driven by the desire to keep my abilities secret or just the determination not to be held up when we were already so close. I was fairly certain I could keep us all warm if it came to it, but I wholeheartedly agreed with either motivation. I had no desire to spend any more time than necessary stuck uselessly on this mountain.

"Aye," Sterling rubbed his chin. "You have the right of it there." He sighed. "I suppose we'll press on then and try to outrun it. I just wasn't expecting anything this bad. Things are deteriorating faster than I realized."

"Outrun what?" I asked.

"The coming storm." He frowned. "Let's just hope it's not a blizzard."

"We just have to get close enough to your village, though, right?" Giselle watched him with sharp eyes. "We must be getting close now, and once we're in the circle of the enchanted object, we should be safe from something like a blizzard."

Sterling nodded, his gaze still on the sky. "Aye, that's right, Your Highness. We might be able to reach the village today even. Depending."

I met Giselle's eyes, and she shrugged slightly. Oliver continued to show a determined face—pressing forward without consideration of failure—but Giselle and I were both significantly more skeptical of our so-far helpful guide. Except there was nothing we could do at this point if he was lying to us.

I could only hope he had no more desire to be caught out in a blizzard than we did.

~

The sky had soon become a solid wall of gray, hiding the sun from view. I itched to light up my hands—just so I could clearly see the path ahead of me—but I carefully refrained, keeping a tight hold on my inner fire.

But as the temperature plummeted, I found myself fueling that inner warmth more and more just to stay warm. It had become an exercise in self-control as I pushed the heat down my arms to warm my fingers, holding it just short of bursting out into the open.

The effort held so much of my attention, that I had stopped watching the weather. So it took me by surprise when the first snowflakes fell. They were soon joined by others, however, and ignoring the heavy flurry became impossible.

Now that I had returned my attention to the others, I could see that they looked almost deathly cold. The tiny sections of exposed skin on their faces shone red, and Giselle's body periodically shook with deep shivers. Oliver kept throwing her concerned looks, but in truth he didn't look much warmer himself.

When we stopped for a brief rest, I approached Giselle, slipping off my glove once her body blocked me from Sterling's sight. Biting my lip in concentration, I slipped my fingers up her closest sleeve until I reached her skin just above her wrist.

"Oh," she gasped, her eyes flying to mine. She lowered her voice. "You're so warm!"

"And you're freezing," I whispered back, equally quiet.

Oliver positioned himself between us and Sterling, glancing

my way, his eyes holding equal parts concern and hope. After my efforts all morning, I was confident I could do this. But I understood his concern. And shared it. I would have to walk a very fine line.

Slowly—painfully slowly—I pushed heat up through my arms and out my palm. I felt a gentle warmth radiate out against Giselle's skin as a soft puff of hot air pushed its way up her sleeve, briefly ballooning out her jacket before it found its way out the other openings.

"Ohhh…" She closed her eyes for a brief moment, a grateful smile on her face. "It's so warm!"

I grinned triumphantly across at Oliver who smiled gratefully back.

"Your control is getting better," Giselle whispered, and I shrugged.

"I've had a lot of practice this trip. I'm fairly certain I would have frozen to death already without…" I gestured toward my middle wordlessly.

"I wish my godmother had given me—" Giselle cut off her words at my warning look. For all we were talking quietly, the less said the better.

I waited a minute before carefully sending another rush of hot air up her sleeve. Then another minute and another burst of heat. Slipping my hand out, I moved to stand casually next to Oliver. Sterling continued to show no interest in us, his eyes focused on the ominous sky, the flurries of snow, and the path ahead of us. I didn't like his frown.

Holding out my hand, I hovered just above Oliver's sleeve, my eyes asking him a silent question. I hadn't hesitated with Giselle, but this felt different, despite my only offering to touch his arm.

He bit his lip, and then a shiver shook him, and he nodded slightly, extending his own hand toward me. Not looking up into his face, I slowly slid my bare fingers up between his glove and sleeve. As soon as my fingertips brushed against exposed skin, the controlled fire inside me roared, and I took a deep breath, pausing while I roughly pushed it down, reasserting my control. I would have to be even more careful this time.

I glanced up into Oliver's eyes, expecting to see confusion at my pause, but his eyes held something else entirely. The coldness that had lingered between us since my agreement with Cassandra had indeed fallen away. Lost perhaps somewhere in the darkness of the night before.

I looked away quickly, already struggling to control the raging inside. Forcing myself to concentrate, I pushed my hand up until my full fingers rested against his forearm.

Slowly, inch by inch, I released some of the heat within me, letting it creep up my arm and then out. I loosened my internal hold even more, and a rush of warm air—stronger than the one I had used on Giselle—rushed up his sleeve.

He sighed, his eyes briefly closing as I felt his body relax. I hadn't realized how tense he had been. I watched his now relaxed face with concern. For just the moment, he had let himself go, and it emphasized how tightly he had been in control before. Just how cold was it, really? I had no way to know how much my ability masked the effects of the weather. If we continued to press on, would we make it to the village?

Just as I thought it, the flurry of snow became more of a solid wall, as if the clouds had suddenly opened wide and dumped all their remaining stores on us at once. Except it kept going and going. I stood between Oliver and Giselle, and I could see them both through the swirling white—just. Sterling was lost to me already.

Until he suddenly appeared from nowhere, so coated in white I almost didn't recognize him. Jumping slightly, I whipped my hand out of Oliver's sleeve and stuffed it back into my glove. If he had noticed our odd stance, he didn't mention it.

"We need to find shelter," he shouted. Even so, the wind

tugged his words away so fast I could barely make them out. "Right now. This is a blizzard, all right."

He produced a rope from somewhere and threaded it through a small loop on each of our packs that I hadn't even noticed before. To keep us from losing each other. Clever.

But my admiration fell away as we began to move. Our pace was so slow I wanted to scream, and yet I had no idea how Sterling in the front managed to find a way forward at all. Several times I saw him jerk suddenly as a tree appeared directly in front of him, too obscured by the white to be seen earlier.

I had been roped between Oliver and Giselle, and my attention was soon focused solely on them. I felt as if we moved too slowly to bear, and yet they walked as if they could barely keep up. Giselle stumbled once and clambered back to her feet so slowly, she nearly got jerked back into the snow by the rope connecting us together.

When she stumbled again and didn't get up, I tugged on the rope attaching me to Oliver. He looked back, a blankness in his eyes that scared me. But at the sight of Giselle he seemed to regain some life, turning to call loudly to Sterling.

I couldn't hear his words, but I had already turned my attention back to the younger princess. She seemed to have abandoned any pretense of getting up and simply lay there in the snow. I dropped to my knees beside her, shaking her frantically.

"Giselle! Giselle!"

She groaned and mumbled something I couldn't hear, feebly trying to push me off.

Ripping off my glove, I stuck my hand back up her sleeve, the cold of her skin shocking me enough that I nearly lost balance myself. She had gotten noticeably colder since our stop.

I wanted to pour all of my heat into her, but I managed to retain enough sense to force myself to move slowly again. This time when the warmth enveloped her, it seemed to only make her shiver harder.

I looked over my shoulder for Oliver, who had approached us and stood just behind me. I didn't have to be able to see myself to know my face would show nothing but fear.

"She's too cold. We can't go on like this," I screamed up at him, battling the wind to be heard.

Sterling appeared next to him. He looked down at Giselle with hooded eyes. When I transferred my gaze to his, he shrugged helplessly.

"I can't find anything in this. We could be right next to a cave, and I wouldn't be able to tell…"

I looked around wildly, but he was right. Solid white surrounded us in every direction.

Oliver looked helplessly between me and Giselle. I could see the conflict within him, and I shook myself. This was ridiculous. What was the point in keeping my secret if the others were going to die for it?

I surged to my feet. "Oliver, help Giselle up. Sterling—" I turned to him. "Didn't you nearly run into two trees just back there?"

He leaned closer, and I had to repeat myself.

"Aye."

I frowned. The tree before that had been off to the left slightly as well. If there was a clump of trees there, it might provide some meager protection at least.

I ripped off my second glove and used my still warm fingers to unlace us from the rope. Sterling looked like he wanted to protest, but at sight of the determination on my face, he subsided. I reattached us all in a new order. Me at the front, followed by Oliver, then Giselle, then Sterling.

Between the two men, they had managed to prop Giselle back to her feet. She swayed slightly but remained standing, and her eyes seemed to have regained some sense. I breathed a sigh of relief.

Her body had made enough of a dent in the snow that the

fresh falls hadn't quite erased the mark of it. Using the slight dip for reference, I moved backward and to what had been our left. A tree appeared from nowhere, and I barely stopped before colliding with it.

I took a deep breath, reminding myself this was what I had hoped to find. I pushed forward until I had passed four trees before stopping and gesturing for the others to huddle close.

We formed a tight little circle, slipping off our packs and allowing them to fall to the snow behind us. Once we were all sitting, I gestured for Sterling to pass me the small number of sticks he still had tied to his pack. I had seen him save some from the night before as well as gather a few more before the blizzard hit. He tried to yell at me that there was no use of thinking of a fire, but I shook my head angrily and gestured more firmly.

Shrugging, he turned and fumbled with the strap before managing to get them free. I wasn't sure I needed them, but they would provide a center for the fire I intended to create, and I figured they certainly couldn't hurt. Piling them haphazardly in the tiny space between us all, I paused for a brief second and met Oliver's eyes.

He looked regretful but resigned.

Pushing my bare hands forward, I sent a controlled burst of fire from my fingertips into the wood.

With a yelp, Sterling almost toppled backward, his pack stopping him from going over completely as he threw himself away from the fire in shock. I ignored him and kept the flames going until the wood finally dried and then reluctantly began to burn.

I stopped for a second to take a breath as the others all swayed toward the warmth. The thick snowflakes kept falling fast, however, and our little fire wouldn't last long on its own. Thrusting my flat palms into the air, I sent out a gust of hot air. It dissipated quickly, but one glance at Giselle was enough to stoke my internal temperature to raging hot.

Scrunching my face, I sent a strong wind streaming from my

hands. I pushed them out in a circle as the wind continued to come, shaping it until it rushed around us in a tight circle. The warm cocoon that now enveloped us repelled the flakes that still fell, giving the little fire a chance to burn steadily.

Three deep sighs sounded, and three bodies slumped against their packs as their muscles slowly relaxed. I, on the other hand, remained upright, every muscle in my body tight and controlled. I had never tried to keep my power going for so long or with so much precise control.

Keeping one hand upward, warm wind still pouring from me, I pointed the other downward, fresh fire leaping from my fingertips to feed our small blaze. It burned brighter and hotter than the sticks would ever have allowed.

I glanced briefly at the others again, concerned for their recovery, but the shock in Sterling's face and the awe in Oliver's made me look quickly away. I couldn't afford any lapses in concentration. Not when all of their lives depended on me.

The minutes stretched on, and I could no longer even guess at how much time had passed. The wind continued to howl around us, shrouding the rest of the world in endless white. For all I knew we were all that was left of Eldon. Of all the kingdoms. Perhaps the ice and snow had already won.

But no. I pushed back the thought, my flames briefly flaring up until I pulled them back under control. Not while I still had breath and strength. I would fight with every bit of fire within me.

But as the endless day stretched on—long since passed into night for all I knew—I could feel my strength failing. And yet the storm raged on, its own strength unabated. I might have started to feel truly afraid, but I had no energy left even for that.

A bigger fight was now being waged inside me. I struggled against my exhaustion, the black abyss of unconsciousness reaching for me with eager hands. I pushed it back, pouring even more of myself into my wind and fire, the rest of the world fading away.

Oliver's voice broke through to me, my name on his lips and his hands on my shoulders. But he pulled back immediately with a wordless exclamation. How hotly was I burning?

I tried to speak, to warn him away from me, but no words would come. And the tiny break in my concentration proved too much. My wind died, and the fire with it, the loss of the bright flames plunging my world into darkness.

Black roared up to meet me, and I fell unresisting toward it. Just as it engulfed me, I felt my body fall into strong arms. And this time they didn't flinch. My heat was gone. I had nothing left.

CHAPTER 19

The first thing I noticed was the cold. It had dug into my bones, and my body shook constantly, despite the warm layers of fur covering me. The cold had been a distant memory not so long ago, but already I struggled to remember how it had ever felt to be warm.

The second sensation was movement. I was fairly certain I was lying down, and yet I seemed to be moving, somehow. Almost as if someone were dragging me along the ground.

Slowly I forced my eyes open. The darkness had gone, but still I couldn't see, everything remained blank—only blindingly bright instead of dark. After a long moment, features began to take shape out of the endless white. We were on the mountain still, and I could see rocks and trees, all covered in heapings of snow.

"What…" My voice came out croaky and weak, so I cleared my throat and tried again. "What's happening?"

"Celine!"

"She's awake!"

The movement stopped with a jerk, and I pushed myself up into a sitting position. My head whirled, and I closed my eyes, drawing a deep breath.

"Slowly," said Oliver's soft voice in my ear, his grip warm and firm beneath my elbow. Without thinking I leaned in toward his heat.

"So…cold," I moaned, reopening my eyes in time to catch him share a concerned look with Giselle. I looked around. They had somehow constructed a sled of sorts using a blanket and some branches, and it looked like they had been pulling me up the mountain.

"How…how long have I been…" I let the sentence drop away as I remembered the blizzard and my endless, timeless struggle to keep the fire burning.

"Did we…did I…?" I looked around again, still trying to get my bearings. Obviously the storm had passed. Unlike the last time I had been awake, the blue sky cast an almost painful light down to reflect against the endless white.

In the snow, at least, the blizzard had left its mark. It covered everything in deep, suffocating layers. I could actually hear some of the trees groaning under the weight.

"Celine," Oliver's voice had dropped so low I could barely hear it. "Your fire. Is it…?"

I gasped, raw fear burning down the back of my throat. I remembered now. I had used it all. Every last drop. And now I was freezing.

I ripped off a glove and held out my hand. I had become so practiced at this that calling the flames required hardly a thought. But nothing came. My exposed skin stung against the cold air. The hand shook so much I could barely push it back into the glove.

I looked up at Oliver, and he must have read the panic in my eyes.

"You were exhausted," he said. "Utterly exhausted. What you did…" He shook his head, the wonder in his eyes filling me with a momentary warmth. "It's no wonder you burned yourself out. You just need to rekindle it."

I closed my eyes, grasping at his words. Could he be right? I turned my attention inward. My chest felt cold and dead, so different from the living warmth I had become accustomed to.

I pushed away the rising fear. I had felt warmth just a moment ago, hadn't I? Where had it come from? Could I get it back?

My eyes flew open as I remembered exactly where it had come from. I hadn't noticed in my earlier panic, but Oliver still crouched beside me, his face close to mine. My eyes fluttered down to his lips. All I would have to do would be to tip myself forward slightly and my own would be pressed against his.

The memory of his embrace in the tunnel filled my mind, and a flush raced across my cheeks. My insides burst into life in perfect time, the fire racing through my body and burning away the chill. I turned away from Oliver, focused now on keeping the heat under control.

"I think it's back," said Giselle's matter-of-fact voice. "Look at her cheeks."

"Yes." I smiled up at her, too happy to be embarrassed. "It's back."

"Well, that's good."

I snorted at her understated words. Without my powers we were just three people against a mountain range, a possibly treacherous guide, an entire village, and a killer enchantment.

Sterling cleared his throat from somewhere further up the mountain. I turned to squint up at him.

"Good to see you're awake. I don't suppose you'll be able to walk now?"

I winced. I couldn't blame him—no doubt he'd been assisting in pulling me uphill.

"How long have I been...?" I gestured at the sleigh and my reclined position.

"A few hours." Oliver glanced up at the sky, as if to check the time by the sun. "You passed out as soon as the blizzard finished, but we couldn't stay in place after it started to get light. We had no cover and not enough wood to burn. Better to keep moving than stay still and undo everything you did for us." He smiled, but I could only imagine how much work it must have been to pull me along. And no wonder I was so cold. They had at least been moving to keep themselves a little warm.

"Are we close?" I looked up at Sterling, and he turned to squint further upward.

"Aye. I think so. This fresh layer of snow makes things look a little different, and it's hard going, but we should reach it before nightfall." He looked down at me. "Especially if you can walk for yourself."

I nodded and gripped Oliver's hand, levering myself to my feet. "I can walk."

I swayed, and Oliver steadied me.

"I can walk," I repeated in answer to his skeptical look. "I can."

He insisted on attaching my snowshoes for me, and I let him, gratefully. My head was clearing, but I could still feel weakness in my limbs, and I didn't really want to crouch down if I could avoid it.

But I found that every minute that passed with the heat back inside me, a little of my strength returned. Within an hour, the others weren't even having to slow for me anymore. Several times I caught Sterling giving me a look I couldn't read. Was he wondering at my quick recovery? Or just generally wondering about my powers?

The others must have talked about it among themselves at some point. Surely. But he hadn't mentioned it to me, and I had no desire to discuss it with him. As we traveled, I did worry about what his knowledge meant, however. We still didn't really know what we were going to face, and we had just lost the element of surprise.

Eventually I threw off the thought. We had been completely out of options. Better to lose one weapon in our armory than to die. And just because he knew about my powers didn't mean he would have any way to counter them. My usual confidence had returned along with the flames that filled me. We had survived the leopards and the blizzard. We would survive what was coming too.

Our overall progress had slowed significantly with the extra dumping of snow, and the afternoon sun was stretching long, before Sterling stopped and pointed toward an enormous boulder with a satisfied smile.

"Ahhh...?" I squinted at it, trying to work out what he wanted to call our attention to.

But Oliver broke into a broad grin and a sliding half-run. He stopped at the rock face briefly and then part of him disappeared.

"Oh." I moved forward, and the change of angle revealed a narrow passage through the rock. No wonder no one had ever found it. You could walk straight past and miss it.

Oliver bent down and removed his snowshoes. His eyes sparkled triumphantly back at Giselle and me.

"There's only the thinnest layer of snow on the ground in here," he called. "We won't need our snowshoes."

I immediately plonked down into the snow and pulled mine off as fast as I could go. Reluctantly I attached them to my pack. We still had to make it back down the mountains again.

Giselle shook her head at me, sliding past toward Oliver with her usual awkward snowshoe gait. As soon as I stood again and attempted to follow her, I realized the cause of her amusement. At the first step, I sank deep into the snow.

I yelped as I toppled, my leg entirely swallowed by the deep powder. I tried to pull myself out, but only seemed to sink further in. I looked helplessly across at Oliver, whose eyes suggested he was trying not to laugh at me, but it was Sterling who stopped beside me.

With a grunt, he reached down and gripped me under my arms, hauling me out of the snow.

"Follow my track," he said, as he took off along the same route the other two had taken.

Sighing, I scooted after him the same way I had slid down the slopes. It required a lot more effort on the flat, but thankfully I only had a short distance to cover.

When I finally stepped off the snow and into the rock passage, I gave a warning look to Oliver and Giselle.

"Not a word."

"I don't know what you mean," Oliver assured me, although his eyes were still laughing.

"You'll learn eventually," said Giselle, sailing past me.

I glared at her back. No wonder my older siblings had found me irritating.

I continued to grumble internally as I brought up the rear of our little single-file procession. I didn't mean it, of course, I was just so relieved to be free of the incessant snow. It made me never want to see another bit of it again, let alone become an expert like the locals.

The rock ended suddenly, and I stumbled into Oliver's back where he had stopped abruptly in the entrance. He murmured an apology and moved out of the way without looking back at me.

As soon as I stepped free, I realized what had captivated them. Spread before us was an enclosed mountain valley. Occasional thin patches of white on the ground were overwhelmed with the green of grass. I even saw some splashes of pink and purple. Here spring seemed to have actually come—at least somewhat.

The sun shone down on a larger collection of houses than I had anticipated, and beyond them I could even see what looked like some small fields. Figures, large and small, moved between the houses, intent on the everyday tasks that occupied villagers.

I shook my head. So this part of Sterling's tale at least had been true. When Oliver looked back at me, I could see he was thinking the same thing. And the earlier triumph in his expression had only solidified. I smiled back at him, unable to help being swept up in his hope. But a moment later, I shot Giselle a more concerned look. I could see from her eyes that she was impressed by the village, but when she saw my expression, she cast a worried look at Oliver's back.

I knew he wasn't fueled by anything so ignoble as a desire to say I told you so. He was merely filled with relief and hope for his kingdom. And I wanted to share his joy, especially since it was obvious a weight had already lifted from him.

But I couldn't help being more wary. We still had to work out exactly how this enchantment protection worked, and if it could help us. And then we had to convince these villagers to give it up.

And when I looked over this perfect village, I saw hope—yes —but I also felt a sinking sensation. The blizzard lingered fresh in my mind, and I couldn't imagine how we would ever prevail on them to give up their protection. And what if we did, and we saved the kingdom, but another blizzard hit in the meantime, and they all died? Could we convince them to return down the mountain with us, at least temporarily?

I looked over the village again and sighed. And even if we could, how slowly would a whole village full of people move? Would we return with salvation for Eldon, only to find Eliam had already completed its coup?

I knew why Oliver wasn't thinking of any of these things. He couldn't allow himself even a moment of weakness in his determination. As heir he carried a weight that I had never known. As seventh-born, it would take a tragedy beyond reckoning to ever make me responsible for my kingdom.

"Welcome to Valley View," said Sterling, striding forward toward the closest of the houses. Oliver followed, his steps long and confident after so many days of carefully picking our way through the snow.

With a sigh Giselle also stepped forward onto the grass, and I followed a beat behind. Except while she kept walking, I faltered and nearly fell. The gap between us widened as I stood frozen, dumbstruck and horrified. As soon as I had touched the floor of this odd valley, my insides had gone cold.

"Come on." Giselle turned back to stare at me in confusion. A quick look at my face had her backtracking to grip my arm.

"What is it?" Her eyes rapidly flitted around the valley and even looked behind us, as if she feared I had spotted some threat the rest of them had overlooked.

"My…my fire," I gasped.

She looked confused. "I thought you said it had come back?"

"It had. And then I stepped in here. And it was gone. Instantly."

"Well, re-light it," she said. "Like you did before."

I shook my head. "I've been trying."

We stood motionless, staring at each other, a slow and horrifying realization dawning on us both.

"Their godmother object," she breathed at last. "The one that keeps away the snow and ice…"

"Well, at least we know it still works against enchantments as well," I said, but no hint of pleasure sounded in my grim voice.

I had feared our loss of the element of surprise. But apparently I should have been afraid of something far worse.

CHAPTER 20

*W*e had managed to spur ourselves into motion by the time Oliver noticed we had fallen behind. His eyes questioned us, particularly once he saw our expressions, but I just shrugged. We would have to tell him later, when we found a chance to shake off Sterling. Now that the mountain man knew about my powers, I didn't want to admit to him they might be gone.

The people we passed nodded greetings at Sterling and cast curious glances at us, but none of them smiled or came over to talk. Sterling seemed unbothered by their reception and led us through the village to a small log house.

The air in the valley was noticeably warmer than it had been out on the mountain, but I still found myself shivering by the time he had a fire going in the empty fireplace. The whole house had an empty, unused feel that told me it was his even before he confirmed it.

"You can all stay with me for now," he said, gesturing to the floor in front of the fire. "Sorry I don't have beds to offer you."

Oliver shrugged and neither Giselle nor I offered any protest.

It would be more comfortable than the floor of a cave which had been our accommodation since we started up the mountain.

"Well, I'll leave you to settle in while I go to rummage up some food," said Sterling, one hand already on the door.

"Wait." Oliver stepped forward, brow furrowed. "Are we just supposed to stay here? We need to meet with the village elders and inspect the godmother object."

Sterling raised both eyebrows, and I narrowed my eyes as I watched him, the thought of my achingly cold middle temporarily receding. It was subtle, but something about his manner had changed. I thought back. Or maybe it had been gradually changing as we moved closer to this village.

"Hold your horses, there. It's almost evening. Too late for calling the elders together today. We'll eat and sleep, and then see what tomorrow will bring." He shut the door behind him.

Oliver remained in place, staring at the wooden barrier. At last he sighed and turned back to us. "I should be happy to see this place so exactly like he described. And tomorrow will come soon enough. But I keep thinking of that army camped outside the palace."

"It might be a good thing if we have a bit more time to think through our approach to the elders," I said, my mind already having circled back to my own loss.

"What do you mean?" Oliver crossed over to join us where we sat in front of the fire.

I glanced at Giselle and then back at him. "Would you like the good news, or…"

"What?" he asked, more forcefully this time. "What is it?"

I swallowed, the words harder to say than I would have liked. "The moment we walked into this valley…"

He leaned forward, his concerned gaze focused on me, silently urging me on.

"The moment I stepped on the grass, my fire disappeared." I placed a hand against my chest. "It's just…just gone."

Oliver rocked back, shock in his eyes. "But what…how…?"

I didn't reply, watching the slow realization fill his eyes.

"So, that's the good news part," I said, my voice weaker than I would have liked. "It seems like maybe this object of theirs really does work to repel magic."

"But without your powers…" I could see the thoughts racing furiously across his face, although he seemed to be struggling to enunciate them.

"Yes, as I said. We might want to really perfect our approach to the elders. Because if we can't convince them to give up the object willingly…"

"Then everyone I love will die, and my kingdom will be destroyed."

He shot up and began to pace the floor. I watched him uneasily. When he put it like that…

My feeling of helplessness grew. I had thought I could save this kingdom—that I'd been sent here to do it, even. But now I was useless. Just like when the leopard attacked Giselle.

"What did you think of the people?" asked Giselle. She didn't appear to have been following our conversation at all, lost in thought about something else.

"What people?" Oliver didn't stop his pacing. He was making me restless. Pacing was usually my thing.

"The people of Valley View, of course. I assume you were both watching them as closely as I was."

Oliver's steps slowed, and I frowned as I felt a fresh stirring of shame. I hadn't been watching the people. I'd been too wrapped up in horror over the loss of my powers. It had felt as if I stumbled through the village naked, and I'd had little thought for anything else.

Or had I? The more I thought of it, the more the people sprang to life in my mind's eye. Apparently some less conscious part of me had been examining them and storing the observations away for later. The thought filled me with a surprising

175

buoyancy. I had only had these powers for a short time, really. Had I been useless before then?

A small smile flitted across my face. Various of my siblings had certainly thought so at different points. But I had never felt that way. So why would losing my powers now make me so? I straightened, determined to still be helpful.

"They looked far more animated than the people back in the capital," I said.

Oliver nodded slowly, his focus still on some distant unseen point.

"But not exactly normal, either?" Giselle made the statement into a question.

"No..." Oliver rubbed a hand along his jaw. "They weren't too friendly, were they? But then maybe that *is* normal for this village. They're very isolated, so they might have developed strange ways."

"Maybe." I scrunched up my face, unconvinced. "But surely their isolation would make them more interested and curious about newcomers. And about Sterling's return, too."

Oliver glanced at the door. "Maybe I should have insisted on going with him. I wonder what they're discussing right now."

I took no pleasure from the unease that had replaced his hopeful enthusiasm, but I couldn't regret it, either. Somehow I suspected we would all need a dose of healthy caution if we were going to make it through this.

"Well, there's nothing you can do about it now," said Giselle, seemingly the calmest of us. "And I can't imagine they'd take kindly to you poking around alone." She wrinkled her nose. "They looked sort of unpleasant."

I nodded thoughtfully. "Or rather as if we were unpleasant." I raised an eyebrow as I surveyed myself. "Not that I can imagine why. It isn't like we've just hiked our way through a mountain range without a bath for...how many days was it, in the end?"

Giselle snorted, and Oliver managed a smile. When he opened his mouth, I held up a hand to stop him.

"Please, no. I'm far too exhausted to cope with any false compliments right now."

"Oh, good," he said. "Since I was merely going to agree that you could use a bath."

I picked up the rough cushion from my chair and threw it at his head too fast for him to duck. It hit him full in the face before he caught it and lobbed it back in my direction. I ducked, and he looked around for something else to throw.

Giselle stopped us with a gagging sound. "Oh, please. That's enough, lovebirds. Now that someone's mentioned the word 'bath', I'm not going to be able to rest until I've had one." She stood up and looked at us expectantly.

For some reason Oliver had flushed and looked away at her scolding rebuke, so I answered.

"Are you expecting me to pull a bath out of my pack? Because I'm pretty sure it was heavy enough that there might be one packed in there somewhere…"

Giselle rolled her eyes. "The villagers must do something for baths. And I for one don't want to face any elders without having had one. Some things are more important than food."

I jumped to my feet in complete agreement. I wanted nothing so much as I wanted to peel off these ill-fitting clothes and sink into some delicious hot water. I would never get used to being cold again after these delightful weeks with my own private heat source.

Oliver looked less convinced. "Wasn't it you who were just saying they're not likely to take too kindly to our poking around?"

Giselle shrugged. "So we won't poke around. We'll just ask someone about a bath."

Since she pulled the door open and marched out, me close

177

behind her, he had little choice but to follow. We hailed the first people we saw, a young couple, and from the expressions of distaste on their faces as they surveyed us, we needed those baths even more than we realized.

To our great joy, it turned out that Valley View came equipped with its own public bathhouse thanks to the presence of a small set of hot springs on the edge of the town. We hurried over to them, Sterling forgotten in our excitement. Oliver warned us to be careful and keep our eyes open before leaving us for the men's bath.

"I don't know about you," I said to Giselle, as I sank into the water, "but I have no intention whatsoever of keeping my eyes open." I let them flutter closed as I heaved a deep sigh.

The water gently circulated in the largish pool, carrying away my grime and replacing it with fresh water. Either nature or an industrious villager had shaped several stone ledges at the perfect height for sitting, and I gratefully let my head tip back against the rim of the pool.

"I have no idea how hot springs can exist in a place like this, but it's the best thing I ever heard of."

Giselle's indrawn breath made me hold up a lazy hand. "No, please don't tell me. Some things really are better with the mystique preserved."

I could almost hear her eye roll, but I didn't care in the least. I was utterly, blessedly warm, and soon I would even be clean. For this one perfect moment I refused to think about anything else.

Once I had soaked enough to regain a little energy, I dipped my head back into the water and vigorously washed my hair using one of the bars of soap provided on a small shelf beside the pool. I watched the suds floating away and wondered how long I could get away with soaking in here when voices made me sit up straight and look over at Giselle.

We probably shouldn't be surprised that at the end of the day some of the locals might want to make use of the bathhouse. And this might be a good opportunity to try to get friendly with some of them.

A group of girls entered, with two older matrons following close behind. They all stopped short at the sight of us, before one of the older ladies prodded the others to keep moving and get on with it.

"The water will be clean again soon enough, I suppose," she said, glancing disapprovingly down into the pool.

I gaped at her and then down into the water. We had been here long enough that our dirt had long since washed away, and the clear water of the pool contained only us.

The girls entered one by one, giving us looks of such disgust that I concluded our earlier state of unwash had not been the source of the couple's distaste. It seemed this village did not like outsiders.

But as I quickly finished my bath, eager to be gone now that we were no longer alone, my confusion grew. These people didn't seem the least lethargic or disconnected. But I had never met such an unpleasant bunch, so eager to see only faults. The way they poked and prodded at each other with their words, pointing out various perceived negatives in each other's appearance, made my teeth ache. I desperately wanted to tell them to stop, but I didn't think it would do our cause any good to get involved.

Still, by the time we had dried and dressed in clean layers, my jaw felt like it had set in position, so tightly was I clenching it. And the older women had been no better. The only words out of their mouths had been complaints. For their day, their work, the girls, each other…

As we walked back toward Sterling's house, I frowned into the sunset. "When you said earlier that these people didn't seem normal, I don't suppose you meant they seemed excessively unpleasant?"

Giselle frowned. "They definitely don't seem normal, do they?"

"What was it Sterling said back at the palace?" I muttered to myself. "That his village isn't like other villages." I was starting to wonder if there was something actually wrong with these people. If that's why they had fled up here. But I had no idea what could turn people like this.

I took a sudden detour, Giselle trailing behind me, to take us close enough to overhear a conversation between several men who stood outside what looked like some sort of small tavern. They each clasped a flagon and appeared to be relaxing after a day's work. And yet just a slow walk past was enough to hear that nothing but complaints issued from their mouths as well.

Giselle and I exchanged glances but refrained from commenting until we were safely back inside Sterling's log walls. Oliver had beaten us back, as had Sterling, who looked less than pleased with our unsanctioned outing. Or maybe the villagers were just rubbing off on him.

"Nice bath?" Oliver grinned at us which made me think he must have completed his wash undisturbed.

"The bath itself was delightful." I eyed Sterling. "But I can see why you were anxious to leave."

Our guide raised an eyebrow. "I'm sure I don't know what you mean."

"Oh, don't you?" But I muttered the words quietly enough not to provoke a confrontation. I was still on edge with the loss of my powers, but turning our only potential ally in this place against us didn't seem like a helpful way to let out my frustration.

Sterling had apparently returned with a hot meal because bowls had already been laid out for us on his small table. We descended on them with nearly as much enthusiasm as the bath, and silence briefly reigned. Only when he had wiped his bowl clean with a large piece of fluffy bread, did Sterling speak again.

"I mentioned something of your situation to a couple of the elders, and they agreed that you can have an audience tomorrow. But they also said that the village will never agree to release the object that keeps them all safe." He glanced up at us, his face hard to read. "Just so you know not to get your hopes up."

CHAPTER 21

*O*f course Sterling refused to say any more about who he had spoken to or exactly what they had said. Meaning none of us slept well. We couldn't even properly talk strategy since Sterling didn't leave again.

By the time we found ourselves standing in the morning sunlight in a grassy clearing at the center of the village, I knew Oliver's nerves were stretched tight. But you wouldn't have guessed it from looking at him. He stood tall, his shoulders back and his bearing every inch the confident prince.

Unfortunately, the group of village elders looked less than impressed. Their expressions reminded me all too forcefully of the girls in the baths the night before. At least they listened silently while Oliver outlined the magical attack on Eldon and our hope that their godmother object could save the kingdom. At the mention of the object, several of them exchanged quick glances, but no one interrupted.

He pleaded with them to let him borrow the object to save the kingdom and promised to return it as soon as possible. I noticed no softening in their faces. Even when he carefully pointed out the consequences to their own village if the rest of the kingdom should fall, they remained impassive.

Any hope I had still clung to faded away as I examined them. I had expected a hardy—and possibly hard—folk to inhabit such a remote location. At worst I had feared that they might have already succumbed as the rest of the kingdom had done. But I had not expected this. Could the entire village really be full of people who saw no good in anything and had no interest in others at all? Who could bear to live in such a way? And surely it could not be natural. But if it wasn't, what exactly was sickening their minds? It certainly wasn't whatever was destroying the rest of the kingdom.

"It is not we who bear responsibility for your kingdom, prince," said the oldest of them when Oliver at last finished pleading his case.

Oliver didn't flinch, although I could see the statement cut him.

"We can offer you no assistance," agreed another of the elders.

"But your object…" said Giselle, stepping forward.

The woman shook her head, her expression cold.

"So you mean you *won't* offer assistance," muttered Giselle, glancing hopelessly at her brother.

"I refuse to believe that you speak for your whole village when you profess so little care for the lives and livelihood of so many," said Oliver, his back still straight and his eyes burning. "I request permission to remain in the village, and to speak with both you and your people again. I believe that with time and consideration, you will see the value of my cause."

Several of the elders narrowed their eyes as if disgusted, but the oldest spoke again. "You may stay for as long as you wish. You will not change our minds, but we have no interest in driving you from here."

Oliver's shoulders slumped the slightest bit, and I could read the subtle signs of relief in his bearing. He had obviously feared we would be unceremoniously kicked back down the mountain the moment this meeting concluded. And he obviously wanted to give us an opportunity to find the object on our own.

"We also request permission to search your village," he said, confirming my thoughts.

I hadn't expected such a brazen approach, but his next words explained it.

"We have reason to believe there may be a stolen royal object here in your village, and we would like to search for it."

One of the elders raised his eyebrows. "A stolen royal object? What sort of object?"

"A mirror."

Sterling shifted beside us, and I wondered if he was merely surprised or if he was offended at the suggestion. The elders all exchanged looks, before the speaker shrugged.

"We know nothing of a stolen mirror. But feel free to ask our people about it. Perhaps one of them has heard something. We won't give you permission to invade their homes, however. If you wish to search any homes, you must receive permission from the owner."

I barely suppressed an eye roll at that. If the thief lived here, he was hardly likely to agree to a search of his home. But Oliver managed to thank them in a voice that almost sounded sincere.

Giselle, who had been watching with a blank face, turned to leave, but the elder spoke again, his words stopping her.

"But know this, princeling."

Oliver's eyes whipped up to meet his, but the older man didn't back down. In fact he leaned forward.

"Valley View does not fall under the sovereignty of your family. Here you are not a prince or princesses, you are merely guests like any other. Guests who are expected to abide by our laws."

Oliver stiffened, and Giselle sucked in an audible breath. Did the man mean to speak treason, or was this village truly so isolated that they no longer saw themselves as part of their own kingdom?

I recognized the fire in Oliver's eyes and could only imagine how one of my brothers would react to such a challenge. I laid a hand on his arm, gripping hard enough to pull his attention from the elders. He glanced down at me, and I glared up at him.

"Planning on getting caught breaking laws, are you?" I whispered at him.

He frowned at me, saying nothing, but I could read the answer in his eyes. Of course not.

"Then let it go. Unless you want to find yourself sent straight back down to the capital. We have no power here to back up your authority, remember?" I let my eyes stray down to where my hand still rested on his arm.

I felt the release of tension before I heard his sigh. When he turned back to the elders, his stance held the same regal bearing, but his eyes no longer burned.

"We have no desire to break laws—either yours or anyone else's. We will conduct ourselves with honor while we remain your guests."

Yes, because we have no other choice, I thought guiltily, remembering that we had certainly contemplated forcing the villagers to assist us. Back when we thought we would have the power to do so.

The elder accepted Oliver's words with a curt nod of his head, before turning to talk quietly with his colleagues. Clearly we were dismissed. I grabbed both Oliver and Giselle and dragged them away before either of them decided to take exception to their reception and treatment.

When we found a quiet spot between houses, I dropped both of their arms and put my hands on my hips. "Well, that went well. What do we do next?"

Giselle frowned, shooting an angry look back in the direction of the now hidden elders. "What, have they ceded from Eldon and just never bothered to inform us? What do they think they're playing at?"

I gestured around our small circle. "Take a look at us, Giselle. We don't exactly have the might of a crown to back us up, now, do we?"

"Still, that's treason," said Oliver, his voice tight. "And this is exactly why we rule. Not for our own gain." He gave a rough laugh with no trace of humor. "I certainly took no pleasure from our hike up here. Did either of you?" He didn't wait for us to reply. "We rule to ensure that the entire kingdom is cared for and preserved. So no one small group can choose to sit back and watch the rest burn." He turned and punched the wooden wall beside him.

I sighed. "I don't think burning is anyone's problem at this point." I couldn't quite keep the bitterness from my voice.

Oliver looked over at me, a frown crossing his face, and I turned away. I didn't need his disappointment adding to the weight of my own.

"Still, their treason does add weight to the idea that they might be harboring the thief," he said.

"I don't know," I said reluctantly. "To me they looked genuinely surprised by your question."

Neither of the other two said anything, and I wondered if they were thinking of the same thing I was. The thought I had tried to push away the whole way up the mountain. What if our trip yielded neither the protective object nor the mirror?

But as I stared at the ground, I felt a sliver of steel creep up my spine. I would not sit around and be useless because I no longer had powers. I would prove my worth.

I straightened and looked Oliver in the eye. "They gave us permission to stay and to speak to the villagers. So that's what we should do. Just because the elders don't know anything, doesn't mean no one else does. And who knows, your ruse might even turn out to be right. Maybe we can find some villagers who don't agree with the elders."

A reluctant smile crossed Oliver's face. "I almost believe it's possible when you say it like that."

I grinned back at him. "I'm good at saying things with feeling. I have a lifetime of experience making myself heard over six older siblings. But I do believe that if there is anything to learn from these villagers, you'll be able to search it out."

"I fear you have too much faith in me," said Oliver, so quietly I almost didn't hear his words.

Giselle grimaced sadly. "Normally I'd agree with Celine. Oliver knows our people well. But there's something different about these people. And I didn't notice anyone putting much weight in our so-called authority." She sighed. "But I also don't know what else we can do but try."

"Exactly," I said, trying to put some bracing enthusiasm into my voice. "That's the spirit."

She rolled her eyes at me but didn't actually protest.

"And what will you be doing while we're convincing people to spill the truth?" asked Oliver.

I looked around, my eyes narrowed. "I'm going to see if I can get a glimpse of this enchanted object of theirs. And maybe find out exactly how it works—if anyone even knows. It would be a pity to hang around here and put all this effort in only to discover it's not going to help us after all. And if I happen upon the mirror in the meantime..." I shrugged. "They did give us permission to search outside of the homes."

I could see that Oliver would have preferred to join me searching for the object, but the same weight of duty which had driven him up the mountain drove him now. As crown prince it was up to him to tackle his people. To see if there was any way they would let him save his kingdom—their kingdom, even if they didn't want to admit it.

We split up, and I soon found myself wandering aimlessly

around. For all my confident words, I didn't actually have the least idea where to start searching for the object. I didn't even know what sort of object it was. For all I knew, it could be something as small and mundane as a necklace.

As I walked, I began to get a sense of the village. It all centered around the open, grassy space where we had met with the elders, the houses fanning out in circles from there. The outside ring seemed to hold bigger buildings, like the tavern we had passed the night before. Another seemed to be a school—at least that's what it looked like when I peeked in the window and saw it filled with children and desks.

The baths stood alone, their position dictated by the hot springs, and the back of the valley held the fields I had seen when we first arrived. Large barns formed a barrier between the rest of the village and the fields, an odd layout that suggested something of a communal nature to the work and property of Valley View.

When I had snooped around the entire area, no one smiling at me, but no one challenging me either, I stopped to think. Godmother objects—especially ones with not only deep historical significance, but also current magical ability—didn't tend to be kept at the back of a drawer or stuffed into a tray of jewelry. So regardless of the object's size, it was likely kept somewhere in a place of honor.

My eyes briefly skimmed the trees that surrounded the valley before I shook my head. No. Surely the nature of its magic necessitated it being kept in the village itself. I know I wouldn't take a chance on placing it anywhere else if I were a local.

I surveyed the village again. The elders had met us out in the open, suggesting they had nothing like a town hall. But that didn't mean they didn't have a ceremonial building of some kind. Perhaps even a small one built with the express purpose of protecting the object.

My eyes scanned the buildings of the outer ring, skimming over the school, the tavern, and several others of obvious purpose such as the blacksmith's shed. Finally my eyes rested on one that looked smaller than the others. Smaller even than the houses.

My view of it was partially obscured as it stood some distance across the village, but I vaguely remembered passing it before. Nothing about it had stood out to me, but now that I thought about it, I couldn't remember seeing much in the way of windows. I had written it off as a storage shed of some type, but it stood on the opposite side of the village to the barns.

Whether my purposeful gait attracted attention or whether it was my close examination of that particular building, this time a man I didn't recognize approached me. He stood for a while just watching me as I circled the small structure. I had been wrong earlier. It didn't have any windows at all. I finally stopped thoughtfully in front of the wooden door.

Now that I looked at it closely, I could see intricate carvings on the door itself and around the lintel. Casting a bold look at the watching man, I strode up the three shallow steps and tried to push open the door. It didn't budge.

I looked back at the man again. "I don't suppose you have a key on you?"

The man finally stirred, narrowing his eyes, his face twisting in distaste.

"That building is forbidden."

I looked at him measuringly. "To me? Or to everyone?"

"To everyone. That building is forbidden."

"I heard you the first time," I muttered, traipsing back down the stairs. As I made my slow way back to Sterling's house, I could feel his eyes burning into my back. Only when I shut the door behind me did I feel his eyes leave me.

The house was empty. I sat inside by the constantly burning fire while I considered what to do about what I had found. No immediate ideas occurred to me.

When Oliver and Giselle finally joined me, I could see by their faces that their efforts had been discouraging.

I winced sympathetically. "Don't tell me. The villagers are all as unpleasant as the few we've had the great joy to meet?"

Oliver slumped into a chair without speaking, his eyes on the fire. There was definitely something wrong with these people. I just couldn't work out what.

Giselle looked from him to me and then shook her head sadly. "It was only our first day," she said, but I didn't hear any hope in her voice. She looked over at me. "As far as we could judge everyone seemed genuinely bemused by our questions about the mirror. And they had even less desire to talk about their object, whatever it might be."

I had no answer for that, so silence fell. After a long moment, Oliver seemed to wrench himself from his gloomy thoughts, focusing on me. "What about you? I don't suppose you have anything more promising to report?"

"Well," I said. "I'm pretty sure I found the object."

CHAPTER 22

Oliver and Giselle's excitement quickly tempered when they heard the full story. Neither of them argued about the likelihood of the object being inside the building, but knowing it was in there didn't do us much good if we couldn't even peer at it through a window.

I promised that I would focus my efforts for the afternoon on the people rather than the village itself. We agreed to leave any direct questioning about the object for the moment. Instead the Eldonians would focus on asking about the mirror, and I would try to extract information about the forbidden building.

"Where's Sterling?" I asked, as soon as we had agreed on a plan, however half-heartedly. My rumbling stomach had pushed our missing guide into my mind. "Have either of you seen him today?"

"Not since first thing this morning when we addressed the elders," said Oliver.

"There are some food stores over here," said Giselle from a small cupboard on the other side of the room. "I guess he's left us to make our own meal."

I frowned. Preparing my own meal didn't worry me, but

191

something about his disappearance didn't sit well. When Oliver looked at me questioningly, I smiled and shrugged off the thought. Sterling had been absent from his village for who knew how long. Was it really surprising he had things he would rather be doing than babysitting us?

The afternoon did not go well. I had decided to take the approach of quickly abandoning any conversation that seemed less than fruitful. That way I could speak to more people and hopefully find one, somewhere, who was inclined to be a little less unfriendly. But by the time I returned to Sterling's house, I felt sure I must have spoken to everyone in the village without finding such a person. For all my hours of effort, I had learned nothing.

Unless you counted that the small windowless building was forbidden. Which I didn't. That I already knew.

One look at Oliver's face told me they had fared no better. The darkness in his eyes scared me. I didn't know what else we could try if this village failed us. And I didn't know how Oliver would take defeat.

Giselle must have seen the same thing in him. Maybe she even saw something similar in my own face. Whatever it was, she kicked us both out of the house. Sterling had still not reappeared, and she said she would prepare some food but not with us hovering around.

"Go for a walk through the valley," she commanded. "You look like you need it, and I certainly don't need you here."

For a second Oliver looked like he would resist, but then he caught me watching him and shrugged. *Why not?* his eyes seemed to say. *It doesn't matter what I do, after all.*

It broke my heart.

Silently we pulled our jackets and boots back on and ventured outside once again. Only this time we ignored the village itself, striding quickly to its outskirts. I wanted to go back through the thin passage of stone, back to the snow—something

I never thought I would say—so that I could feel flame on my skin again. But Oliver led me the other way, deeper into the valley.

We passed the barns in silence, skirting the fields beyond. Young growth appeared in the plowed earth, and the sight was at once comforting and jarring. Life goes on, it said. But at the same time I knew that only here in this valley had spring taken hold. Winter had gripped the rest of Eldon with icy fingers and refused to relinquish its grip. And the aching pain in my healed ankle—absent in all these weeks with my own personal heat source—reminded me of it with every step.

I didn't even realize I'd sighed until Oliver reached over and took my hand. He had never done such a thing before, and I stared at our entwined fingers for a moment, wondering if I should pull away. But I couldn't bring myself to do it. I had thought he was falling apart, and yet a strength seemed to flow into me from his firm clasp.

We walked past the fields and into a small grove of trees tucked up against the surrounding cliffs. Only once we had passed out of sight of the village did he sigh, his body releasing tension I hadn't even realized it held.

He dropped my hand and I flexed it, hidden within the folds of my jacket-skirt. I had always prided myself on my strength, so why did I feel strangely empty now, and cold, without his warm fingers in mine? I forced my hand to still. I would not be weak. I would not be helpless. I didn't need my power, and I didn't need anyone else. I would find a way to save us.

Oliver turned suddenly to meet my eyes, and my thoughts fell away. Fear gripped me. Because I could read too easily the same determination in his eyes. Without thinking, I closed the space between us, grabbing the front of his jacket in both of my cold hands.

"What?" I asked. "What are you planning?"

My words seemed to take him by surprise, and he hesitated

for a moment. Finally he reached up to place his hands over mine. I didn't let go of the jacket.

"We're not making any headway here. There's no sign of the mirror, and we can't even get them to give us any information on their object. Let alone the object itself. It's obviously a powerful object since it's nullified your powers, but that means we can't force them to help us. I've been so sure I needed to bring this object back to the palace, but then I realized I was wrong."

I stared up at him, trying not to allow myself to hope that he'd actually thought of another way. But it wasn't hope I saw looking back at me in his eyes. It was despair. I trembled, and his hands dropped from mine, circling around me instead in an embrace I barely noticed.

"What do you mean?"

"There's no reason it needs to be *me* that brings the artifact back to the palace. You and Giselle could do it just as well I'm sure."

My mouth wanted to protest, but his eyes silenced me. *What is he planning?*

"I can understand why the villagers wouldn't want to risk their object. And they've made it clear they feel no loyalty or allegiance to me or the crown. So I need to show them they can trust us. That we *will* return it. I've been wracking my brain trying to work out how to do so, when I realized the answer is simple. I'll offer myself in exchange. I will remain here—as a hostage of sorts, I suppose—until you return with the object."

He forced a smile that didn't quite reach his eyes. I knew the prospect of staying back and leaving us to defeat this enchantment on our own must be killing him.

"You will come back for me, won't you, Celine?"

His attempt at lightening the mood didn't work. I shook my head quickly, and his expression dropped.

"No," I said, more strength in my voice than I expected. "I won't come back for you."

His eyes searched mine, and I wondered what he saw there.

"I won't come back for you because I'm not leaving you in the first place. Without that object—and without me—you won't survive here. None of you will. We saw that on the mountain. We have to convince them all to come down with us."

"But they never will, Celine," he said, fear in his voice. "It's only been a day but already I can see that. These people will never follow where I lead. They will never give me the object or come with me down the mountain."

I remembered the elder's words about sovereignty. Did Oliver think this refusal from the villagers was an act of defiance against him? Was that what had given rise to this mad plan? Did he mean to sacrifice himself?

I shook him. "You cannot stay here. I will not leave you to die here alone."

Oliver's breath caught, and a different look crossed his face. One that made me pause and forget for a moment all about enchantments and godmother items and the killing power of a blizzard.

"I wish it could be true," he said, his words a whisper. "I wish it could be that you will never leave me."

This time it was my own trembling that made my hands shake his jacket. "I will not leave you."

One hand slipped up from my waist, somehow free of its glove, to trace the lines of my face. "I wish it were true," he said again. "But even without all this, you are a creature of fire and heat, Celine. You were before ever your godmother got involved. Why do you think she gave you such a gift? You could never be happy here, in a kingdom of snow, trapped in a palace like ice. How could I ask such a thing of you?"

I couldn't breathe, but somehow I found the breath to speak. "You wouldn't have to ask."

Even as I said the words, I wondered if they were true. Would I stay here for him? Would I condemn myself to a lifetime in this frozen kingdom? But the answer was already burning through my veins. Here in this valley where my gift had been stripped from me, I still felt heat rushing through every part of me. It jumped from his hand to my face, and it seemed to center around my heart.

Love. The word whispered in my mind, echoing through me until it grew into an all-consuming shout. I never dreamed when I sailed from Palinar that such a thing could be possible. But I hadn't met Oliver then. Not truly. I could never have loved the icicle that the enchantment had made him.

But the real Oliver—the one I had seen since our eyes met on that first day when Lord Treestone's men attacked—that Oliver burned just as brightly as me. He might be prince over the ice and snow, but for all his words about my fire, one just as strong burned in him.

It drove him, while still only partially freed from the cloying fog of enchantment, to track us through the forest and scale a castle alone, little more than a shadow. And it drove him now to fight, and to sacrifice himself, to save his people and his kingdom. A kingdom he knew inside out. I had seen it in my weeks in Eldon. Oliver was no prince who hid himself away in his palace, above the people he was called to serve. He was certainly confident in the icy marble halls—a figure of assurance and authority—but he was also at home in the southern woods, in the tunnels of the capitals where he could read the tunnel markings like any local civilian, and on the ice-filled mountains themselves where he could snowshoe like an expert and track a snow leopard without pause.

The shout reverberating inside me spilled out of my eyes, and I saw his own light up in response. His hand dropped from my face, returning to my waist and pulling me hard against him. His eyes blazed back into mine, but still he hesitated.

"Are you asking?" His voice sounded ragged, and it took me a moment to recall our long-ago conversation.

I nodded, unable to speak, and then our lips met, mine angled up to meet his as he pressed his face down to mine.

His kiss reached all the way down to my toes, filled with too many emotions to separate. Our love and longing swirled with our desperation and fear and despair. I knew, without a doubt, that if we had stood anywhere but this valley we would both have gone up in flames by now. None of my attempts at training would have been a match for emotions like this.

If only our biggest problem was his icy kingdom and my aversion to the cold. But we both knew it was not. And our desperation fueled a kiss that tasted too much of goodbye.

I clung to him still because I was afraid if I let go I would fall. I had promised myself I would be strong, but some things I could not withstand.

When Oliver at last pulled away, he rested his forehead against mine, both of our breaths ragged. It hurt to look at him, so I closed my eyes.

"You're so beautiful," he breathed against me. "Sometimes you seem too bright to be real."

I laughed shakily, unsure how to reply. I was beautiful enough, it was true—although not like my sister, Celeste. All the women of my family were. But my beauty had done no good against the snow leopard. And it did us no good now, when we stood so close to something that could save us. For all my efforts to be more—for all my brief taste of true power—I had been reduced once again to a beautiful princess. He said he saw brightness in me, but in truth my fire had failed us.

I tasted fear in my mouth when I remembered what he planned to do. How he planned to sacrifice himself because I had failed to protect us as we planned.

Shaking my head, I pulled back, out of the warm circle of his arms. He looked at me, his brow furrowed and eyes confused as if waking from a dream.

"What is it?" he asked, his gaze never leaving my face. Once again I wondered what he could read there.

"I said that I would not leave you, Oliver, but what of you? Will you truly leave me?"

Pain twisted his face. "I must."

"No!" I slashed angrily at the air with my hand. "This is not the way. This will not save us. Your kingdom needs you fighting, not waiting uselessly!"

I saw my words hit him like a physical blow, but I wouldn't take them back. I could feel every nerve humming. I had to make him understand. This village was poison, for all it looked so idyllic. I could sense it—had sensed it since we stepped through the rock. I didn't know where the poison came from, but nothing good would come of lingering here.

"I wish there were another way," he said, "but I cannot see one."

I took two stumbling steps backward, his haunted eyes piercing me. Had I been cold when we started this walk? Every part of me burned now. And yet still no flames leaped to my command. I closed my eyes, drawing deep breaths, trying to think of something that might convince him.

But when I opened them again, he was gone. I sank down onto the forest floor. For all I apparently burned so brightly, I had not been enough. I could not save us from whatever poisoned Valley View. I could not take the object by force. And I could not keep Oliver from walking away. What use was my fire now?

CHAPTER 23

J don't know how long I remained curled there, but eventually the cold seeped through into every part of me, driving out any lingering warmth from our embrace. Even in this protected valley it wasn't warm enough to stay outside and still for so long without a fire.

But the cold wasn't the only thing that had taken root inside me. I didn't need fire, I could save us all without it. I had promised myself I could, and I would not back down now.

I suspected the elders wouldn't even accept Oliver's proposal, but I didn't want to take the risk. I could save him before he even approached them.

I just needed the object. And I knew where to find it.

As I strode back toward the village, new energy flowing through me, I made my plans. Dark was already falling, but I would wait for full black. Then I would force my way through that door and take the object that could save an entire kingdom. These people would thank me one day, when they had been forced away from this noxious place.

Once I had it, we would run for it, straight back down the mountain. The villagers would undoubtedly pursue us—they would have to. But by then it would be too late. I would send Oliver and Giselle ahead with the object, and I would stay behind, just out of range. I would protect us with an inferno impossible to penetrate no matter how well these people knew their mountain. And somehow, with me as the buffer between us, all of us would make it down the mountain. Once we were back in the palace with the object, we would have the royal guard to protect us from the incensed villagers and their treasonous ideas.

I was fired up, ready to act now, but I made myself wait. Full dark still hadn't fallen. And a loud grumble from my belly reminded me I hadn't eaten yet, so I reluctantly returned to the house. Calmly sitting down to eat felt too much like being locked back up in Lord Treestone's castle, but I needed every advantage I could get. Food would only strengthen me.

When I appeared, Oliver quickly looked away, his eyes guarded, his fists tightening briefly. I carefully focused on Giselle instead who looked curiously between us. Eventually she shook her head and turned back to the food.

"I'm not going to ask," she muttered as she served it into bowls.

I appreciated her forbearance.

Although I forced myself to sit and eat, Oliver didn't seem to have the same capacity. Whether it was his coming sacrifice, or our encounter in the trees, something tormented him enough that he could sit still only for a minute. After thrusting himself back from the table and striding to the fire for the third time, he was met with a glare from Giselle.

"Sorry," he said, sounding guilty. "I'll go." And before either of us could protest, he had disappeared out the door.

"What did you do to him?" she asked, her voice halfway between exasperated and amused.

A flush rose up my neck, and I couldn't answer her in kind.

"Well!" she said after a moment of silence.

I pushed my bowl away and leaned across the table. "I don't

know when he'll be back, which means you have to get ready for all of us."

"What?" Giselle seemed confused by the sudden change of topic, her blue eyes uneasy at the light in mine.

"We're getting out of here—tonight. So you need to be dressed and packed for a hasty exit." I gave her a significant look, and she frowned.

"What exactly are the two of you planning?"

"I'm going to save us before your brother does something stupid. And I'm not waiting any longer." I stood to my feet and pulled on my jacket. "So just be ready."

Giselle stood and joined me, although she made no move to pack our bags or dress herself.

"Why do I get the distinct impression that *you're* the one about to do something stupid?" She eyed me warily. "What are you planning to do, Celine?"

"I'm stealing the object. And then we're going to make a run for it."

Her eyes grew wide. "What?!? We've never even seen the object. Are you mad?"

I laughed, but the slightly wild sound didn't seem to reassure her. "Perhaps."

She continued to glare at me, but her disapproval did nothing to erode my determination. "We know where the object is, that's enough."

"Yes, it's in a forbidden hut. Remember? And you don't have your powers anymore."

I frowned at the mention of my fire. "I don't need powers, Giselle. I survived without them for eighteen years. Even in the midst of an attempted coup and a rebellion."

She didn't look convinced.

"And, anyway, once we've got it, you can take it ahead. To free my powers."

Giselle narrowed her eyes. "If we make it that far." She

gripped my arm. "This is crazy, Celine. At least wait until Oliver gets back. Let us all talk this over. What if you get in there and there's more than one object inside? How will you know which one it is? And what if they catch you? You remember what the elder said about obeying their laws. Do we even know the penalty for disobeying them? Oliver and I won't be able to protect you."

I brushed her concerns aside along with her hand. "I'll know. And I won't get caught. You'll see. Just be ready to run."

Before she could stop me, I thrust open the door and pushed out into the night. Excitement filled me, tingling in every part of my body. She would see. And so would Oliver. So would anyone who had ever doubted me. I was Celine of Lanover, and I didn't need a godmother's gift to keep the people I loved safe.

I soon slowed my stride, however, remembering the need to stay out of sight. Thankfully my goal stood nowhere near the tavern or the baths, the two buildings that seemed to attract nighttime traffic. I slipped from shadow to shadow, staying away from lighted windows or the occasional villager making their way home. I should have waited longer, but I couldn't risk Oliver returning and trying to restrain me.

When I reached the building, I realized I also should have checked Sterling's house for tools of some sort. I tried the door, just in case, but of course it remained locked. So now I stood in the dark with empty hands, staring at a locked door.

My eyes traveled to my useless hands and then down to my feet. After a moment of consideration, I shrugged. It seemed I only had one choice.

Planting one foot firmly, I pulled the other up, glad to be wearing pants instead of skirts, and smashed my heel against the door, just below the latch. It didn't move, but I thought I heard a faint splintering.

A grin stretched across my face as I drove my foot again and again against the same spot. For a moment I forgot everything else as I vented all my anger and frustration on the wooden panels. Finally, with a louder splinter and a crash, the latch gave way, and the door swung inward.

I stood for a moment, panting, satisfaction surging through me. But slowly it faded, a flaring pain in my ankle replacing the surge of energy. I shouldn't have used my previously injured leg. And now an unwelcome unease accompanied the physical pain.

How much noise had that made? I glanced around, but no one emerged from the shadows to tackle me. I looked again at the broken door. There would be no hiding this. If I couldn't identify the object, or if it wasn't even here…

But I shook off the thought. Such doubts would do no good now. And why else would there be a windowless hut, forbidden to all? It would be here.

I stepped inside. My first thought was that I should have brought a lantern. Without windows, the hut remained in almost complete blackness. Something I should have foreseen.

But you didn't stop to think, did you? said a voice in my mind that I squashed just as I had the earlier thoughts. I was here now.

I pushed the door as wide as it would go, letting in the faint gleam of moonlight. A small table stood close enough to catch some illumination, and I could just make out the outline of a candle. My groping fingers found the nearby tinder box and after much fumbling, I managed to light it. I was far from expert in the task, and I was still complaining to myself when I turned to survey the room.

Ice instantly washed over me. The inside of the hut was as simple as the outside, with the exception of the carved door I had just partially destroyed. But it was no display room. In fact, the inside looked exactly like the storage shed I had first imagined it to be.

Several wheelbarrows, one missing a wheel, leaned haphazardly against one another in one corner. And at least half of the single room was taken up with various pieces of broken furniture all piled on top of each other.

Godmothers were known for enchanting ordinary objects, but I had never known one to enchant a broken chair. And no one would store an essential magical object in such a place. Several of the mismatched piles looked like they might collapse at any point, crushing anything that happened to be beneath them.

An unpleasant tingling rushed down from my scalp to my toes and back up again. If it wasn't kept here, where was it? And what had I done? This had all been for naught.

A drop of hot wax dripped onto my hand, and I yelped and jumped backward, only just managing to keep my grip on the candle. My gaze flew from the small flame to the wide-open door. I tried to remember what this building faced onto. Was it angled so that anyone would see the light, so out of place in this particular spot?

I needed to get out of here before someone discovered what I had done. I blew out the candle and let it fall to the floor. Running, I burst from the door, almost tripping down the few stairs in my haste.

As my eyes sought out a path in the unfamiliar darkness, they fell on the shape I most feared. A human shape. Not on the village side of the hut, but on the other side. Someone lurked on the very edges of the village, barely visible in the gloom of the night.

My feet took off running before my brain could catch up. I fled back toward Sterling's house, not bothering to keep to the shadows because the sound I most dreaded had fallen on my ears. A shout from the shrouded figure. And then the pounding of multiple feet.

I should have run out of the valley entirely, but I was pointed the wrong way, my pursuers cutting me off from the narrow passage and escape. Without thought I continued on my current path. Only as I neared Sterling's house, my breath now coming in sharp pants, did it occur to me that I couldn't lead them here. I had to keep running. Find somewhere to hide until I could circle back and be free of this wretched place. Once I hit the snow line, none of them would be able to hurt me. Or so I hoped.

But even as I made the desperate plan, I neared the house, almost brushing against its wall, and the door flung open, blocking my forward momentum. Oliver leaned out, gazing beyond me, clearly looking for the source of the commotion. But it took less than a second for him to see me, my face no doubt blanched with fear.

It seemed to take even less time for him to take in the whole scene, understanding rushing across his face and fear filling his eyes. I tried to duck around the door to keep fleeing, but he grabbed my arm, pulling me inside and slamming the door behind us.

He still wore his boots and jacket, so he had either just returned or had been on his way out to find me. *If only he had found me in time,* a miserable voice inside whispered. *If only he had stopped me.*

But the fear in his eyes held no room for recriminations. Instead he scrabbled at the clasps of my jacket, pulling them apart while I stood there stupidly, trying to understand what was going on. As soon as they were undone, he ripped the garment from me, throwing it into a heap in front of the fire.

It hit the floor just as the door handle turned, and he thrust me back toward a chair, his hands rough and his eyes on the doorway. As I hit the seat hard, understanding rushed through me. I leaped back to my feet, but the damage had already been done.

Several men had pushed their way into the room, and the sight that confronted them was two girls sitting by the fire and one man, dressed for the outdoors, standing panting by the door.

"No!" I cried, even as three of them moved forward to grab Oliver's arms. He didn't resist, whether for our sake or simply because he was outnumbered, I didn't know. But I could see several more men milling outside, talking in angry voices. We had no chance against them if it came to a fight. Not without my fire.

Someone else stepped inside just behind the men, and my brain finally caught up with me. The figure I had seen watching the hut was a familiar one. The same who now entered the house —Sterling.

His eyes traveled from Oliver, held securely between the villagers, and me. Relief rushed through me. He had been there. He had seen me. The truth would now be exposed.

But his eyes skated back over me, landing once again on Oliver. And the expression on his face was one of satisfaction.

"My apologies for bringing a lawbreaker into your community," he said to Oliver's captors.

I rushed forward, my mind scrambling to make sense of it all, and wrapped my hands around one of Oliver's arms. The man on that side pushed me back, and Oliver turned on him, his eyes furious and his stance strong despite the restraining hands.

"Don't touch her!"

"She'll be safe enough," said the elder who had warned us only that morning. "It's not she who has broken our laws." His eyes held no mercy.

I opened my mouth to correct him, if Sterling would not, but Giselle kicked me so hard in the shin that I nearly fell, already off balance. I wobbled against the younger girl, and only two of the men even spared a glance for the overwrought women as they hauled Oliver away.

I got a final glimpse of him, looking back at us, and the relief in his eyes made me crumple to the floor for the second time that day. He had not hesitated to sacrifice himself for me. And I—I had destroyed everything.

After several deep, shuddering breaths, I scrambled back to my feet.

"We…we should go after them."

Giselle, her face white, and her hand shaking, glanced from me to the door. "Do you know where they'll take him? Did you see a prison in your explorations?" She bit her lip and wrung her hands. "We might make things worse."

I looked around, trying to make my mind work rather than circling endlessly back to Oliver's final expression.

"Why did you stop me? You should have let me tell them the truth!"

"And have you both hauled off? We have a better chance of freeing him this way. Especially if they send him out of the valley."

I wanted to storm off into the night. To demand to know where Oliver had been taken. To demand to see him. But I hesitated. What if Giselle was right? What if I made it worse? I didn't know their customs or laws, I had been too busy in my useless quest for information on the object to ask. And we were only in this predicament because I had already rushed foolishly into something today…

"It was Sterling," I whispered.

"What?" Giselle looked at me in confusion, clearly having the same difficulty in ordering her thoughts that I was having.

"He was out there in the night, watching the hut. I think he was waiting for one of us to try…" I took a deep breath. "I think the whole thing was a set up."

"Did you…did you find it? Was it there?"

I bit my lip. "It was just a storage shed. Like it looked from the outside. But one that had been locked and forbidden. Why would anyone forbid access to a storage shed? Unless they wanted to lure someone into breaking the law."

Giselle swallowed. "You mean Sterling wanted you to break the law?"

I shook my head. "Not me. You saw what just happened. Sterling knew I was the one to break into that shed, but he said nothing. It was Oliver he wanted. He must have thought he was the most likely to do something rash." Tears filled my eyes. "He underestimated me. And then he got lucky that Oliver is too noble for his own good."

Giselle gaped at me. "But what does Sterling want with Oliver?"

The two of us stared at each other wordlessly. Because neither of us had an answer to that question.

CHAPTER 24

*W*e didn't sleep. Instead we took turns pacing and glancing anxiously at the door, until we both ended up huddled together on the floor in front of the fire.

We had agreed that at dawn we would venture out and find the elders. Demand to know where Oliver was being kept and what his punishment was to be. But the hours dragged endlessly, and with every one that passed, the heavy weight of my stupidity and arrogance grew. This was all my fault.

Dawn brought no lessening of my guilt. But at least we could finally act. Silently we picked ourselves up and left the house.

Even though they refused to acknowledge his authority, I could only hope the villagers would hesitate to deal too harshly with the crown prince of the kingdom in which they sheltered. Except, of course, that these people had already shown they didn't think like other people. I bit my lip.

As we left the house, I saw our full packs lined up next to the door. The sight drove a fresh shot of pain through me. For all her disapproval, Giselle had obeyed my orders. She had been ready to flee with the object.

As the sun rose higher, we made our way to the central

square. I don't know if I had expected to find the full council of elders in attendance, but I didn't expect to find it empty, with no sign that anything at all had happened.

Blinking, I took in the entire village. Nothing I could see looked out of place. People moved about their daily business, as they had done the morning before. None even looked at us with any special curiosity.

When a woman passed close by, I reached out and grabbed her arm, forcing her to stop. She looked at my fingers with distaste, but I didn't let go.

"Where's Prince Oliver? Where are they holding him?"

This time she looked at me in surprise, and the emotion seemed genuine. "Didn't you hear? He broke our laws."

"Yes, I know," I said, barely restraining my impatience. "But where are they holding him?"

Her brows lowered, and she looked between me and Giselle. "Holding him? What do you mean?"

I held back the urge to shake her with difficulty. "Prison, jail, the stocks...whatever it is you use for those who break the law."

"Oh, we don't hold them," she said.

Her words surprised me enough that my grip slackened, and she managed to pull herself free. I turned frightened eyes on Giselle as the woman marched off, her gait indignant.

"They can't have...surely they can't have...already..." I couldn't seem to get the words to come. Giselle looked equally stricken.

When the elder from the day before appeared, as if from nowhere, I rounded on him so fiercely I was actually baring my teeth. He looked unintimidated, his gaze hooded and impossible to read.

"Where is he?" I demanded. "Where is Oliver?"

"He broke our laws," the man said, calmly.

"Yes, we know," snapped Giselle, her patience clearly wearing as thin as mine. "But where is he?"

He looked between us. "He is gone."

I fell back a step, my heart stuttering. Surely he couldn't mean…

"You dared kill the crown prince of Eldon for breaking down a door?" asked Giselle, and I had never heard that tone in her voice before.

He shook his head once, and I managed to breathe again.

"No, of course not. We do not kill. But neither do we keep lawbreakers among us. Those who transgress must leave immediately."

I tried to comprehend his words. If Oliver had merely been banished, I felt certain he would have found a way to sneak back in by now to find and reassure us.

"I don't understand. Where has he been taken?"

The man's eyes strayed to Giselle, although I was the one who had spoken. "We told you that we do not fall under your sovereignty. But you never asked who it is that we serve."

A horrible, creeping cold swept over me. "Who do you serve?"

His eyes bored into mine. "She calls herself the Snow Queen."

PART III
THE SNOW QUEEN

CHAPTER 25

I screamed and threw a chair so hard against the wall that one of the legs broke off, bouncing across the floor. Giselle flinched, but she didn't scold me.

"That traitor! That lying piece of manipulative scum. I'll—" But I broke off, unable to think of a suitable punishment, and settled for throwing a plate against the wall instead. When it shattered, something in me shattered with it, and I sank onto one of the remaining chairs.

Sterling's treachery ran even deeper than we had feared.

"I always knew there was something off about him."

"Yes, but we couldn't possibly have guessed this," said Giselle. I could see the horror in her eyes, but she held it in much better than me.

"So you've really never heard of this Snow Queen?" I shook my head. The whole thing seemed too incredible to believe. "I seem to remember someone mentioning her but only as a nursery story."

"Well…" Giselle hesitated, and I pounced on it.

"So you have heard of her!"

"Not in any real way. Not as a real person. But you're right."

She chewed on her lip. "I have vague memories of hearing the servants talk about her as a threat to keep children in line. You know. Behave or the Snow Queen will freeze your heart. Eat your vegetables or the Snow Queen will freeze you where you stand." She shrugged. "I always thought they meant it as a sort of humanizing of winter itself."

I stood back up and paced across the small floor.

She shrugged apologetically. "I certainly never heard anyone say, *Hey, you know that woman who lives high in the mountains with the power to control snow and ice? The one with a whole village to serve her? You know—the Snow Queen.*"

I slumped back down, as unable to keep pacing as I was to keep sitting. I tried to take stock of what we had learned.

Valley View served not the King of Eldon but this so-called Snow Queen. They provided her with food and supplies and kept her existence a secret from the world. And Sterling was not a villager, but a long-time servant of this queen. He carried her commands between her distant Palace of Ice and the village. And any lawbreakers were sent back with him, to serve the Snow Queen in whatever way she saw fit. None of them ever returned to the village.

"What do you think she does with them?" asked Giselle, as if reading my thoughts.

I threw up my hands. "I have no idea. Turn them into giant sculptures of ice to decorate her throne room?"

Giselle paled even further, and I felt instantly guilty.

"No, of course she doesn't," I said quickly. "Ignore me. I'm sure she has them doing the usual servant things. Preparing her food, cleaning her rooms, tending her fires." I considered. "Well, maybe not that last one. Not if she lives in a palace of ice."

Giselle's eyes widened. "Surely it's not really made of ice. Surely it's just a name…"

I shrugged. "I wouldn't put anything past her at this point. Would you?"

Giselle's thoughts seemed to have wandered down a different track. "So do you think this magical object we've been chasing even exists?"

I rubbed at my temples, briefly covering my face as I considered her question and my own foolishness.

"Yes," I said at last. "Something is protecting this village from the weather. And something is blocking my powers. But I don't suppose it all happened the way Sterling described it. We've been able to tell since we arrived that there's something wrong with this place. With these people. But it doesn't seem to have anything to do with ice. No one seems frozen…"

I swallowed. "I didn't think it was the same thing as what's infecting the rest of the kingdom. But clearly it's all coming from this so-called queen. Which means while the object may work against enchantment, it clearly doesn't work against this strange ability she must have to destroy people's hearts and minds. Which means it would never have worked to free the palace anyway. And if I had listened to my instincts warning me about Sterling, maybe I wouldn't have been so quick to do something so stupid…"

Giselle looked away, apparently not willing to absolve me, and I couldn't blame her. Because it hadn't been trust in Sterling that had led me astray. It had been my own pride and over-confidence. I had let myself rely too much on my new powers. And then, when they were stripped away, I had been so determined to prove my strength—to prove how useful I could be all on my own without powers or even help—I had behaved not with strength but with recklessness. And someone else had suffered the consequences. I deserved far worse than Giselle's condemnation.

"So why bring us here at all?" Giselle sounded bitter. "If you're right, and it's Oliver he wanted—or rather she wanted, I suppose —why not take us straight to her? We wouldn't have known he was leading us away from the village."

"I've been thinking about that. I can't know for certain, of course, but I think that was probably his original plan. Only the weather was worse than he expected. We were in a bad way after that blizzard, and he must have decided we needed to rest and resupply."

Giselle looked at me grimly. "And the blizzard did something else, remember. It exposed your powers. Maybe he thought his queen wouldn't be so pleased if he showed up at her ice palace with a girl who can lob fireballs in tow. He must have had to improvise. Try to come up with a plan to separate us from Oliver."

I groaned. "And we played straight into his hands."

Giselle glared at me.

"Well, I did, at any rate" I corrected quickly. "Me, and Oliver's stupid nobility." I thought it over, remembering the way Sterling had disappeared when we first arrived. "What did that elder say? That we hadn't asked? I think Sterling commanded them to lock that hut and forbid all access to it. On the Snow Queen's orders, of course. He probably told them not to give us any information on the object, and not to tell us anything about anything unless we specifically asked. Easy enough instructions for everyone to follow, but safe, too, since none of us would ever have thought to ask about a Snow Queen."

I groaned. "We were too busy asking about the mirror which was likely never here at all."

How strange that I had been so right to mistrust Sterling even though it now seemed as if he couldn't be responsible for the thing that had made me doubt him in the first place. Because if his queen wanted Oliver alive, it didn't make sense for him to have caused the cave in.

Silence fell between us as we both pondered the most important question. If it was Oliver the Snow Queen had been after all along, then what did she want with him? I had a sinking suspicion it must have something to do with his being the heir to the throne. Perhaps she had grown tired of ruling a distant mountain and a single village. And if she offered him a marriage alliance in exchange for lifting the curse on Eldon, would he agree?

Would he have any choice?

"What do we do now?" asked Giselle, and for once I remembered that she was only fifteen and years younger than me.

I hadn't actually considered it, but I found I knew the answer all the same.

"We go after him, of course. We get him back, and we melt this ice palace to the ground."

Giselle met my eyes and actually smiled, her expression ferocious. "Well, what are we waiting for then?"

~

The elder had been able to tell us only that the Snow Queen's Ice Palace lay to the north. Or, in other words, up. We didn't bother questioning anyone else. If no one taken there ever returned, it seemed fruitless to hope any of the villagers would know the way. And I couldn't imagine they'd tell us even if they did.

At least they didn't try to stop us leaving.

It took longer than I would have liked for us to prepare, but Giselle had insisted that we both sleep and eat, at least a little, before starting out. Reluctantly I had to admit that she was right. We wouldn't get far on a sleepless night and empty bellies. And we'd sleep better here in the house—despite the destruction I'd wreaked on it—than we would out in the snow.

And then, of course, there was the matter of our packs. With only the two of us, we had to abandon many of the supplies we'd used on the way up to Valley View. I had never been so conscious of the fact that Sterling and Oliver had carried the heavier packs. So even more time passed while we unpacked and laid everything out, carefully choosing which things we most needed.

Despite our early start to the day, it was well into the after-

219

noon when we finally set off. My feet seemed to bound forward, eager to be on our way, but I had enough experience now to know that wouldn't last. Not for long, anyway. The mountain and the snow would soon sap my energy and weaken my muscles.

But it wasn't only the desire to be off after Oliver that drove my steps forward. I couldn't wait to be free of this valley. Since none of us had seen any other way out during our time here, Giselle and I had agreed to backtrack to the narrow rock entrance and go from there. I just hoped we could find some sign of Sterling and Oliver's passage to guide us after that. Because if we couldn't...

But all my doubts fell away as we stepped clear of the rock passage and out into the deep snow, the frozen landscape still piled high from the recent blizzard. Giselle immediately sat down to strap on her snowshoes, but I just stood there.

I closed my eyes, already full of more emotions than I knew how to handle. The inferno that burst into bloom inside my chest raced eagerly down my arms and sprang from my fingertips in dancing flames. I swirled my fingers, forming the fire on each hand into a ball, and hurled both of them at distant trees.

They hit with a bang and sizzle, shaking clumps of snow from the branches. I laughed, and Giselle applauded.

"We needed some good news," she said, still fastening the clasps of her shoes.

Grinning back at her, I thrust out my palms and sent a rush of hot air racing away from me. The trees in front of us bent and creaked, more snow falling to the ground.

"Whoa there," said Giselle, climbing back to her feet. "Let's not bring the forest down around us."

I nodded, my momentary elation subsiding as I remembered our situation. I quickly sat and attached my own snowshoes, my thoughts turning dark.

"He'll be ready for me, you know," I said. When Giselle looked at me blankly, I added, "Sterling."

Understanding crossed her face.

"I knew we didn't want him to find out about my powers." I wobbled a little as I stood, my legs taking a moment to remember how to walk properly in the strange contraptions.

"Well, I for one am glad you didn't let us die," said Giselle, but I could see the worry in her eyes.

I gestured at the valley behind us. "It doesn't seem promising that this Snow Queen can apparently dampen my powers."

Giselle winced, but her eyes were thoughtful. "The enchantment on that valley is obviously of very long-standing. And this Snow Queen clearly is no follower of the High King. She isn't a godmother. She must be fueling her magic with objects she has somehow acquired, twisting them to her purposes. As you said, there must be an object hidden in the valley somewhere. One that works against enchantments, but not against her control over people. So, one that wouldn't have helped us," she added before sighing.

"So far I'm not feeling encouraged." I made a face at her.

She rolled her eyes back at me. "My point is that just because this object deadened your powers, doesn't mean any of the ones at her palace will. I can't see why she would want to nullify enchantment there. Her palace would probably melt around her ears."

I grinned, cheered by her logic. Fire danced across my fingertips. "I think I might be able to help with the melting thing."

Giselle smiled back at me. "I'm counting on it."

To my utter gratitude, we easily found tracks leading further up the mountain. I didn't know what method Sterling had used to compel Oliver's obedience, but it looked—as far as my limited knowledge could tell—to have only been the two of them. The track they had left behind them didn't look packed enough to have been used by any others.

And the existence of the broken trail raised my spirits for the first time since I had burst into the storage hut. It was even better than I had hoped since it both showed the way and eased our own journey. For the first time I began to think we might actually have a better than decent chance to make it to this distant palace.

"As long as it doesn't snow," I muttered, too low for Giselle to hear.

By the time darkness fell, forcing us to stop, I felt more relieved than I cared to admit. I had thought I was starting to grow accustomed to the exertion on our earlier journey, but apparently even two idle days had caused all my muscles to rebel.

We succeeded in finding a cave to shelter in, at least. It was shallower than I would have liked, but a great deal better than nothing. And at least I didn't have to worry that a snow leopard might have made her den in the distant reaches of the cave.

I hadn't even thought of gathering wood as we traveled, so we had only a meager fire that wouldn't last the night. A much smaller problem than it otherwise would have been without my powers. We ended up curling up to sleep back-to-back so that my internal fire could keep us both warm. And from the way we overslept, it worked all too well.

Once we saw how far the sun had already risen, we raced to pack up and get back on the trail, neither of us speaking much. I looked out of the cave with trepidation, but no fresh snow had fallen. I heaved a sigh of relief as we resumed our journey. I had no idea how far ahead they were. They had left in the middle of the night, so perhaps they weren't even stopping for darkness. Some fresh enchantment drove them on, perhaps. Either way, I didn't have any hope of catching them before they reached this Snow Queen. But that didn't mean I wanted to waste any time either. Who knew how quickly she would want to seal an alliance?

~

For reasons that didn't contain any logic, I had expected the scenery to change past the village, but it continued to look much as it had further downslope. The snow was thicker, courtesy of the blizzard, and some of the paths were a little steeper, but otherwise the trees looked the same—tall firs interspersed with the occasional bare trunk of something else—and the mountains still rose around us.

We saw no sign of any snow leopards, and I suspected they had all fled lower, like the one Oliver had been forced to hunt down. We did find a couple of deep valleys with drops so steep we couldn't even slide down as we had previously. Instead we had to pick our way down what felt like rock faces, using our boots instead of our snowshoes.

We took our time on these, although the burning inside me always increased at our extra slow pace. But I let off the pressure by throwing the occasional fire ball at the opposite slope rather than hurrying. We couldn't afford for either of us to fall. Neither Giselle nor I would be able to drag the other either onward or back to safety. Not on our own.

The second night we couldn't find a cave, so had to make do with a small depression in a cliff face. We had gathered some wood as we walked that day, but I suspected we would have been in trouble without my powers.

The next night we found a deeper cave, perfect for our purposes. A fact I assured myself of by exploring its full length with blazing fire springing from each hand. We were the only occupants. We slept much better than the previous night but woke to a sight that filled me with dread.

Snow. Gently falling from the sky, flakes so soft and light they danced on the light breeze before hitting the ground. But hit the ground they did.

Giselle and I exchanged a loaded look, but neither of us spoke.

Instead we packed and attached our snowshoes with fumbling haste. The path was still visible—for now. But I had no idea what we would do when it disappeared.

The morning passed in a blur, a race against the falling flakes, with all my attention focused on the disappearing trail ahead of us. To make it worse, our progress slowed as the packed path gradually filled with fresh powder. My eyes barely left it, afraid that if I moved them away, I wouldn't be able to find it again when I looked back down.

At some point my neck began to spasm, but I barely noticed. My eyes ached from the strain of staring at the bright white of the snow, but still I tried not to blink. The lines were so faint now, our progress so labored and slow.

I blinked, my eyes watering, and when they reopened, I saw only a flat expanse before us. I swiveled my head desperately, pushing ahead. There. I saw a packed down line, the path appearing faintly before me again. I breathed a sigh of relief and tried to pick up the pace. I knew Giselle followed close behind, but I had no attention to spare for her.

Several minutes later, I blinked and lost the path again. This time I couldn't find it. I stopped, my eyes still glued to the ground, my heart beating faster.

"Can you see it?" I asked. "Can you see the path?"

Giselle shuffled up beside me, close enough to touch my arm. Gripping it, she squeezed, making me look up at last from the snow.

"I don't think it matters anymore." Her voice was a breathless whisper.

I followed her gaze and gasped.

Ahead of us and slightly to one side, a tall structure rose from the distant slope. Steep towers and impossible curves and long arching bridges.

I drew in a shaking breath. "I could have sworn your brother said your palace was one of a kind."

Giselle slowly shook her head. "He'd never seen this one." She whistled softly. "And I think this one might actually be made of ice after all."

"Welcome to the Palace of Ice," I said softly. "Domain of the Snow Queen."

CHAPTER 26

The palace had looked shockingly close, but as with the mountains themselves when we first started this journey, it didn't seem to get any closer for a long time. It didn't help that our pace had slowed even further now that we had to break our own trail. We took turns at the task, swapping regularly and taking much more frequent breaks.

I occupied myself by keeping my internal fire running at full heat, carefully balanced just below breakout level. I kept expecting it to wink out when we approached too close to the palace, and my fear easily fueled the constant burn.

But finally, finally the palace did begin to creep closer, and no icy fingers reached out to steal my fire. At some point the snow had stopped as well, the latest fall only deep enough to cover Sterling and Oliver's trail. I no longer begrudged a single aching, tired muscle from the pace at which we'd pushed ourselves the last few days. We'd made it just in time.

The now clear blue sky began to slowly change, tinging with pink and orange before deepening into indigo. I frowned at the palace which now loomed over us, close but not close enough. We wouldn't make it today, after all.

Giselle seemed as reluctant as I was to stop, but neither of us wished to face the Snow Queen in the middle of the night, either. So when Giselle noticed a small cave off to one side of our current track, we reluctantly changed course. I had been far too distracted to gather wood, so we picked up what we could now. As we worked, I felt the silent presence of the Ice Palace casting its sinister shadow over everything. I found myself facing away from its fantastical shape as often as I could, but it took me some time to realize what was bothering me.

"There are no animals," I said.

Giselle looked up from breaking off a small branch and peered around with a frown.

"It's so silent." I swept my own gaze around the area but saw nothing to refute my statement. "When was the last time you heard a bird, even?"

Giselle's brow crinkled in thought, but she couldn't come up with an answer.

"I'm sure I haven't heard one since we saw the palace," I said. "I couldn't work out what was bothering me so much at first."

I noticed a slight tremble to Giselle's hand as she reached for a couple of twigs that had broken off her branch and fallen to the snow. I bit my lip. I shouldn't have said anything. The whole situation was unnerving enough.

So when Giselle later gave a wordless cry from the mouth of the cave where she had gone to fill a pot with snow, I jumped up immediately from the small fire which I had been tending. As I hurried to join her, various terrifying possibilities raced through my mind. But when I staggered to a stop in the cave entrance, my mouth fell open. I hadn't expected this.

"That's…"

"Beautiful," she breathed, not taking her eyes from the sky. "I've never seen anything like it."

"I don't remember seeing it last night…" I couldn't blame her for her wonder.

"We were in a deeper cave," she reminded me. "And I don't remember coming out after dark. But perhaps this only happens here. Part of the enchantment of this place."

Enchantment seemed the right word for it. I had never seen or even imagined such a thing in any of the kingdoms I had visited. Spectacular ribbons of violet and turquoise and emerald streaked through the dark night sky, throwing reflections of color down onto the white snow. As we watched, the ribbons pulsed and danced across the heavens.

"You don't think they could hurt us, do you?" asked Giselle, after we had stood there for endless minutes in entranced silence.

I shook myself slightly and looked at her. But irresistibly, my eyes were drawn back to the incredible phenomenon.

"Surely not?" I whispered.

"It's hard to believe something so beautiful could come from someone as evil as the Snow Queen."

"Perhaps it doesn't," I said. "Or even if it is the result of one of her enchantments, not everything about them is bad. Think of the one that protects Valley View from the storms and snow. Her magic is a corruption of the objects of the godmothers, so it must have had some good purpose originally."

Giselle nodded, her eyes still riveted on the sky. "I can't imagine how I'm going to sleep now."

It was a long time before we dragged ourselves away to cook some food, and then we brought it back to eat at the mouth of the cave. Eventually we lay down to sleep there, back-to-back, leaving our little fire to die out on its own and relying on my heat to keep us from freezing.

Neither of us thought we would actually be able to sleep, not with the outline of the Snow Queen's palace black against the unending beauty of the sky. But eventually our long day of exertion overcame us, inexorably drawing us down into sleep.

～

I woke with a start, Giselle mumbling and twitching in her sleep beside me. A cold, clear day greeted me, the sky returned to its normal shade of blue. The stillness made the absence of other sounds stand out. Nothing flew through the sky or rustled in the trees. And not a sound emerged from the palace which, unlike the day before, now seemed closer than I remembered.

If I didn't know better, I would believe us all alone up here, confronted with an empty building of ice. But we weren't alone, and we'd do well not to forget it.

The reassuring warmth of my inner fire still burned, unaffected by the proximity of the Palace of Ice. It reassured me, somewhat, but I still remembered how easily it had been taken away. And how foolishly I had then behaved. I had worried that the powers had changed me, but in my efforts to prove I was the same person I was before them, I had overcompensated and rushed into action without proper thought.

The truth was that they had changed me. As had the rest of my experiences in Eldon. And I had to work out how to take all the new parts of me and make myself into a stronger whole. Because, with or without my powers, there was no going back to who I was before.

And now my fire had returned—and I was glad for it—but I couldn't make the same mistakes. My new power was merely a tool. It didn't define me, and it wasn't what made me strong. My mind, and my determination, and the hours I had spent building my skills were just as valuable. As long as I remembered to use them.

Quickly I prepared some food and cleaned up our little camp, my mind lingering on the many unknowns about to confront us. When Giselle appeared, sleepily rubbing her eyes and claiming some breakfast, I was staring down at our packs.

"I think we should leave them here," I said.

"Good morning to you, too," she murmured. She took a bite. "Leave what?"

"Our packs."

When she looked surprised, I raised my brows. "Do you want to face unknown dangers from a bizarre palace built of ice and a woman claiming to be some sort of queen of winter with a giant, heavy pack on your back?"

Giselle blinked at me, obviously still struggling to think so early in the morning. "I can't say that I do, now that I come to think of it."

I nodded once. "Exactly. If we leave them at the back of the cave, they should be safe enough." I bit my lip. "I hope."

It would be a deadly trip back down the mountain after we rescued Oliver if something happened to our packs while we were gone. Especially since he hadn't taken his when he left Valley View, so we would have to share Giselle and my meager supplies between the three of us.

But that was a problem for later. We had to actually rescue Oliver first. And while I would love to think it was just a matter of marching into the palace, burning the place down, and marching back out with Oliver in tow, I didn't really expect it to be so easy. Who knew how long we would be gone?

Giselle's stiff posture as she broke a trail ahead of me told me she felt as unsure as I did. But neither of us said anything. Since neither of us had any intention of abandoning Oliver or Eldon, there was nothing to be done but press forward.

I just wished my mind didn't insist on dwelling on all the awful things Oliver might have endured since being brought here. What would this Snow Queen do to him if he refused her wishes? My heart sped up a bit. And what if he agreed?

Shivers shook me only to alternate with bursts of heat so intense I could barely control them whenever I remembered Oliver's arms around me and his lips against mine. Surely he would not agree to marry this woman who was tearing his kingdom apart. Assuming marriage was, indeed, her goal. Surely he would not.

The closer we got, the more incredible the ice palace became. The blue-green color reminded me of the marble used in the royal palace of Eldon, but it was different, too. Translucent in a way the marble couldn't match.

A long sloping staircase emerged from the snow and led up to huge double doors. I didn't exactly want to barrel through the front entrance, but I could see no other openings at ground level, and our progress with the snowshoes was so slow that I hated the idea of trying to circle the structure looking for another way in.

When Giselle fell back to let me take the lead for a while, she noticed my eyes fastened on the still-distant doors.

"We might as well," she said. "Somehow I don't think we're going to slip into this queen's domain without her noticing, whichever entry we use."

I winced. "I suppose you're right." I glared at the ornate entrance, adding in a mutter, "Doesn't mean I have to like it."

I was still taking my turn at the front when Giselle's sudden indrawn breath made me pause. I scanned our surroundings looking for a threat. I sighed when I spotted a dense flurry of snow approaching like a moving wall. Great. Just what we needed.

But when I began to push forward again, Giselle stayed frozen in place. I looked back at her and then back toward the incoming snow, examining it more closely.

"Wait, is that…" I looked up at the blue sky, still as clear as when I had opened my eyes this morning.

"It's not coming out of the sky," breathed Giselle, her fear clear in every word.

"Well, magical or natural, we're too close to the palace to get caught in a blizzard now," I said grimly, pushing forward again. I glanced back over my shoulder. "Giselle! Come on!"

The younger girl shook herself from her daze and hurried across the snow to join me.

231

"There's something about it," she called, as she half-slid, half-ran. "I don't think we want to get caught in it."

I didn't stop again to ask what she meant because I felt all too certain she was right. But despite our increased pace and the nearness of the palace, the distant flakes rushed far too quickly to meet us. I tried to push my legs faster, but I could already see we weren't going to make it.

The strange flurry approached us, moving horizontally to the ground and broad enough to stretch up above my head. The dense heart of it was still a little distance away, but the first flakes, dancing in front, had nearly reached us.

They came at us from the side, a strange whistle of wind driving them along, and one flew past just in front of me. I tried to keep moving, although my body wanted to freeze in shock. It had been huge, and the flake had glittered strangely as it passed.

A scream from behind made me whirl around, nearly falling as my snowshoes tangled. Giselle was still moving forward, but a small stream of red ran down her cheek from a long, narrow gash along one of her cheekbones. While I watched, trying to understand what had happened, a sharp pain raced along the arm which faced toward the encroaching snow.

I stared as the flake whose icy tip had cut clean through my layers to pierce my skin continued on its way, gusting up and then down in the strange breeze.

"Don't stop," screamed Giselle, waving me onward. "They're not snowflakes—they're iceflakes. And their edges are razor sharp."

I had never heard of such a thing and, judging from her face, neither had she. I scrambled to face myself forward again, ignoring the sting in my arm and the warm trickle I felt making its way down my sleeve. The cut hadn't been deep, thanks to all my protective layers, and I had no time to tend it now.

As I hurried forward, slipping and sliding awkwardly in my haste, more iceflakes flew past. They appeared like perfectly formed—but huge—snowflakes. Except now that I looked more closely, I could see the hard lines and glitter of ice instead of the soft white of snow. I had never seen such a thing before and, given the heavier weight of ice, the wind that blew them shouldn't have been strong enough to lift them in such a manner.

Giselle gasped and moaned, and I gestured for her to come up beside me. "Get ahead," I yelled at her, continuing to gesture wildly as she pushed past me, panting and gasping.

As soon as she entered my line of sight, flame rushed to fill my hands. I sent it streaming between us and the oncoming wave of iceflakes. The hiss of steam overpowered the wind as the flakes melted. But even as I sent out another burst, a flake danced up and over it, driven by the unnatural breeze, to swing down toward my nose.

I jerked my head from its path and snapped my hands into fists. I had reacted without thinking again. Fire wasn't what was needed here.

Still pressing forward, my snowshoes sliding desperately across the snow, I thrust out my palms. A hot wind rushed from them, and I gestured around us. Like I had done in the blizzard, I created a whirlwind of air around us, with us in the still center. My wind overpowered the breeze that drove the flakes, and they spun away from us, some melting in the sudden warmth.

It was working. Except we were still rushing madly toward the palace doors, and keeping a circle of air around two moving people was far more difficult than keeping it around four immobile people. I battled to stop it from sweeping us away, along with the flakes. And we both now looked as if we were involved in some sort of mad dance, ducking and weaving to keep away from the flakes that made it through my imperfect shield.

The last stretch before the ice stairs seemed to extend forever, the densest part of the flurry having now hit with flakes coming at us from every direction. When Giselle reached the first step, she flung herself at it, only to slip and fall back into the snow. Snowshoes weren't made for climbing ice stairs.

I threw myself down beside her, gripping her arm to keep her from rising.

"Take them off," I shouted above the roar of my wind and the fury of the flurry. My hands remained out, my wind tightening around us. It was infinitely easier to control now that we were sitting still.

For a moment I forgot Giselle in my concentration, until I felt a tugging at my feet. Looking down, I saw that she had stripped off her own shoes, and now struggled to free my boots. I thrust my legs out in front of me to make her job easier, and she smiled at me with tight lips. She had a rip at her shoulder and on both legs, and red still dripped sluggishly down her face.

As soon as she had finished, she tugged me up to standing, my wind coming with us. But as she stepped up onto the first step, she nearly slid back again. I risked a glance downward and saw that the first few steps, the ones within reach of my hot wind, had started to melt, water dripping off them as they lost their shape.

"Jump over them," I shouted, steadying Giselle from behind. I tried to lift my wind slightly as she leaped forward. Keeping it off the stairs but still low enough to protect us was a delicate balance I didn't think I could achieve while running up stairs.

Eventually I gave up the effort and let my power rip at the stairs. We would just have to move faster than the wind could melt them.

"Go! Run!" I screamed at Giselle, who hesitated above me, looking back down to track my progress. She turned and dashed upward, and I followed.

I kept my eyes beneath me, watching each step, my whole focus on the next stride upward. So when the next step failed to materialize, the ice stretching out instead into a flat platform, I fell. Sliding forward across the smooth surface on my knees, I felt my grip on the wind slacken and then die. Giselle looked back at me, her eyes jumping to the flakes that rushed in to fill the quickly stilling air.

Sprinting the last steps, she grabbed at the icy handle of the door and tugged with all her might. The door swung open so smoothly that she nearly joined me on the ice. Regaining her balance, she swung it wide and then held it there, beckoning for me to join her.

Slipping and sliding, I forced my feet under me and ran as fast as the ice would allow, not slowing as I barreled through the doorway. The clang of heavy ice against heavy ice made me stop and turn. Giselle stood with her back against the now closed door, her breath heaving.

"Without your power, those would have cut us to ribbons," she said, her wide eyes meeting mine.

"What did I say?" I asked. "Welcome to the Snow Queen's domain."

CHAPTER 27

$\mathcal{I}$ had barely regained my breath before I swung around, fire balls bursting into life in both my hands. The run had drained me, but too many emotions flooded me to have any difficulty accessing my power. And whatever greeted us in here, I wanted to be ready.

Except nothing greeted us. The bare hall of ice stretched out on all sides, the ceiling far overhead. But it held no furnishings, no decorations save from the carved ice of the walls themselves, and no people at all. Nothing threatened me, and slowly I let my hands drop, the fire burning out.

Giselle's breaths softened and slowed behind me, returning to normal before I heard the sound of her boots scraping against ice.

"Well, this is…somewhat unexpected," she said when she at last reached my shoulder.

High windows, made of ice so thin it resembled glass, let in the sunlight. But the golden rays provided no heat, posing no threat to the frozen structure.

"Where do you think everyone is?" She looked around, as if expecting people to start popping from the walls.

"I have no idea." I reminded myself I should be pleased we hadn't been met with armed guards, but I felt unnerved all the same. "I suppose we should go and find someone. Well, one person in particular."

The reference to her brother made Giselle start, as if she had forgotten him in the madness of this place. "Yes. The sooner we find Oliver, the sooner we can leave."

She headed straight for the broad staircase on the other side of the hall, and I followed without question. Inside my heart was sinking, however. Upstairs meant the royal suites. And I didn't like to think of finding Oliver there, even if Giselle thought it the most likely place to look for him.

But this strange palace didn't seem to follow a usual layout. We passed through room after room, the corridors and apartments creating a warren, one leading into another into another, until I had no idea where we were anymore. Many rooms held no furnishings, but we found a massive dining room containing an ornate table made of thick ice, with more than twenty matching chairs.

Giselle shivered when she saw it. "Can you imagine eating here?"

A blond head with burning blue eyes filled my mind. Had Oliver been forced to eat meals here? Not surprisingly, I hadn't seen a single fire since we'd entered, and the air burned so coldly against my skin, I was surprised I wasn't steaming. Did some enchantment keep the inhabitants from freezing?

I looked over at Giselle as we entered another long corridor. "Are you cold?"

She shot me an odd look. "No, Celine. I'm walking through a palace made entirely of ice, the home of someone who calls herself the Snow Queen. I'm feeling toasty warm. Must be all those bonfires burning everywhere."

I rolled my eyes, and she rolled hers straight back.

"Yes, I'm cold."

"But, how cold?" I persisted. *"I'm about to turn blue, and I'm seriously concerned I may lose my fingers and toes,* cold? Or, *this is unpleasant, and I could probably do with an extra layer or a nice fireplace,* cold?"

This time Giselle took the question seriously, considering her answer.

"Closer to the second, I think. Which is surprising now that I think about it. It must be part of the magic of this place." She reached out to run her fingers along a wall and shuddered.

"Well, that's reassuring, I suppose." I eyed a graceful column as we passed but kept my hands to myself. "And not only for Oliver's sake. Perhaps this Snow Queen is a bit more human herself than she might like us to believe."

"I wouldn't count on it," Giselle murmured, staring with fascination at an intricate chandelier of ice hanging from the ceiling.

I couldn't imagine the point of it since I felt certain it would never hold candles.

"Oh, I'm not counting on anything," I said. "Believe me."

"Good," said Giselle.

Despite her lack of further comment, I winced. I hadn't forgotten that she had told me not to go to the forbidden hut back in the village. Or that I had frozen when the snow leopard attacked. For every time I had saved her, there was another occasion where I had let her down. Neither of us could afford for this time to be anything but a success.

No matter how many rooms we explored, we found no other people. In fact, we found nothing at all that wasn't made of ice. Nothing that made the palace look lived in at all.

Although the layout was different, it reminded me a little of what the Eldonian palace could have been like without the warm touches of velvet and wood. Back before the hand of the servant-turned-queen, Estelle, transformed it. No wonder she had decided to take on a decoration project.

When we found the first room that contained something

other than ice, my thoughts were once more directed back to the true palace. The display room reminded me forcibly of the Eldonian one, although this one held fewer jewels and more domed pedestals. The domes were made of the thinnest of ice, instead of glass, of course. But there was no mistaking the similarity.

My eyes skimmed over them all, noting how many were empty. Waiting for future treasures? Or the home of objects currently in use? I peered at one that held two combs, simple in design but elegantly carved. The stand was clearly made to hold three, and I wondered if they were useless without the third or whether each of the combs held a different enchantment.

Glancing back at Giselle, I jolted and called a wordless warning. She started and looked at me guiltily, pulling back her hand just before touching one of the domes.

"Who knows what powers these hold?" she said. "One of them might help us defeat this Snow Queen."

"Yes, it might," I said. "But it might just as likely kill us. And how are we to know the difference? They've all been tainted by her, remember. However good their purpose may have been originally."

Giselle paled even further than her already chilly coloring, and we both hurried from the room. Not long afterward, we stumbled across a second room that held something more than ice. And once again the room seemed to mirror something from the true palace. This time something that was common to most palaces. A portrait gallery.

"Well," said Giselle, after we strode silently down its length. "This is different."

"It's..." I didn't know quite how to finish the sentence. I'd never seen anything like it.

"Self-obsessed, would you say?" Giselle suggested.

I nodded wordlessly. Where a normal royal portrait gallery held the painted likenesses of generations of royals, this gallery portrayed only one person. Painting after painting of a single woman in various poses.

Her hair at first glance appeared white but, as I examined one painting more closely, I realized it was white blond, as leached of color as the rest of her. Even the blue pigment of her eyes was so pale that I could see the red of her blood vessels shining through. Everything about her face made me shiver, an unnatural quality to it that I suspected had more to do with the model than any lack of skill in the artist.

"Celine!" Giselle's sharp cry drew my attention away from what could only be yet another image of the Snow Queen herself.

Giselle had wandered away, reaching the end of the gallery ahead of me, and was fixedly regarding something there. I hurried to catch up, eager to see what had caught her attention.

"This one isn't the Snow Queen," she said as I reached her.

I came to a sudden stop, my mouth falling open. "No," I finally said slowly, "it most certainly is not."

It was, however, a recognizable portrait. Here at the end of the gallery, a single painting depicted someone other than the Snow Queen. A large image of the long-dead Queen Estelle. The image was well done, there could be no doubt of her identity. But, at the same time, she looked different. Determined still, but nothing of the sweetness showed. If anything, her face held a hint of calculation that didn't quite sit naturally.

"But why..." My question trailed off as Giselle pointed at something beside the portrait.

Like the painting of the queen back in the capital, this one hung beside a domed pedestal. Only this one wasn't empty. It held shimmering folds of material that I thought might be a cloak. An old-fashioned design that I had seen in old portraits.

"What does it mean?" I asked, after looking back and forth between the pedestal and the painting several times.

"I have no idea," said Giselle. "But I get the sense there's a story here. And that one of those objects back there might extend life. Because this feels personal. I think this Snow Queen woman knew my great-grandmother."

Our pace increased after that, both of us even more on edge than we had been before. The continued emptiness of the palace was more than eerie, and I could only hope that Valley View had an unusually law-abiding populace and not that the Snow Queen made a habit of disposing of lawbreakers on arrival.

I reminded myself that Oliver was a crown prince. And that the Snow Queen's servant had expertly manipulated him here. She must have some purpose for him beyond death. If assassination had been her aim, Sterling could have achieved it on our journey up the mountain easily enough.

Finally, on the second level, we found a bedchamber that actually contained a bed covered in blankets and furs. A pack sat in a corner and several items of male clothing lay draped across a chair. Although none of it looked familiar, Giselle and I still looked at each with excited eyes. We were not alone here.

Unfortunately, we found no further such evidence. An enormous suite looked as if it must be meant for the queen herself but, if so, she apparently had no need for real blankets. And I couldn't quite determine if the gowns that hung in the wardrobes were made of material or ice.

The Snow Queen might once have been human, but surely she could not count as one anymore. Not if this was her bedchamber.

Soon after that we found a small staircase that led straight down. A servant stair, no doubt. Giselle's energy seemed to rise as we descended lower.

"If there is anyone here, it makes sense they would be down in the servants' quarters. We should have started by going down instead of up."

I didn't entirely share her enthusiasm, but I did feel a faint stirring of hope. Surely anyone forced to work for years in such a strange and unnatural place would be glad to see us and eager to help us defeat the Snow Queen.

A glow of warmth around my hands attracted my attention, and I quickly clamped my fingers into fists. When had I begun to flame?

I watched a single drop of water run down the wall and shuddered. I had every intention of burning this place to the ground before I left, but not while we were down in the lower levels. My eyes tracked back up the staircase. How many tons of water stood frozen above us? Exploring this place had not been wasted effort. I needed to assure myself no one remained inside before I could bring it down.

My fists clenched tighter. No one but the Snow Queen, that is. If she was made of ice instead of flesh, she could melt along with her palace. Anyone who would willingly freeze an entire kingdom of people needed to be stopped.

The servants' quarters we found looked no more lived in than the guest suites upstairs. And a long empty room that looked like it might be meant as a laundry held nothing at all. The last bit of hope for this level had dwindled to almost nothing when a sound hit my ears. I looked up.

"Was that...?"

"I don't know," said Giselle. "But I definitely heard something."

Together we broke into a run, heading up the corridor in the opposite direction to our previous progress, following a quiet rhythmic sound that continued to echo through the silence. We pushed through a wide door, shoulder to shoulder, and stumbled into another large room.

The emptiness of this place had gotten under my skin more than I realized because the need for caution hadn't even entered my head. Giselle seemed equally affected, actually grinning at the sight of a man calmly chopping potatoes. Until he raised his head, and we got a look at his face.

I stepped immediately away from Giselle, fire balls springing to life above my now outstretched hands.

"Very impressive, Princess Celine," said Sterling, his voice calm and slow. "No less so than the first time I saw them. I was hoping we wouldn't see you here, but I rather suspected we might."

His otherwise emotionless voice seemed to carry the faintest undercurrent of mockery. I narrowed my eyes.

"You shouldn't have doubted me."

He gave a small bow, his hands not leaving the vegetables. "My sincere apologies. I shan't do so again."

"No," I said. "I won't be giving you the opportunity." My fire balls bounced slightly, as if eager to be set loose, and yet I couldn't quite bring myself to throw them at a man calmly chopping potatoes. However much of a lying traitor he had turned out to be.

"Where's Oliver?" Giselle demanded from a half step behind me.

"With Her Majesty, I suppose," said Sterling, looking back at his task.

"You suppose?" I slammed both my fists down onto the table, my fire extinguishing as I balled my hands. But enough warmth remained behind that the table steamed around my skin.

Sterling's eyes returned to mine. "I believe she means to keep him with her always."

Something about the way his eyes tightened ever so slightly and his mouth quirked gave me the impression that he knew I felt more for Oliver than friendship and enjoyed the pain his words might cause.

I kept my expression tight, refusing to let him see the pang that his statement sent through me.

"We'll see about that."

"Yes, I suppose we shall." The methodical chopping sound

resumed. When both Giselle and I remained frozen in place, he looked back up.

"You're too late, you know. You can't win here. Not even with all your..." He waved the tip of his knife toward the steaming table.

"You know nothing of my power," I hissed.

"No, I don't suppose I do," he said thoughtfully. "But I have some experience with Her Majesty's power. And she has already gripped your precious princeling in more ways than one. I don't think you'll find he even wants to leave."

I swallowed, struggling to keep my face neutral. Surely he could not have been re-infected already? But then we were now in the heart of her powers. Who knew what she could do?

Drawing a breath, I forced a shrug. "Then we'll just have to convince him."

Sterling also shrugged and resumed chopping, but his eyes strayed back up to me, a gleam of curiosity and something else in them.

"Is it an object that you wield, princess from beyond our lands? Because it seems the godmothers have gifted you, indeed."

I narrowed my eyes, watching him closely. His eyes roved over me, as if searching for a significant piece of jewelry or other object likely to hold such power. And I recognized the second emotion in his eyes. Avarice.

Sterling wanted my gift. Badly.

"No..." I said slowly, seeing no reason to lie. "I carry no object. The gift is in me."

"Ah. Pity." He turned away, but not before I saw the disappointment in his face.

Where was it I had seen Sterling before Eldon? Marin, he had said. Another distant memory surfaced. Of Palinar, before the wedding. Princes Jonathan and Dominic had asked me to keep an eye out for a man who had escaped during their final battle to free Palinar from the usurpers who had attempted to claim it. A man they believed had taken an enchanted object and fled into Eldon before the fighting began. A man who had already helped someone escape from a prison in Marin. Sudden understanding washed over me.

"Back in Valley View, they said you have long served the Snow Queen," I said. "And yet I saw you in Marin. You serve her by seeking out enchanted objects, do you not? To grow her collection."

He stilled for a moment. "Impressive. Your understanding is quicker than I expected." When he looked up to meet my eyes, there was no shame or regret in his own. "Certainly that is my role. Her Majesty can no longer leave her snowy realm to search them out herself."

Was that love in his eyes? Did he love this Snow Queen? But, no, that wasn't quite it. Obsession then, perhaps? With her, or with the power she wielded?

"How can you?" I asked, the words bursting from me. "How can you serve such a person?"

He looked up at me, something like scorn in his expression. "Her Majesty wields power such as you can't even imagine. She provides resources I could never hope to match on my own. And she is generous with the power she does not need." His words cut off suddenly as if he'd said more than he intended.

I eyed him with narrowed eyes. So he got to keep some of the objects, did he? I thought of the empty pedestals in the display hall. What had he done with them?

After a moment of silent chopping, he continued, as if unable to help himself. "But soon that will all change. Soon she will wed the princeling and descend from her mountain fastness to take her true throne. Soon all of Eldon will be hers. And then she will have even more power to bestow upon her truest servants."

My heart seized at his words, although I had already suspected it.

"Oliver would never marry this queen of yours," said Giselle, disgust heavy in her tone.

"Won't he, lass?" Sterling gave the ghost of a laugh. "I don't think you'll find he has any interest in gainsaying her. And once he is king—which will be soon enough, I imagine, given the state in which we left the capital—there will be no force to prevent the spread of her authority."

I struggled to breathe, leaning heavily on the table as I fought to shrug off the weight of his words. That would never come to pass. Never.

"I thought you said she couldn't leave this mountain," said Giselle. I had expected her to be horrified at his casual reference to her parents' death, but she sounded merely angry.

"No," he said, drawing out the word, as if he enjoyed the conversation. From the look of this place, he didn't get many. "I said she couldn't leave her snowy realm. But you saw how her power spreads already. Soon all of Eldon will meet that criteria."

My mouth actually dropped open as the full extent of her plan crashed over me. I had suspected she wanted Oliver and his throne. But I had thought the winter and the frozen people a means to that end, not an end in itself. I looked around the large, mostly empty kitchen. I needed no more evidence that this was a queen who would happily rule a kingdom almost devoid of people.

"She can't really mean to kill everyone and turn Eldon into an icy wasteland," I managed to choke out.

Sterling looked at me, almost quizzically. "Why ever not?"

"But...all the people," said Giselle, coming to lean on the table beside me as though her legs had grown weak. "She can't!"

"I think," said Sterling, "you'll find she can. And I suspect a few of the strongest will survive. She might even lift their enchantment enough to let them serve her." He stopped to ponder his words. "Yes, she might well do that."

I wanted to burn the kitchen down around him at his words,

but curiosity restrained me. He seemed to be enjoying speaking freely as his true self rather than the front he had shown us previously. And I had questions I wanted answered.

"The cave in," I said. "That wasn't you, was it?"

I had expected him to look confused, but instead he looked contemptuous.

"Of course it was me. Her Majesty wouldn't have entrusted the task to anyone else, I assure you."

"But she needs Oliver," said Giselle. "You just said that. Why would you try to kill him?"

"Kill him?" Sterling's knife continued to descend in methodical rhythm. "Of course I didn't intend to kill him. I would have ensured the rock landed on his head if that had been my aim. I merely wanted to trap him for a while. To weaken him enough to allow—" He cut himself off abruptly, eyeing us briefly. "Suffice to say I had a means of getting him up the mountain, but it required him to be a little less energetic. And since the queen's enchantment wore off unexpectedly, I had to improvise another way."

He looked at me. "I suppose you were responsible for that. I don't suppose you'd tell me how?"

He paused, but I said nothing, and he sighed. "No, I didn't think so. After your unexpected escape from the tunnels, I'll admit I became a little cautious. I don't like having elements at play that I don't understand." He eyed me again, and I glared at him.

After a moment, he continued. "But it eventually became clear that I had no need to force Oliver up the mountain. His desperation had grown to the point that I needed only to spin the truth a little, to give him an appealing enough story that he would follow me of his own volition. I didn't even have to make most of it up."

I closed my eyes briefly. The most convincing lies always held some measure of truth.

"You told us a story about an orphan girl turned princess." After seeing the bizarre portrait gallery, I couldn't help myself asking him about it. "Was that part true? Did you speak of Queen Estelle?"

He looked between us. "You've been in the portrait gallery, then?" He shook his head. "I suppose even the most powerful of us have our weaknesses." The thought seemed to give him pause, and he fell silent.

"What is the connection between them?" I prodded him. "And what was the object beside her portrait?"

For a moment I thought he wouldn't answer, but then he shrugged. A shadow filled his eyes, and he seemed distracted still by whatever earlier thought had made him pause.

"As you guessed, the deserving orphan girl from my story was Estelle. And she was real enough. She was also the servant in a noble household. A household with a daughter her own age."

I could already see where this was going, but I didn't interrupt.

"The servant girl was much beloved by all who knew her. Except for the noble girl who was jealous of her despite their stations."

"Let me guess, the noble girl is the Snow Queen," said Giselle, with a disbelieving look. "And I suppose she told you all about her jealousy."

Sterling gave us a wry smile. "I am not without intelligence, you know. I can read between the lines as well as the next man. And, as I said, we are none of us without our weaknesses."

"Was there really an enchantment on the royal family?" I asked.

He shook his head. "No, that part I made up. I needed to link the story to the village. To give a reason for them to possess an object that protected them from both snow and enchantment. Estelle was given a magical cloak by her godmother. One that would reveal her true self when she wore it. So she might attend a ball at the palace, and be seen for who she truly was."

He looked disgusted. "What a ridiculous use of such power. Truly, power is wasted on the godmothers."

"And yet Estelle's pedestal is empty," I said. "And the one here bears a cloak. I suppose the noble girl stole it?"

"It is all rather predictable, is it not?" he said. "She hated the idea that her own servant might be judged more worthy of being a princess than her. But she was a different person then. It would be many years before she became a queen worth serving. But even now, when Estelle is long dead, she cannot let go of her completely. She keeps the portrait and the cloak, a constant reminder. But perhaps when she rules over Estelle's kingdom—when it has become an icy wasteland that serves only her—perhaps then she will at last be able to put it all aside."

I wanted to be sick at the calm way he said the words, at how coldly he viewed the horrifying story about his chosen ruler.

"The servant girl became a princess anyway," I said, trying to understand how the noble girl had ever become the Snow Queen. "So Estelle didn't need the cloak in the end."

"No." Sterling looked thoughtful. "I suppose that only enraged her noble mistress further. And when she tried to use the garment herself, it didn't work how she had imagined. Even her only family turned away at the sight of her true self."

He said the words with no more emotion than he had said anything else, but in spite of myself I felt the force of them in my gut. Didn't we all fear that somewhere deep inside? That if people saw our true selves, they would turn away in disgust? However dark her heart had been as a girl, could I wonder that it had only become more twisted?

Giselle must have seen the reluctant pity on my face because her next words seemed directed as much at me as Sterling. "A sad tale, certainly. But whatever she suffered then, she isn't that person anymore. I would say she's long since forfeited her humanity with the choices she's made and the magic she's used.

She might have twisted godmother objects, but she seems to have twisted herself even more."

Sterling actually laughed at that. "It's an apt parallel. Only the objects have kept her alive so long, and it's hard to know where they end and she begins. I have long pondered on it. She searched many years for an object that would remove her crippling emotions. Strip her of the grief and anger and make her strong. She told me long ago that she eventually found a locket. The second of her many magical acquisitions after the cloak. The locket was enchanted to guard the wearer's heart. That seems to have been the start of the ice theme."

He glanced down at the frozen bench beneath his knife. "I suppose when what you wish to guard against is actually your heart itself—when you direct such an object against itself in such a way—it is bound to have unexpected results." He looked up at us. "But you won't see that object on display anywhere. Even I have not seen it. She keeps it close to her always, I believe."

Something about the calm way he spoke such monstrous things about his own mistress ignited my fire again without conscious thought. It sizzled against the ice table, and I sent it shooting along the surface to consume his potatoes.

He jumped back with a yelped exclamation, and I cut off the flames, standing tall again.

"You can stay here if you want," I said, turning to leave the room. At the door I paused, looking back. "But I intend to melt this place to the ground, so you might want to consider leaving before that happens."

I didn't wait to hear his response before stalking out of the room.

$\mathcal{I}$ was done skulking below stairs. As usual for a palace, a set of servants' stairs stood just outside the kitchen door, and I stormed up them. I could hear the patter of Giselle's feet behind me, but I didn't stop to look back or speak to her.

The staircase led us up to a small antechamber. We had yet to explore the state rooms on the main floor, but I easily recognized the purpose of this space. Maybe because I had stood in the equivalent stone room in many other palaces.

I pointed across at a door on the other side, larger and more ornately carved than the one we had just entered through.

"I think that's the throne room. Or a banqueting hall, at least."

Giselle worried at her lip beside me. "Do you think she's in there? Do you think *he's* in there?"

I snorted contemptuously. "She sounds like the type to sit around on her throne all day, don't you think?"

I strode forward and put my hand on the door, but a soft protest from Giselle made me pause. I looked back at her.

"Do you think…Are you sure that's a good idea?" she asked.

I paused, forcing myself to truly consider her words. Now was not the time to let reckless emotion drive me. If the Snow

Queen was holding solitary court inside, with the man I loved chained to her side, did I really want to go bursting through these doors? I tried to think of other options, craftier ones, but nothing came to me. I could feel down to my bones that there was no escaping a confrontation with this woman—or whatever she was.

"No," I said at last, in answer to Giselle's question. "But I don't have any other ideas. And I'm sick to death of all this snow and ice. It's time to end this."

With the final word, I thrust my full weight against the door and walked through into the throne room of the Snow Queen.

The vast hall looked much as I had imagined, lined with tall windows down both sides, a high, vaulted ceiling far overhead. On the far end a large dais held an imposing throne carved in whorls of ice. The traditional second throne was missing, leaving no doubt there was only one ruler in this frozen kingdom. Instead a tall figure stood beside whoever sat on the throne.

I stood too far away to make out either of their faces, but I could well imagine who they both were. I strode forward without checking to see if Giselle followed me. If she wanted to keep out of this fight, I wouldn't blame her. Not after the iceflakes that had guarded the outside of the palace. Who knew what horrors guarded the queen herself?

But nothing came forward to challenge me as I made my steady way across the empty floor. Even with my focus on the figures ahead of me, I noticed something different about this floor. It wasn't completely smooth like those in the rest of the palace, and the light reflected differently from the ice.

A hissing voice behind me told me Giselle had followed, and that she'd noticed me glancing at the floor.

"It looks like the surface of a frozen lake."

I stilled briefly in surprise before striding on. Why should it surprise me at this point that the Snow Queen would build her palace on a frozen lake? She clearly had no fears this place was going to melt.

But she should be afraid, a voice inside me murmured, accompanied by a comforting swell of warmth in my middle.

As I got close enough to see their faces, my eyes were drawn irresistibly to Oliver. He watched me approach, but his eyes didn't connect with mine. This wasn't the Oliver I knew, the one I had come to love. This was the Oliver I had first met in Eldon. A vise gripped my heart and squeezed, nearly causing me to stumble.

Yet again, I lost control of my fire which sprang unbidden to my hands.

"Ah," said a voice like the clanging of bells. "The little fire girl. How fascinating."

My eyes snapped to her face, and for the first time I saw the woman who had been slowly destroying this kingdom. The kingdom Oliver loved so much.

A crown, several times taller than any I had ever seen, perched atop her head, the steep points rising up in shards of ice. Her strange coloring looked just as it had in her portraits, and she made even the frozen version of Oliver beside her look flushed and alive.

Her cheekbones cut as sharply as her pointed crown, her features beautiful, I supposed, if not for the red in her eyes and the absence of color. But nothing about her looked natural, and the sight of her made me want to shiver, not admire.

But the prince at her side showed no such revulsion. He showed no emotion at all as he watched me and his sister draw closer and closer. I longed to run forward and send my power racing through him, as I had done so long ago at the palace. But when I went to take another step, the queen waved a lazy hand, and a waist-high wall of ice sprung up before us. I only just stopped myself from crashing into it.

"I think that is far enough," she said. "I am not so fond of fire, you see." The bells of her voice sounded musical, but also grating.

A clanging that reverberated in my head and set my teeth on edge.

"I can well imagine, Your Majesty," I spat the last two words at her. "I'm not so fond of ice, myself." My hands—still burning—reached out to melt the ice that blocked my way. But before I could do more than release a few puffs of steam, my attention was drawn sideways to Giselle.

Something on the far side of the room had captured her attention. She strode down the long wall of ice, making no effort to bypass it, and after a quick glance at Oliver, I dashed after her.

"What are you doing?" I hissed, glancing back at the throne again. The Snow Queen remained seated, watching us with a small smile on her face.

When we finally reached the side wall, I frowned. Apparently it hadn't been coincidence that had led her to sprout the wall where she had. Not when the only decoration we had seen in the entire palace outside of the portrait gallery hung on the wall in a direct line with it.

"Look," said Giselle, her expression fascinated. "I recognize it."

I sighed and actually looked at the object in front of me. The elaborate gilt frame held nothing, its large oval interior bare, revealing the ice wall behind. I couldn't imagine the purpose of such a thing. There could be no need to highlight that this building was made of ice. The palace itself did a more than adequate job of that.

But when Giselle reached a hand forward, as if to trace the distinctive markings of the frame, I pulled her back, noticing it wasn't completely empty after all.

"Careful," I said. "That looks like it could cut." I glanced back at the throne again, my mistrust growing at the smug look on the queen's face.

Now that I had seen the tiny shards around the inside edge of the frame, I realized what this was. Or at least had once been. A mirror. And now that I knew it was a mirror, I realized the frame did look vaguely familiar.

"It's our mirror," said Giselle, shock and anger in her voice. At least she didn't try to touch it again.

"But it's broken." I struggled to think clearly. My desire to get to Oliver overwhelmed my mind. I needed to free him. Every time his blank eyes fell on me, it cut like a fresh wound. I had never imagined he would look at me that way again.

"The royal mirror of Eldon. Our royal mirror. The one we've been searching for. It might be broken, but this is it." Her voice turned sad. "Or it was. I suppose I'll never get the chance to see it now." She spun around to face me only to push straight past, stalking back toward our original position. "I may have only seen it in that portrait back home, but I'd recognize it anywhere."

I hurried to follow her, struggling to grasp the fact that the mirror we had pinned so much hope on had already been destroyed. Not that we needed it to tell us the source of the curse now.

"I see you are observant, little princess," said the queen when we faced her once again. "How do you like my mirror?"

"It's not your mirror, it's ours." Giselle almost spat the words. "And you've broken it."

"Yes." The queen sighed, her eyes straying back to the frame. "I was most disappointed at the time, but it has turned out far better than I could have hoped." She reached out a languid arm and patted the prince beside her.

I actually growled, wanting to leap over the ice and rip her arm off. She smiled at me as if she could read my thoughts, and I forced myself to calm down. She had wanted us to see that mirror. And I wanted to know why. Was it purely to taunt Giselle with what she had stolen from her family?

"What did you do?" demanded Giselle. I had never seen the younger girl look so regal.

"I tried to use a second magic item to enhance its power. To infuse something of myself into it."

"The mirror can only be used by the royal family of Eldon," snapped Giselle.

To my surprise, the queen nodded in agreement. "So it seems." Her gaze strayed again to the empty frame. "It did not take kindly to my attempts." But then she laughed, and I had to stop myself pressing my hands to my ears as the sound echoed painfully in my head.

"But it seems that something of me transferred into it after all. And then I discovered the power in the shattered pieces—no more than specks of dust in some cases." She smiled again. "Such clever little shards, as it turned out. Able to worm their way into a person's heart and make it as frozen as my beautiful mountain. Such powerful magic in those royal mirrors!"

Giselle swayed beside me, looking sick. I gripped her arm to steady her and glared at the queen.

"If you're trying to say this all happened by accident and wasn't part of your plan, I don't believe you."

"Not *originally* part of my plan," she said. "Once I understood the power of the shards, naturally I knew my time had at last come to act. For years beyond counting I have waited, amassing the right tools, ready to spread my snow and ice down the mountains." Her terrifying eyes seemed to glow. "And I knew my moment had come. I began to send down my winds, each of them carrying such precious, invisible cargo. Sent first to the capital and then out into the rest of the kingdom. Only the farthest southern regions have yet to feel my wind blow."

I shivered. How far would her winds extend once she reached the capital? Eliam was right to fear the encroaching cold.

"The magic is slow to work," she continued. "But that gave me time to study it. To perfect it. I have learned how best to use the power."

This time her gaze flicked not to the mirror, but to Oliver. So that was how she had managed to freeze his heart again so quickly. I understood Sterling's words now.

The thought of the traitor made me want to spit. He was far more dangerous than I had supposed. He might even be the only servant who served her with a free heart and mind.

"Why are you telling us this?" asked Giselle. "Is it just that you've missed having a chance to gloat?"

The queen laughed again, sounding genuinely amused. "Of course not. I have no need to gloat. I merely hoped to rid myself of the tiresome necessity of a battle. I hoped you would see how impossible it is to resist me. I hold an entire kingdom in thrall, after all."

"Enough!" I said, sending a stream of fire into the partial wall of ice in front of me. "I will free Oliver's heart as I have done before, and then we will leave. And once we're gone, I will melt your precious palace, and your throne, and all of your enchantments with them."

I strode forward through the newly created gap, steam rising around me. I expected to have to burn through much more than one thin half-wall, but the queen made no move to prevent me approaching Oliver. I watched her out of the side of my eyes, not trusting in her seeming acquiescence. But even when I placed my hands flat against his chest, she made no move to intervene.

As soon as I felt his broad chest, still warm with life beneath my hands, thoughts of the queen fell away. The fire from my anger was nothing compared to the inferno that raged inside me now. Freeing him would be easy. I pushed warmth down through my arms and out my hands, keeping it just short of bursting into actual flame.

"Oliver! Wake up!" I repeated the words I had used once before.

I expected him to glow, as he had then and Giselle after him, but the warmth instead seemed to leach out of me and disappear into him without making him any hotter. I tried again, with more force, but when nothing happened beyond singeing his outer shirt, I stumbled backward.

"I don't understand," I said, my eyes on his. He had not reacted to my presence in any way, and I was finding it hard to breathe.

It was the queen who answered. "The prince is not infected with a single speck of dust blown into his heart on the wind, little girl. He has a shard placed there by my own hand. He will not be so easily freed."

I shook my head, refusing to believe it. Oliver wouldn't give himself up so easily. He would fight.

"Oliver," I said, keeping my voice low, and pretending the queen wasn't there. "Oliver, please. It's me. It's Celine. You can fight this. You must try!"

"I can see it's you, Celine," he said, the sound of his voice shocking after his previous silence. "I haven't lost my mind, you know."

The voice was his, certainly, but his tone was cutting and cold. I had never heard him speak like that, not even in Marin when we had first met. I stumbled back another step while he surveyed me coldly from head to foot. I had never been so conscious of being in such physical disarray before. I was very far from the perfectly dressed princess who could shock a room into silence.

"Although, now that I see you again," he said, "I can't work out what it was I saw in you before." He shook his head in disbelief. "I seem to remember I even thought you beautiful."

I sucked in a breath, unable to believe the words I was hearing.

"Can't you see she's enchanted you, Ollie?" cried Giselle, following me through the gap in the ice, but staying off the dais. "Please, you have to fight her."

He turned his cold eyes on his sister. "Oh, be quiet, Giselle. You're always following along where you're not wanted, pushing in no matter how much we try to keep you away. When will you learn that you only make things difficult for those of us who actually have important things to do?"

Giselle gasped, her mouth falling open as tears welled in her eyes. I backed down the stairs of the dais so I could put an arm around her shoulders. I directed my glare where I knew it belonged—at the Snow Queen. These words didn't come from Oliver. He loved both his sisters—but his younger sister, especially.

"Don't listen, Giselle," I whispered. "Don't listen to her poison."

The younger princess wiped an angry arm across her eyes and straightened. I squeezed her shoulder before pulling away to stride forward again. It was time to try something more drastic.

Remembering the way he had surprised me in the cave, I barreled forward to grip his face, pulling it forcefully down to mine.

CHAPTER 29

A spark seemed to leap from me at our touch, but his lips remained cold and unresponsive.

Pulling back, he pushed me away, and I once again stumbled backward away from him.

"Did you not understand me before? I do not want your kisses, Celine. I suppose it must have amused me to dally with you when there was no one else around, although now I can't imagine why. Whatever my reason previously, I'm no longer interested."

I screamed, rounding on the Snow Queen and throwing fire ball after fire ball at her head. She reacted instantly, throwing up an arm and pulling a shield of ice from the base of the dais. My fire balls burst against it, shattering the ice, but as each one made a dent, she waved again, bringing up a fresh layer of ice to strengthen it.

I circled around her, moving away from Oliver, as I looked for an opening in her protective layer. If I couldn't burn this ice from Oliver, I was going directly to the source. But as fast as I could throw my fire, she raised her shield to match.

Wheeling back around, I changed tactic. Dropping the fire, I let my anger and pain burn brighter and brighter inside me. When it reached a peak, I thrust my palms outward.

A gale force wind, the type that had blasted rocks from a blocked tunnel, shot out and smashed against the queen's protective wall of ice. With an angry shriek, the queen leaped on her throne and vaulted over the ice as it fell before my onslaught, crashing into the seat where she had sat a moment before.

With a feral grin, I directed my palms toward her, and the wind swept her up and pushed her body against the wall behind us.

"Prince!"

She managed to yell the word despite my wind stealing her breath.

Oliver nodded once and stepped between us. I snapped my hands down, cutting off the air before it could do more than sweep back his hair. The queen straightened slowly as Oliver eyed me with disgust.

"Always so impetuous, Celine, that's your problem. Always ready to rush into some ill-thought plan with no consideration of others. And why would you consider them? When you're so sure of yourself. So brash. You hurt others with everything you do. I can't imagine why your kingdom allowed such wild behavior in a princess. I would have expected them to beat some sense and manners into you long ago."

I had thought I knew this wasn't really him. Had thought myself armored against the Snow Queen's poison. But his words beat against me and wormed their way into my heart. I had told Giselle that the words were not his, but the Snow Queen did not know me like this. Her magic mirror was broken. She had not been watching me, living with me for weeks. It was Oliver himself who knew my faults. Who had seen my confidence spill over into dangerous, willful stupidity.

I swayed and fell to my knees. Tears blurred my vision. So this was how Oliver truly saw me, once my beauty had been stripped away by the magic. I tried to remember the words he had spoken among the trees of Valley View, to hold on to the moment we had shared, but I couldn't actually remember him saying anything. Other than that I was beautiful. And that I burned with fire. Both true, but neither the foundation for love.

Blinking, I saw vague movement, but only Giselle's scream gave me the warning to throw myself sideways. My vision cleared as gleaming icicles stabbed through the space where my body had recently been. As the queen stalked toward me, I twisted and sprang back to my feet.

I tried to call fire to my hands, but my insides had gone cold. I almost fell down the stairs as I backed off the dais. The queen continued to stalk toward me, only now she was smiling, her face twisted out of any semblance of beauty. Oliver remained behind, apparently uninterested in further intervention.

"It's not true, Celine," said Giselle, her sudden presence warm at my back. She gripped my elbow and dragged me backward away from the advancing queen. "Ollie doesn't mean any of that. It's like you said to me. It's just her poison speaking."

"But Giselle…" I choked on the words as I remembered the snow leopard, and Valley View, and every stupid thing I'd muttered unthinkingly under my breath. Only the night before, I had scared her with my thoughtless words.

She continued to pull me back, maneuvering us through the gap in the queen's ice wall.

"I love your confidence," she said. "And so does Oliver. The true Oliver, anyway. You saved us all from the blizzard, remember? We would be dead if not for you. And you nearly killed yourself doing it. You were unconscious, and Oliver was nearly beside himself. I've never seen him like that."

I tried to cling to her words, to regain some of that confidence she spoke of. The confidence that had always driven me into foolish scrapes.

"Even in my fog," she continued, still moving us backward,

"even when my heart was frozen, I saw something in you. Back in Marin. During the Princess Tourney. The piece of me that still survived recognized that you had the strength to save us. That's why I invited you to visit."

I regained my feet, moving away from her dragging grip. "But it was Emmeline who invited me."

"Because I asked her to." Giselle smiled up at me, but her eyes were afraid. "And now I need you to use that strength. It's time to save us, Celine."

As she said the words, she pushed me to one side and spun me around. The sudden movement pushed me out of the way of another burst of icicles and left me standing in the middle of the throne room, facing the queen.

The Snow Queen laughed mockingly, the sound bouncing through the room and echoing from the ceiling.

"Inspiring words, I'm sure. But if your Oliver once saw those things in you, he will never do so again. Because I have discovered that the mirror fragments work differently when placed in the eye rather than in the heart." Her smile grew even broader. "It is not only his heart that is frozen now. And a splinter in the eye means that the bearer will see the world as it truly is." Her smile dropped away. "Ugly. They will see only the ugly truth about everyone and everything they see."

I stared at her in horror. Giselle had been right. The Snow Queen had chosen to dwell in the darkest parts of herself for so long that she had lost the person she must once have been.

"Valley View," I gasped. I finally had the answer to what poison consumed that place.

The queen smiled again, as if she approved of my joining the pieces together. "My experiments there were so very fruitful. I couldn't have my servants losing the will to grow my food. But neither could I risk them being corrupted by outside forces—such as you—who might come up the mountain in search of the source of my new winter." She looked insufferably pleased with her foresight. "I'll wager they saw nothing of worth or value in any plea you made on behalf of the kingdom."

"Well, that explains that," muttered Giselle, now sheltering behind me. "Those poor people."

Without warning, I whipped both hands forward, sending two fire balls soaring toward the queen. She ducked, but one of them clipped her crown, knocking it from her head.

With a screech of fury, she stooped to grab it, but had to leap the other way as I threw my next attack at the crown itself. One of my fire balls landed with precise aim, exploding the ice of the crown. Giselle and I ducked, shielding ourselves from the flying shards while the queen screamed again.

She staggered back to her feet, thrusting her arms out to either side and pulling them slowly upward, as if dragging a great weight. Spears of ice shot from the floor in every direction.

Giselle screamed and almost knocked me over as she threw herself from the path of one that erupted just behind her. I stumbled before regaining my feet and dancing away from her.

"Get to the door," I shouted and watched her turn and run, weaving and stumbling as the spears continued to burst from the ice in a widening circle around the enraged queen.

Part of me wanted to flee after Giselle as fast as my legs would take me, but a bigger part pulled me in the opposite direction. I ran, sending my fire balls ahead of me to shatter any spears I couldn't avoid. More and more of them thrust up toward the ceiling, and a deep groaning sounded through the hall.

I stumbled before running on. Had that been...? A groan sounded again, and the next spear that burst upward was accompanied by a terrifying crack. I saw the ice split ahead of me and put on a fresh burst of speed.

Another crack webbed out and then another, and Giselle's earlier words seemed to echo in my ears. *A frozen lake. A frozen lake. A frozen lake.*

At last I reached the dais and the calmly disinterested prince.

Rushing up, I grabbed his arm and looked around for another exit. Any exit. But I could see none. So, with a groan of my own, I tugged him back toward the frozen lake, now covered in towering spears of ice and crisscrossed with threatening cracks.

Oliver allowed me to pull him along but made no effort to hurry. Apparently he could no more be bothered resisting me than he could in attempting to save himself in the first place. Surely he could see that this entire place was about to crumble?

"I never liked this room," he said, as calmly as if we were on an afternoon stroll through the forest.

Apparently he did know what was happening.

"Hurry up!" I snapped, losing my patience. "Or we're both going to die."

"Do you always have to be so dramatic, Celine?" he asked, deep weariness in his voice.

I staggered to a stop as a fresh groan sounded around us. Whirling, I grabbed at his jacket with angry hands.

"Yes! Yes, I'm always dramatic! And I'm overconfident. And I say what I think. But you love me, Oliver! You said you loved me!"

But even as I said the words, I remembered once again our conversation among the trees. The word love had echoed so loudly in my head then. But had he actually said it? He had kissed me, yes. But had he spoken of love?

I looked up at him, suddenly afraid as I had not been before. Had I once again leaped into something that I didn't truly understand? The mirror fragment had twisted him, yes, but had it truly changed his heart? Or was it never actually deeply engaged at all? Did I only see in him what I wanted to be there? A reflection of my own feelings.

"Please," I whispered, pouring every ounce of my heart into my words. "Please tell me you love me, Oliver. Because I love you. I love your strength, and your heart, and the fact that you burn just as brightly as I ever have."

This time I was soft and gentle as I stretched up onto my tiptoes, ignoring the chaos of ice around us, and pressed my lips gently to his. Instead of a spark, a deep heat poured out of me, carrying all of my love and longing with it.

When I pulled away and looked at him, tears shone in both his eyes as he stared down at my face. As I watched, they spilled over, running down his cheeks. And something bright in them—no more than a speck on either side—caught the light, winking and shining as it ran down his face and was gone.

He gasped, his gaze still locked on me.

"I see you again." His words sounded amazed. "You're so full of beauty it almost hurts to look at you." And something in his gaze told me he didn't mean my ripped clothes, disheveled hair, or terror-filled features.

But as a smile broke across my face, the loudest groan yet made me spin around, suddenly remembering where we were. We'd made it only halfway across the throne room, the door still far out of reach.

A scream of rage made me look back at the dais. While we ran, the Snow Queen, it seemed, had made her way back to where her heartless, uncaring prince was supposed to be waiting. Her eyes were fixed on us through the jungle of ice spears, and I could see she knew what had just happened.

For the second time she raised her hands, but this time she brought them both swinging back down. A resounding, splintering crack rolled over me, and then the ice at my feet shifted, and I fell, Oliver torn from my grasp as we were both hurled into the freezing water below.

CHAPTER 30

*P*ain. That's all I could feel at first. Pain everywhere, burning into every nerve. And not with the friendly burn of my fire. This was the burn of freezing ice.

But then the desperate pain in my lungs overwhelmed all the others, and I kicked upward toward a glimmer of light. My head burst into the open air, and I gasped a deep breath, kicking to keep myself afloat as a chunk of ice slammed into me, nearly robbing me of breath again.

I scrabbled at it with my hands but couldn't find a grip. Pain. Needles of pain everywhere, trying to drag me back down into the depths.

Fear filled my frozen mind, and with it came a rush of heat. Memory of my power returned, and I pushed the warmth down into every part of my body. The sweet relief stilled my limbs for a moment, sending me sinking back under again. Pushing hard, I re-emerged into the air, wisps of steam rising from my body.

Looking up, I could still see the ceiling above me, but everywhere else I looked, the throne room had become a churning lake full of chunks of ice, big and small. I could only hope Giselle had made it out before the ice cracked.

But Oliver...Oliver had been with me. I twisted in a full circle, looking for his head amid the ice. I could see no sign of him.

I took a deep breath and dived under the water, grateful that it was as clear as it was cold. Still, I had to twist and turn for agonizing seconds before I got a glimpse of him.

I dived down, arms outstretched, and managed to hook my hands under his arms. Straining with everything I had, I pushed toward the surface. We hardly seemed to move. Letting go with one hand, I gripped desperately with the other and pushed my empty palm downward. A jet of air shot out of it, propelling us upward so fast I nearly lost Oliver.

When I catapulted out of the water, I was only just clinging to one of his arms, dragging him behind me. As soon as his head hit the air, he coughed and spluttered, sucking in a breath and then another. But as soon as I let go, he sank straight back down again.

I swallowed a curse and dived after him again. The water must have frozen his limbs, preventing him from swimming. My questing hands found him quickly this time, dragging him up for another gasping breath from us both.

This time I held on, placing one hand against his bare neck and pushing as much warmth into him as I dared. He gave a shuddering sigh of relief, his eyes fluttering briefly closed. But I held on, still pumping warmth into him. Only when he also began to steam, did I let go, turning in the water to look for a way out.

"Do you see—" I turned back, but he had disappeared again without a sound.

"What—" I cut off my own words to dive back under the water yet again. Frustration drove me as I kicked down toward his sinking body. This time I used my wind again to propel us upward faster than I could swim. When we broke through into the air, I kept a tight grip on Oliver, looking around for a large enough piece of ice.

When I spotted one, I gave a final burst of air through the

water, pushing myself up and out completely so that I sprawled forward, landing hard on the ice. I gasped, scrambling to gain some balance and keep an arm gripped onto Oliver as well. I lay flat, clinging to the part of him that had been partially dragged behind me. My momentum and grip had been enough to pull the arm I held and the attached shoulder onto the ice.

Slowly, I inched forward until I could get a better grip and then slowly pulled back again, dragging him after me. Once his body had made it out, I collapsed, leaving his legs to dangle into the water. It was the best I could manage on the floating ice.

I sent another burst of warmth into his skin, maintaining the flow until steam rose all around us.

"What is it?" I asked when I pulled away. "Why can't you swim?"

He just shrugged. "It was so cold."

"But—" I stared at him, my frustration almost boiling over. He didn't meet my eyes.

Sudden understanding filled me, and my heart sank. His tears had cleared the shards from his eyes, had let him see good and beauty in the world again. But the Snow Queen had done a thorough job this time and had placed one in his heart as well. He had lost all initiative. He had no drive left, not even to save himself from drowning.

I crawled over, my body near exhaustion, and clung to him. Earlier I had made it through to him, even in his enchanted state. We were supposed to have won. This second blow felt like too much.

But I couldn't give in, couldn't let the Snow Queen win. Not now, not after everything we'd been through.

"You have to fight it, Oliver," I cried. "Like before. Remember who you really are. You can save yourself!"

He sighed and reached up to caress my face, but no spark of defiance filled his eyes, and he made no effort to move. I felt the cold again seeping up from the ice under us and from where his legs still dangled in the water. A fresh burst of my warmth drove it away, but it crept back again, faster this time.

My power wasn't enough. My words weren't enough. I had nothing left to try.

But my heart refused to give up. Even without my powers, even without my mind, my stubborn determination wouldn't let go.

"You have to wake up, Oliver," I said into his chest, still gripping at his jacket. "You have to. Because I'm not letting you go, and I'm not ready to die." Fear filled me as I felt us both slipping closer to death. How long could we survive floating in the Snow Queen's melting throne room?

But love burned more strongly in me than fear. I would not give up Oliver to her icy power. Not even to save myself. Tears dripped down my already sopping face, falling onto his chest with a fresh burst of steam.

But these weren't my normal tears. Scalding hot, they burned instantly through the material of his jacket, sinking down to the skin beneath. I lunged for the freezing water around us, scooping some up to splash wildly over the bare patch of his chest, afraid of the burns I would see there.

But the skin appeared smooth and unharmed. I didn't even realize I was still crying until I saw fresh drops sizzle down onto his skin. Impossibly they sank down toward his heart.

With a cry and a gasp, he jerked upward, flinging me from the ice and back into the water. For a moment I could see nothing but bubbles and steam as I thrashed to right myself and find the air again. I burst up, gasping, to see Oliver staring down at me in wonder.

"Celine!"

I didn't need to hear more than my name to know he was free. Truly free. The tears streamed faster down my face, but they had changed now into tears of joy.

"Celine." His tone had transformed, his eyes wide in wonder. "Look."

As my tears hit the surface of the lake, steam rose, almost obscuring our view of each other, although I bobbed just beside his block of ice. And it was spreading, racing out across the surface of the water.

He had pulled himself fully up onto the floating chunk, kneeling on all fours to peer toward me, and he reached into the water to feel it.

"Ouch!" He pulled his hand back quickly. "It's hot!"

The temperature didn't bother me, but something caught my eye.

"Look at the ice." All around me, I could see the chunks of ice melting in the now hot water, the smaller ones disappearing completely.

The ice Oliver crouched on was large and thick, but I thought I could see it thinning. Soon he would be dumped into the water, and from his earlier reaction...

"We need to get out of here. Now!" I said.

"But how?" he looked around, trying to get his bearings in the room that had become a lake. Pushing himself up a little higher, he pointed. "I can see the door. Over there."

A distant cry reached me above the steam, although I couldn't make out the words.

"It's Giselle," said Oliver. "She just saw me. She must have made it out before the lake cracked."

I remembered how I had propelled us onto the ice in the first place. "Hold on," I said, my voice determined. "We're going to her." I released my air beneath the water.

"But how—" Oliver flattened onto the ice as I landed partially on top of him, causing the block to lurch and rock beneath us.

"Oof! Sorry." I scrambled off, as the ice tipped dangerously. "You watch where we're going, I'll provide the power."

When I thrust both hands back under the water and blasted a

trail of bubbles that sent us careening across the surface, he laughed. We smashed into another large block and both nearly ended up back in the water.

"Whoa, steady there. Maybe a bit slower," he suggested, positioning himself as flat as he could while still allowing himself some visibility across the choppy lake. At least the obstacles were getting fewer as more and more of them melted away.

I had wondered if we might stop melting once we got away from the hot patch where I had fallen into the water, but it seemed to have spread, great billows of steam and vapor rising toward the distant ceiling on all sides.

I faced behind us, using all my control to slow the stream of air and keep us moving forward in a controlled way. Oliver called out directions, and I moved my hands left or right, maneuvering us around any remaining blocks liable to tip us over. And all the while our own block grew smaller, pushing us closer and closer together until Oliver was crouched half over me.

A sudden wild cackle broke my concentration, and we lurched dangerously. Looking up, I saw the Snow Queen, her white-blond hair whipping behind her and her dress billowing as she appeared to float across the surface of the lake.

As she got closer, I saw that she actually rode a block of ice, just as we did. Only she stood straight on hers, apparently having no problem with balance or controlling the movement of the chunk.

"Hold on," I screamed again, restarting my wind and loosing my control. We flew across the surface of the water, but still she seemed to be closing the distance.

She laughed again, sounding a little mad, and threw an icicle spear in our direction. I pushed us sharply to one side, avoiding it but nearly tipping us both into the water.

"Steady, Celine," said Oliver. "We're nearly there. A straight shot now."

We had approached close enough that I could hear Giselle

more clearly, screaming both our names. Our block had grown even smaller, and I dangled half in the water now, to give Oliver more room.

My eyes focused in on the block carrying the queen. Despite her control, it seemed she couldn't fight the heat of the water. It, too, was being eaten away, growing smaller and smaller. Already it was smaller than ours, although she needed less space to stand on.

My bubbles shot us forward, and I didn't dare break concentration to look over my shoulder and see how close we were to the door. The ice shrunk again, forcing Oliver to rise up fully onto his knees or dangle half in the heated water. With him upright, I had to slow our progress, and the queen approached even closer, her arms stretched out toward us, a feral grin pulling at her face.

She stood on only a thin circle of ice now, but it was enough to hold her up. Oliver grunted in pain as he slipped, one leg falling into the water. I put on one last spurt of speed, trying to outrun both our melting boat and the pursuing queen.

But our block of ice had become so thin and light that I misjudged it, and the power of the blast made us shake from side to side, both of us sliding off and into the steaming water.

CHAPTER 31

*O*liver's cry of pain sliced through me. I thrashed back to the surface, trying to find him and the edge of the lake among the steam and the splashing water.

Another cry, this one of relief, drew my eyes over to the door, which now stood on the edge of the lake, giving entry to the antechamber that still stood beyond it. Despite overturning us, my final push had gotten us close enough it seemed.

Giselle, the one who had cried out, knelt at the side of the water, reaching down to pull her gasping brother onto the solid ice beside her. I kicked out toward them, anxious to see how badly Oliver had been burned, but a sizzling splash of water pushed me to one side.

Turning, I saw the Snow Queen. Still balanced precariously on a thin film of ice, she threw another icicle at me. This one I dodged, throwing myself to one side, and it hit the water with an equally loud splash, quickly melting into nothing.

I dodged another one, managing to bring up one hand and send a fire ball back. This time it was the queen who had to dodge, half-crouching on her meager platform. The action

274

seemed to break her concentration enough that she slipped, one foot falling into the water.

Her scream pierced the room, shaking chandeliers of ice down from the ceiling. They crashed into the water, one landing so close that it swamped her remaining block before sending me tumbling beneath the surface.

Pushing back up into the air, I looked for her. I heard her before I saw her, her horrible screams shaking the walls. Her block of ice appeared to have melted completely, and she thrashed wildly in the water, almost fully submerged.

I glanced back at Giselle and Oliver. I absorbed that he seemed to be moving easily, his face clear of any serious pain, before my eyes were drawn back to the queen's desperate cries. The water steamed in the cold room, but it didn't boil. And despite the discomfort that prolonged immersion must have brought, Oliver seemed to have survived his dunking intact.

And yet the Snow Queen screamed as if we held her down in a pot of boiling water. As if she was...

"Melting!" cried Giselle. "She's melting!"

There was no other way to describe what I was seeing, though it seemed impossible. Like the chunks of ice had already done, the queen herself was slowly losing her shape, becoming smaller and smaller as the features that made her human disappeared, reducing her to a vaguely human shape. And at the center of that shape, in the place where her heart should have been, I saw a small metal object.

Even as my mind registered that it was a simple locket, the remaining part of her chest melted away, and it slipped beneath the water. Her face remained for another breath, held above the water and contorted into an expression of anger and pain and madness. And then even her head had sunk beneath the water and disappeared.

I gasped and swallowed and swallowed again. Had the locket *replaced* her heart? No wonder Sterling had never seen it.

"Celine!" Oliver's voice pulled me from the horror that had overwhelmed me at the terrible sight. "We need to get out of here."

I kicked out toward them, no ice left now to impede my path. When I reached the edge, they both held hands down to help, but instead I sent a burst of air through the water behind me, shooting up and into Oliver's arms.

He grunted and staggered backward, just managing to keep us both upright. He looked down into my face and moved as if to press his lips to mine, but Giselle's sharp voice made him pull back.

"There's no time for that!" she yelled. "I think we need to run. Oliver do you know the way?"

I pulled back from him and looked around. The heat in the water had reached the walls of the throne room, and they had begun to melt, water streaming down to join that already in the lake. Looking across at a distant wall, I saw the dim glint of the mirror frame as it slid free of the wall and fell into the water with a splash.

Perhaps it was coincidence, but at the exact moment it disappeared beneath the surface, a screeching crack resounded above all the other sounds of the disintegrating palace.

Giselle and Oliver were already backing away from the edge of the lake, pulling me with them.

"This way," Oliver yelled, and I stumbled after them, forcing my exhausted limbs to yet further effort.

We slipped and slid across the wet floor, barely avoiding chunks of ice that fell haphazardly from higher up the walls or from the ceiling. Thankfully it wasn't long before we burst into the empty entrance hall. The front doors beckoned across a large floor.

We all put on a fresh burst of speed, Oliver's long legs moving him ahead. He reached the doors and ripped them open, swinging them wide before turning back to search for us. Ahead of me, Giselle stumbled and fell, slipping as she tried to regain her feet.

I shook my head and grabbed her hand, running the last few steps with her sliding through the thin layer of water behind me. As I shot out past Oliver, he reached down and swung his sister back to her feet.

But when we all stopped to look down the long staircase leading up to the door, we realized we would all have to slide. Already the melting stairs had lost definition, one merging into another in a steep incline. Plonking down, I pushed off, the others close behind me.

"Wooooooo!" I screamed as I slid down the newly-created slide, the snow at the bottom rushing up to meet me. All of my pain and terror and horror and exhaustion expelled in one long wordless exclamation. Oliver yelled behind me, and then Giselle's higher voice a beat behind.

When we all tumbled into the deep, soft snow, I just lay there for a moment, too spent to even push myself to my feet.

"That last part was actually sort of fun," said Giselle, her voice breathy, and her eyes glassy.

I shook my head at her, too tired for any verbal response.

"What?" she asked. "We're all alive, aren't we?" And then she laughed, and it sounded slightly hysterical.

Oliver shook his head at her, but he was smiling. He pulled me up, and reluctantly I let him.

"I would feel more comfortable if we put a bit more distance between us and this melting palace," he said.

I wanted to protest, but he was right. I didn't want to stay near this place for a moment longer, either.

"Look!" Giselle held something up, her voice triumphant. "Look what I found."

I forced my eyes to focus and saw that she was holding our two sets of snowshoes. Quickly she began to lace hers on, and I tried to make my fingers and arms follow suit, but they didn't seem to be working properly.

Oliver knelt to attach them for me, letting me lean against his shoulder as he worked. I breathed a sigh of relief, all my energy focused on staying upright.

When he had finished, we took off, poor Oliver falling into the snow with every stride. How were we going to get back down the mountain when he didn't have snowshoes? But my brain was too tired to focus on anything other than moving forward.

Briefly I wondered if the flurry of killer iceflakes would reappear, but to my relief, nothing darkened the late afternoon sky. I didn't think I had the energy to protect us from anything else.

"We left our packs in a cave just over there," I heard Giselle say. "I think that should be far enough, don't you think? Because if we don't stop soon, I think the two of you are going to keel right over."

I didn't protest, relieved at the idea of a dry cave and food after a long day without any. But as I stumbled the last few steps, a surge of energy filled me at the unexpected sight of another person. Perhaps I did have something left after all.

For a horrible moment, I thought it was the Snow Queen herself, somehow re-formed. But then I blinked, and a different familiar figure appeared. Not the Snow Queen, but her loyal lieutenant.

"Sterling!" Oliver's shout made the other man falter and nearly trip.

He was emerging from our cave, and I suspected he had just been looking through our packs for anything of value. From the surprise on his face as he looked over his shoulder, he hadn't been expecting us to emerge alive from the rapidly disintegrating palace.

His expression as he took off running gave me the remaining strength to send out a blast of air. Catching him square in the back, it sent him sprawling face first into the snow.

I swayed from the effort, but held up my hands, ready to send another blast. Oliver and Giselle had both taken off running toward him, however, so I refrained. Giselle, faster because of her snowshoes, reached him first and promptly sat down on his back, pushing him further down into the snow.

He mumbled something in protest and stirred feebly, but he couldn't gain any traction against the soft snow. Only when Oliver arrived did she pop back up so that he could reach down and wrench the other man to his feet.

"Going somewhere?" Giselle asked sweetly, as Oliver pulled Sterling around to face us.

Sterling glared at them in silent anger, but when his gaze moved to me—standing a way off still, but with both arms extended, ready to fire—he slumped.

"No, I suppose not," he said.

Between my exhaustion and the discovery of Sterling, I hadn't mustered the energy to look back at the Ice Palace. But standing in the mouth of the cave at last, I saw the tallest of the spires droop, dripping and melting into oblivion, steam rising as water raced down its sides.

As I watched, the last remnants of the structure crumbled in, leaving in its place a great lake, bigger than the frozen one we had swum through. Its surface roiled and steamed, but it didn't seem to be expanding any further, solid ground and snow standing firm between us and what had once been the Snow Queen's home.

"It was beautiful, you know," said Giselle, who I hadn't heard come to stand beside me.

I gave her a disbelieving look, and she shrugged.

"Well, it was. But that doesn't mean I'm not glad to see it gone."

I sighed, my eyes drawn back to the lake. "I suppose it was beautiful. But I prefer your palace. The real one. That's made of stone."

Giselle smiled. "Me too."

Reluctantly I retreated back into the cave where a silent, bound Sterling sat beside a small fire. He had helpfully brought some wood with him, so I had only needed to provide the briefest burst of flame to get it started.

Swaying, I sank down to sit on the opposite side of the cave to him, admitting to myself I was more than glad we wouldn't be relying on me to keep us warm all night. Dim embers still burned somewhere inside me, but I felt too drained to whip them into any sort of serious heat.

Despite myself, I found my eyes straying to Sterling's still form. He had a full pack with him—which had turned out to contain some of our own things as I had suspected—and not only snowshoes but a second spare pair as well. Finding him had been fortuitous. But what had driven him from the Ice Palace so fully prepared? He couldn't have put all that together after it started melting, especially not when he had been ahead of us.

Had he taken my words in the kitchen seriously, after all? It was true that something about his manner had seemed to change during our conversation.

When I realized he was staring straight back at me, I shifted slightly, turning myself away. Oliver had already declared that we would take him down the mountain with us, to be secured in the palace where he could await judgment from the king. And that was good enough for me. I wanted nothing more to do with a man who had let his thirst for power lead him to assist in nearly destroying an entire kingdom. And, if he was the man Prince Dominic had asked me to watch out for, he might have had a hand in nearly destroying Palinar as well.

Giselle, who had entirely escaped the icy and then burning waters of the lake, had more energy than either me or Oliver, so she volunteered to prepare food. By the time she brought some to me, I could barely keep my eyes open to eat it. Only my complaining stomach kept me upright for long enough to get it down.

The light of sunset hadn't faded from the sky when I at last lay down, but a little light wasn't going to be enough to stand between me and blessed rest. My eyelids closed, and sleep claimed me.

~

When I awoke, it took me several moments to orient myself. Two figures slept around the still-smoldering fire, and the darkness of the cave suggested it was still night. But light flickered outside the mouth of the cave, and I thought I could hear faint movement.

In another moment I remembered everything of the day before and that we had Sterling with us. I sat up abruptly, focusing on the other sleepers. The small one was clearly Giselle, and the other...he stirred and moved in his sleep, and I realized it was Sterling, sleeping restlessly due to his bindings.

I got up, no longer feeling sleepy, and crept silently from the cave. Oliver sat just outside, his attention on the sky—the source of the flickering light.

He looked up quickly at my approach and smiled, but the expression held sadness as well as welcome.

"I've been here several nights, but I don't remember seeing these before. But then I wasn't really looking."

I sat down beside him, nestling against him when he reached out an arm to invite me close.

"You can't blame yourself for what the Snow Queen did to you. I'm just glad you can enjoy it now. And that it's still here. I just knew that something so beautiful couldn't be part of that woman's evil."

"I can't describe to you how bleak the world was once she

leached all the beauty from it," he said, and I noticed his eyes were on my face now and not the sky.

I flushed, hoping the reflected colors would disguise it. "I can't imagine a world without beauty."

"I wish I didn't remember any of it," he said, and there was anguish in his voice now. "But it's all there, just like last time. Dream-like, but not gone. And the horrible things I said to you keep running over and over in my mind."

He shifted slightly so he could look down at me more easily. "I'm so sorry, Celine. I wish there was something I could do to show you that none of it was true."

"There is," I said, a smile creeping up my face.

He regarded me with creased brow, uncertainty in his gaze, so I rolled my eyes, grasped his face and pulled it firmly down to mine. He started slightly, but then seemed to catch on, his own arms sliding around to pull me close and his mouth warm and responsive against mine.

Fire roared inside me, but after everything I had gone through—everything we had broken through together—this time it remained firmly under my control. Which was something of a relief, given the circumstances.

When he finally pulled away, I made a soft mew of disapproval, but he just laughed softly and guided my head down to rest against his chest.

"I don't deserve you, Celine," he said with a soft sigh.

I shook my head against him. "Don't be silly. Of course you do. I'm in love with you which means you must be quite exceptional. I'm not that easy to please, you know."

His body shook with silent laughter. "Why do I have the feeling you're going to keep me on my toes?"

"Because you're very wise. Like I was just saying."

His arms tightened around me. "But are you sure, Celine? Are you sure you could ever be happy here in Eldon?"

I paused to really consider his question. We were talking

about the rest of my life, so it wasn't the time for impulsive decisions.

It was true I still hated the cold. And there were many things about my home I would miss. The sun and the heat, for one. Along with the flowers everywhere and the long, sandy beaches. But when I tried to imagine going back there—returning to a life without Oliver—my mind turned away, unwilling to form the images.

And our earlier embrace had stoked the embers within me, revived by his presence and a good sleep. Would I ever truly be cold again?

I felt him go tense as he waited for my answer, the silence drawing out between us.

"I could be happy here," I said at last. "If I had your love." I twisted so I could look up at him. "Do you love me, Oliver? Truly?"

His arms tightened around me again, a ghost of pain flitting through his eyes. "I love you, Celine. I swear I do. I really didn't mean those things I said in that throne room."

I shook my head quickly. "I wasn't thinking of those." I hesitated. "Well, not exactly. I knew you were under the evil influence of that corrupted mirror. But it made me realize you'd never actually said the words to me. I assumed, after Valley View, but…"

His brow creased, his mind obviously racing back. "Didn't I say it? I felt as if I did. I was bursting with the effort of keeping it in, since I was convinced you would never want to stay in Eldon, even if it were free from the curse. But after you nearly killed yourself saving us from the blizzard…" He swallowed and shook his head. "Don't ever scare me like that again, Celine."

"I'll do my best," I said, grinning up at him. "But no promises."

He shook his head with a rueful chuckle.

I settled back against him, overwhelmed by what I saw in his eyes. A delightful warmth seemed to have reached into every part of me, and I couldn't tell if it came from my magic or from this man, or perhaps some combination of the two.

"Celine," he said into my ear, "just in case there's any doubt—you are brave, and bold, and clever, and true, and I have never enjoyed spending time with anyone as much as I do you. I can't imagine ever wanting anyone else to be my queen. I love you."

I stilled at his words, taking them in. Then I looked up at him cheekily through my lashes, creasing my brow in confusion.

"So…is that a proposal, Your Highness?"

"Celine," he growled my name, tightening his arms around me and shaking me slightly. "You know it is."

I grinned up at him. "Maybe I do," I conceded.

"And your answer…?" He sounded impatient, although I couldn't imagine how he could truly doubt it.

"Yes, of course," I said. "I mean, I'm the youngest of seven, I never thought I'd get a chance to be a queen."

"Celine!" He sounded half-amused, half-irate, but when I pressed my lips up against his, the colors of the sky reflecting against our faces, everything else melted away except for our love and this perfect moment.

CHAPTER 32

I thought our return journey with a prisoner in tow would be painfully slow, but the extra snowshoes for Oliver more than made up for it. Plus, I hadn't factored in just how different it was going mostly downhill.

We kept Sterling attached to two of us at all times by a handy length of rope we found in his pack. Oliver took his pack, as well, so that even if he somehow managed to make a run for it, he would find himself stranded on the mountain without supplies.

Several times he attempted to speak to me, reminding me that he had made no move to obstruct me back in the Ice Palace.

"Far from it," he said. "I even answered all your questions."

I merely narrowed my eyes and turned away. So that's why he had been so forthcoming. He had hoped to hedge his bets, to curry my favor in case I did manage to best the Snow Queen. She had never deserved his service, but his lack of loyalty still disgusted me.

Now that I had rested, my power had returned to full strength, and I took every opportunity to demonstrate that to him—another deterrent against any attempt at escape.

Giselle, who had taken her brother's and my betrothal without a blink, watched me at target practice during one of our breaks. She had chosen a distant tree as the target, and I was casually lobbing fire balls at different parts of it as she called them out.

"Base." Throw.

"Top branch." Throw.

"Trunk, halfway down." Throw.

She grinned at me. "I think you're getting better. And no wonder Oliver wants to marry you. No one will ever dare attack us again. Not when we're going to have a queen who can produce fire balls from thin air."

"Giselle!" A moment later a snowball hit her shoulder, thrown by her irate brother.

"That's not why I'm marrying her! If you go saying things like that around her family, they might decide to withhold their permission!"

"Why?" asked Giselle, all innocence. "It sounds like perfectly sound reasoning for an alliance to me."

He laughed reluctantly before muttering. "Far too sound. They might decide they want her to make an alliance with a more powerful kingdom than Eldon."

"Relax," I said, smiling at him. "My parents wouldn't dare say no to me."

Giselle laughed, the sound echoing through the small valley where we had stopped. "Now that sounds all too believable."

I didn't bother to wad the snow into a ball before dumping a handful down the back of her neck. She shrieked and pulled away.

"Now, don't you start, Giselle," warned Oliver. "I want us to make Valley View sooner rather than later."

"Start? Me? But she—" Giselle spluttered the words, still trying to scrape snow out of her hood.

"Yeah, Giselle." I stood and shouldered my pack. "No more wasting time. We need to get moving."

I grinned at her narrowed eyes and slid away before she could get any ideas about retaliation. "I'll break the trail for a while."

Oliver let me lead for a few minutes before he came to take my place, probably already sick of the slow pace I was setting. I stayed close behind him, near enough to talk as we shoed along.

"You know my family would never really refuse their consent, right?" I asked. "They would never try to push me into a different alliance."

He glanced over at me, and I saw enough of a shadow in his eyes to realize that some of his concern at least was real. I reminded myself that things were different here in these kingdoms.

"You don't need to worry," I repeated. "I know that these lands turned their back on the ancient laws, and on the High King and his godmothers a long time ago. That's how the darkness was able to grow so strong. But things are changing. Marin and Palinar have already been freed. And now Eldon. The godmothers themselves gifted me with the tools I needed to help you."

I paused, considering. "They must have seen something in you, even under all that ice."

He shot me a confused look. "In me?"

I nodded. "The High King decrees that a kingdom must be ruled by love. That's why his godmothers work so hard to find true love for princes and princesses." I threw him a significant look. "And that's why I know my family would never stand in the way of our betrothal. They respect the laws of the High King and would never obstruct a betrothal based on true love. But romantic love is not the only love, you know."

I gazed down the mountainside. "A ruler must also love his kingdom and his people. And you were ready to sacrifice yourself for yours. What could be truer than that?" I shook my head. "And you have shown nothing but understanding and forbearance with those who have wronged you and yours—first with Lord Treestone's abduction and now Valley View's treason. I know you're not going there now to look for vengeance. The godmothers must have known you would follow the ancient laws if given the chance. They must have seen that you would rule with love. And so they sent me."

He looked back at me, a warmth in his eyes that made my insides surge in response. "And how could I not serve someone who so clearly has my interests at heart? I could never doubt the godmothers when they sent me you."

I smiled and would have responded if a shout from Giselle hadn't interrupted. When I turned to look, she was pointing at a boulder that I realized looked all-too-familiar.

It felt almost surreal returning to Valley View, but we had all agreed we needed to stop by the village. And their hot baths and real beds were only a small part of that decision. If the Snow Queen's power was really broken, Valley View would be the first indication. And if it was...Well, the inhabitants needed to be warned that their long-standing protection might not be so intact anymore.

The hubbub our arrival caused far exceeded my expectations. It was hard to believe it was even the same place, although the buildings all looked the same. Clearly something, at least, had changed.

Each of the elders wanted to shake our hands, assuring us that they saw things much more clearly now, and had no wish to act against the true rulers of Eldon.

The regular villagers were rather more exuberant and less controlled. They fell on Sterling, carrying him off to be locked up for the night.

"We have a handy storage shed," one of them said with a rueful smile. "And we just finished fixing the door and lock."

I winced, but the man only laughed. Apparently life with a

mirror speck in your eyes was far from pleasant, and their loyalty to the Snow Queen had evaporated along with the enchantment itself. And it seemed to have transferred onto us, who they saw as their rescuers.

When we finally extracted ourselves and retreated to Sterling's house, Oliver and Giselle both looked almost giddy with excitement.

"It looks like all of the Snow Queen's enchantments melted with her palace," said Oliver, at the same moment as Giselle said, "I wasn't sure if the mirror shards would outlast the queen herself, but..."

"The mirror was destroyed as well," I said. "I saw the frame and remaining shards fall into the lake."

"Then that means..." Giselle didn't finish the sentence since Oliver swept her into an exuberant hug.

I looked at Sterling's bed—now available for one of us to use, two if Giselle and I were willing to squeeze together—and sighed. There would be no convincing them to stay an extra night in Valley View now. At least they were both still enthusiastic to revisit the baths, and this time the chattering girls who half-filled it when we arrived were full of compliments and enthusiastic questions.

The next morning, we once again faced the elders in the center of the village, but this time at their request, and with most of the village in attendance. They apologized for their earlier reception of us, explaining how thunder-struck they had been when they woke up several mornings previously to all wonder why they had turned us away.

"It's like a dream," said the elder who had previously condemned Oliver. "I can remember it, but not understand what could have led me to think such terrible thoughts."

We had explained briefly on our arrival, but we gave them the full story now. I could see from the concerned looks they threw each other, that the significance of the Snow Queen's destruction wasn't lost on them.

"I realize that you would be justified in bringing an army back up the mountain to punish us for our treason," said their spokesman once Oliver finished speaking. "But I plead your mercy. We have long traded supplies with the Snow Queen in exchange for protection from the weather, but she was always merely a distant figure, remote in her mountain palace, causing no harm to anyone that we knew of. We thought her content in her realm of ice, another one like us who preferred the isolated places of the world."

He frowned. "And once she infected us, we were helpless to fight against the poison she had begun to spread. When Sterling arrived and gave his orders as to how we were to answer your request, as well as the stranger one about locking our storage shed and forbidding anyone from entering, we didn't even think to question it."

Oliver nodded. "I well remember what it is like to be caught under her spell. I wish for no vengeance upon you or yours." He hesitated. "But I am afraid this haven will no longer be safe for you. Know that you will be welcome in the capital or elsewhere in the kingdom."

The spokesman sighed. "The same thought has occurred to us. But already since our eyes have been opened, we've noticed a new warmth in the air. Spring is returning, as it should at this time of year. And soon it will be summer. We have time to think on our options and evacuate our people before winter returns again."

Oliver nodded. "I wish I could offer to stay and help with your deliberations, but we must hurry back to the capital."

The elders all nodded, and many of the villagers came forward with gifts of food or wood for us to take with us. Apparently the freeing of their minds was worth the loss of their village. And I couldn't blame them. What good was such a place if you couldn't see the beauty in it?

~

The rest of the return journey went even faster. The Valley View elder had spoken truly. Spring had come in one big rush. It hadn't snowed once since we left the Snow Queen's lake, and the further we descended, the shallower the snow on the ground became until eventually we had to stop and remove the snowshoes.

I had almost forgotten what it felt like to move freely, striding forward and leaping over rocks in only my boots.

"You look happy," said Oliver, watching me as I watched a mother bird scold her hatchlings. I had wandered away from the others while they rested, captivated by my surroundings.

I smiled, gesturing around me. "How could I not be? There's so much green! I even saw some flowers back there."

He laughed. "You know this is what spring and summer here are normally like, right? It's not supposed to snow all year long."

I grinned up at him. "I suppose I must have known it, but it's different to see it." I lowered my voice, my next words just for him. "I have no doubts I could be happy in such a place. It's beautiful. Even the mountains." I gestured back up the way we had come where the distant slopes rose far above us, still crowned in white.

Oliver swung me up and spun me around while Giselle—who had followed him, leaving Sterling tied to a tree—watched on and rolled her eyes.

When he put me down, I clung to him, wanting to soak the moment in. I had been thinking of many things as we walked, and not all of them had been pleasant.

In the frozen throne room, back on the mountain, it had been easy to focus on my anger and on the evil the Snow Queen had wrought. But I couldn't forget her story, and I couldn't help a small twinge of sympathy. After all, were we so very dissimilar? I, too, had been arrogant and foolish and had attempted to take a magical object that didn't belong to me. And it had nearly destroyed a person I loved. If things had turned out differently, could I have ended up like the Snow Queen?

After much thought, I had rejected the idea. We might be the same in some ways, but we were different in others. None of us were perfect, all of us made mistakes. It was how we responded to those mistakes that mattered the most, surely. Whether we took responsibility and did our best to make restitution. Whether we recognized our faults and sought to correct them.

I had learned my lesson—or I hoped so, anyway—and tried to turn away from the selfishness and pride that had driven me. Whereas she had only compounded her wrongs, destroying herself and others in the process. I could not regret what I had done to her. It had been done in defense—of both me and the people I loved.

But neither would I forget. Darkness lingered all too close, and far too often in our own hearts. I never wanted to forget my capacity for making bad decisions. Because one day I would be a true queen, and I would have a responsibility to my people. I didn't want to let them down again.

While I had been thinking, Oliver had been gazing down at me, his hold slowly tightening. When I squeezed him back, he smiled and strengthened his own embrace.

"Have I told you today how much I like having you around?"

I grinned back at him. "I can't remember. I guess you'll just have to say it again."

"Um, really?" Giselle said. "You know I'm still here, right? Honestly, this is all a bit much."

I laughed guiltily. I had forgotten her presence. Disentangling myself from Oliver, I saluted his sister and adopted a formal tone. "Noted. I will attempt to keep all conversations of a serious nature and expressions of physical affection for private from now on."

Giselle rolled her eyes. "I'll believe that when I see it. Traveling with the two of you gets worse by the day. We can't reach the palace soon enough."

"Well, the sooner we get back to walking, the sooner we'll get there," I said cheerfully, knowing she was probably right, but somehow unable to regret it.

CHAPTER 33

The next day we reached the capital. I had expected Oliver and Giselle to almost fly down the last part of the trail, but instead they seemed to slow. I could read the reason in their eyes. For all their hope, there was fear as well. Had the invaders retained enough willpower to complete the coup? Would we find a capital ruled by Lord Treestone as a tool of Eliam? Or, much worse, would we find a capital full of people who had wasted away, stripped of the will even to live? Had we destroyed the enchantment in time?

But the bustle of the mountain city itself as we moved through it was enough to reassure me, if not them. People seemed to fill the external roads, drinking up the bright sun and newfound warmth in the air. And none of them seemed bowed down with the weight of an invasion.

A rustle of voices followed behind us, our presence clearly causing a stir, so I wasn't surprised when we reached the gate into the palace and found a group gathered to meet us. My eyes latched first on Lord Treestone and Cassandra, with Alexander close beside, flanked by several guards in the colors of Eliam. My heart seized. Perhaps the coup had happened, after all. But a scream from behind me told a different story.

"Emmeline!" Giselle almost tripped in her hurry to fling herself into her sister's arms.

"Giselle!"

Both girls cried, happily ignoring their tears as they talked over the top of each other.

King Leopold gestured several Eldonian guards forward to take charge of Sterling so that nothing would hamper Queen Camille as she pressed her son into a warm hug. She seemed to be crying as freely as her daughters.

I met Cassandra's eyes, and she smiled. Relief filled me. Whatever had happened here, it appeared to have happened peacefully.

I stood back a little, watching the family reunion, feeling out of place and tingling with nerves I hadn't expected. But this was my future father- and mother-in-law, and I hadn't truly met them before. What sort of impression of me would have lingered in their dream-like memories? I hadn't exactly put out much of an effort to please or impress when I had stayed here before.

But Oliver quickly detached himself from his mother, pulling me forward and tucking me under his arm. His mother's eyes flew quickly between us, and then she broke into an enormous smile and fell upon my neck, crying all over me.

"Sorry," mouthed Oliver over her head, but I just smiled and shook my head. Who could resist such a welcome?

Everyone on every side wanted answers, of course, but when the queen eventually stopped crying, she insisted that we all get inside and comfortable first. And given the length of the story, I could only be grateful.

We were made to talk first, when the time for stories finally came, although our explanation was peppered with questions and exclamations from the others. Everyone wanted to remember what it had been like from their own perspective, and no one had imagined anything like the Snow Queen or her Palace of Ice.

But we made it through the story eventually and finally were able to demand a more cohesive version of events from their side. It turned out that the weather had turned so bad that Lord Treestone had been forced to lead the Elamese contingent to the palace not long after we left.

"We would have frozen otherwise, camped out in the open like we were," he said with an apologetic look at Oliver.

"And it's a good thing we did," said Cassandra, who had somehow wormed her way into the meeting.

Her uncle gave her a repressive look but nodded. "We found no opposition whatsoever, and soon realized we would be needed in the role of caretakers if we wished to prevent a mass tragedy."

"Basically, we had to cook all the food and keep all the fires burning," said Cassandra. "For the entire city."

"However did you manage that?" I asked.

"We had to cram as many as we could fit into the palace," said Alexander, speaking for the first time. "And anyone who didn't fit we sent to the biggest of the noble houses further up the mountain." He shook his head. "My men had a time of it trying to round everyone up from those blasted tunnels, I can tell you."

"And you might find some missing silver," said Cassandra, although she didn't look apologetic. "Some of those who were sheltering here looked less than honest to me, and I wouldn't put it past them to have filched something on their way out. Once they all woke up, of course."

King Leopold didn't look too pleased, but Queen Camille merely shrugged.

"A small price indeed for all our lives."

"Unfortunately, by then," said Lord Treestone, continuing the original thread of the story, "it was clear that the evil was coming from the northern mountains. But the weather had grown so bad, no one could follow you. There was nothing for us to do but wait and hope we could keep everyone alive."

I examined his face, glancing between him, Cassandra, and the Elamese colonel in charge of their troops. As they had approached the palace, they too would have been infected, as my own servants had been. How much had their slow descent into an enchanted state affected their decision to do nothing but stay alive? Somehow I suspected none of them would admit it had been anything but true helplessness and altruism that drove them. And we could all only be grateful they had maintained initiative long enough to gather together the locals and keep them alive as well. I, for one, had no desire to challenge their motives.

"And then one day everyone just woke up," said Lord Treestone. "We had no explanation for it, although we understand now, of course." He inclined his head toward where I sat on a small sofa with Oliver. "When the weather began to ease almost immediately, we realized that something had happened to break the enchantment. Naturally we ceded control back to Their Majesties, but we have lingered under their gracious hospitality in the hope of your return and an explanation such as we have just received."

King Leopold inclined his head regally toward Lord Treestone, and I suppressed a smile. Clearly everyone had decided that the best approach was to ignore everything that had happened while under the enchantment. An approach of which I heartily approved.

The colonel thanked us for our efforts and said he would make plans to start the march back to Eliam the next day.

"My own monarchs will want to hear the news as soon as possible, I'm sure." He glanced over at Alexander. "But we will leave a couple of representatives as a delegation of sorts, to lend all support possible for the upcoming royal wedding."

He bowed toward my sofa, and I realized with a jolt that he

meant my wedding. A giddy rush of excitement filled me, although I noticed that a fleeting look of annoyance crossed Alexander's face at the clear implication that he was to stay. Still, his lack of desire to attend my wedding couldn't damp my joy, and the mention of the event successfully derailed conversation on any other topic as Queen Camille immediately began to discuss the necessary preparations with great enthusiasm.

It was a long time before I left to find my way back to my old room, my stomach full and my mind still whirling with plans and possibilities.

"Do you know the way back on your own?" asked a familiar voice at my elbow, echoing the words from my first night so long ago.

I turned to regard my betrothed, looking up at him through my lashes just as I remembered doing on that distant-seeming occasion and echoing my own words. "I don't suppose you would be willing to show me?"

When he bowed and offered me his arm, I laughed and threw myself against his chest for a stolen kiss. When the sound of an opening door made us spring apart, I took his arm and laughed up at him again.

"Could you have imagined back then that it would all end like this?"

"The details? No. But even in the half-haze of that night, I had already formed the strong impression that you were someone I didn't want to let go."

I bumped him with my shoulder. "You had not!"

"Of course I had." He smiled down at me, glancing behind us before pressing his lips briefly down over mine. "Don't tell me you've forgotten what kind of an entrance you make, Princess Celine? How could I not be captivated?"

I flushed, remembering now his expression when I appeared that night.

"And somehow," I said, "despite everything, I knew you were

the one I wanted to make an impression on. I think that's why I managed to free you that night. Something in me was drawn to you from the moment the curse began to lose its grip."

"One day I want to visit Lanover and see the kingdom that created a woman like you, Celine," he murmured against my hair.

I gazed up at him. "One day I'll take you. And I want to see more of your kingdom. I want to see all of it. There are so many things I want to do with you."

"Then it's a good thing we have the rest of our lives," he said as he pulled me against his heart and kissed me again.

EPILOGUE

"*Well*, what do you think?" I asked, emerging from my dressing room and throwing my arms wide. The first of the guests coming in for the wedding were due to arrive at any moment, and I had put some effort into my dress. We would be welcoming them at a betrothal feast in my honor, after all.

I had worked with the palace seamstress on a new gown for the occasion and was more than satisfied with the result. The rich blue silk hugged my torso, held in shape with subtle boning, before sweeping out at my hips into the fullest skirt I had ever worn.

Emmeline regarded me with wrinkled brow, as if my question required serious thought. "It looks very suitable," she pronounced at last.

"Suitable? Suitable?" I stared at her aghast. "You can't be serious." I turned beseeching eyes on Giselle who appeared to be smothering a laugh.

"Come on, Celine," said a new voice from the doorway. "You know you look incredible."

"As always," agreed a second, nearly identical, voice.

"I do, don't I?" I laughed, almost tripping in my haste as I rushed over to throw my arms around both of the new arrivals. "You came! You made it!"

"Of course we did." Sophie laughed as well. "Were you worried we would be lost at sea?"

"I'm just so glad you're here." I lifted onto my toes and spun in a circle, blue material billowing around me. "I'm getting married!"

Lily threw Sophie a concerned look. "I don't think we've ever seen her like this. Should we be worried?"

Sophie elbowed her in the side. "Don't be mean. It's beautiful."

"Well, I want to meet the new Prince Oliver," said Lily. "Because he must have changed a lot. I nearly fell off my chair when I read your letter saying you were betrothed to marry him and madly in love."

"You will soon enough," I said, pulling them both around. "But first let me re-introduce you to two of our fellow Princess Tourney contestants. You might not recognize Princesses Emmeline and Giselle now."

Giselle grinned and came forward to greet the twins. "We weren't exactly good company back then, I'm afraid."

Emmeline joined her, shaking her head. "Although perhaps we should be glad of it. I can't imagine going through such an ordeal with my emotions intact."

"It wasn't the most fun we've ever had," I said, remembering the unpleasant months after we first arrived from the Four Kingdoms. "But that's all in the distant past now." I glanced at Sophie who glowed with happiness. Marriage seemed to suit her. "And it all worked out for the best in the end."

I left them all to chat while I wandered away to pick jewelry to match my gown. What would the twins make of my soon-to-be sisters-in-law? I had been making an effort to get to know Emmeline, although it still caught me by surprise when she said things Giselle would never say.

"They're so different from each other!" whispered Lily, sidling up to me while Sophie engaged Emmeline in polite conversation. "I mean, I figured they'd be different from how they used to be now the curse is lifted, but I really didn't see that coming."

I shook my head. "Eldon has been full of surprises."

"Oh yes," said Sophie, breaking off her conversation to join us. "I want to hear all about it."

"About what?" I asked, all innocence.

"About everything, of course." Lily rolled her eyes. "You said there was a Snow Queen in your letters which seems to me like a horrible thing to include if you didn't intend to spill the whole story. We've been dying of impatience ever since."

"Very well, then," I said, relenting. "But you'd better let me ring for some refreshments because you've only just arrived, and this isn't going to be quick."

~

"And so we became officially betrothed," I finished, beaming at them both. "I want you both to be my attendants, of course. Alongside Emmeline and Giselle. I hope you'll agree, even though you're already married yourselves."

"Of course we'd love to," said Sophie. "But what about all your sisters? Aren't they coming?"

"Well, Cassian and Tillie were just here for your wedding, so they won't be trekking back. They'll keep things running at home so Frederic and Evie can come with my parents." I grinned at the thought. I'd always liked Tillie, but Evie was a closer friend. Maybe because of everything we'd been through together. A little like it was with Giselle and Emmeline, I supposed.

"William and Celeste can't come either." I winked at the twins. "No doubt they're far too important to be gone when so many other royals are already traveling. But Cordelia and Ferdy are coming, and hopefully Rafe and Marie as well. I can't wait to see them all again."

I smiled. I was always smiling these days. "Celeste is absolutely green at being left behind. At least from the sound of her letters. She's dying to come sniffing around all these new kingdoms. I figure once everyone else gets back, she'll come up with an excuse to visit."

My eyes fell on the material draped over one corner of the room, still waiting for my final approval before work began on the attendants' gowns, and I remembered the original question. "So I'll have Evie and Cordelia as well, and that will make a nice even six." I beamed at the twins.

"You're clearly enjoying planning this wedding far too much," said Lily, mock fear in her voice. "I'm not sure what we're getting ourselves into."

"Can you enjoy your own wedding too much?" I asked. "I don't think so. And I plan to wrest every ounce of enjoyment out of it that I can."

"Celine," said Sophie, her voice clearly conveying that her mind was on neither weddings nor enjoyment. "I don't think you said what happened to that Sterling fellow."

"Oh, nothing in particular," I said, surprised at the turn of her thoughts. "I was actually going to suggest you all go down to the holding cells at some point and check if he's the man Jon and Dominic were after. The one from Palinar."

"But you searched him thoroughly, right? And you have him under extra security?" Lily had instantly picked up on her sister's concern.

"Umm…" I regarded them uneasily. "I think it's just the usual security?"

"Because if he is the man from Palinar," Sophie said, "then the godmother object he took with him when he fled is the one that allowed Cole to escape from two different prisons."

My eyes widened, and I swallowed. "He would have been

collecting it for the Snow Queen, I'm sure. In fact, he was probably only ever helping Cole so he could get his hands on it. But all the objects were destroyed with the Ice Palace."

"Are you sure?" Lily asked. "Because we never got a good look at the item, but it must be something small since Cole managed to sneak it into two cells with him."

I thought of his bulging pack, and my heart sank. He hadn't run out of that palace with empty hands. Would he have dared steal any godmother objects from his queen?

"I'll take you there now," I said, jumping up.

"But Celine, your dress," said Giselle, but I brushed her comments aside. Now that the twins had raised the possibility, I didn't want to lose a moment checking on the security of the prisoner.

The twins hurried after me as I raced through the corridors. I stopped the first footman we passed, sending him to fetch Oliver, but I didn't wait, telling him to send the prince straight to the holding cells.

When I burst through the doors, my dress filling half the small room, two startled guards leaped to their feet and hastily bowed.

"Your Highness," one stammered out. "Can we help you?"

"The prisoner," I said, breathless. "Is he secure?" Sterling was the only one currently being held there.

They exchanged confused looks. "Of course, Your Highness. Would you like to see—"

Before I could agree that I would like to see for myself, the door crashed open again, Oliver only just pulling up before he collided with the twins.

"What—" His question cut off as his eyes fell on me and slowly widened.

I stared at him in confusion until Lily elbowed me.

"The dress," she whispered, a laugh in her eyes, and I looked down at the blue silk. I had forgotten I was already dressed for the banquet. I suppressed a flush of pleasure at his reaction, forcing my mind back to the issue at hand.

"The twins have just reminded me that if Sterling is the man from Palinar, he may have had access to an object that allowed two previous prison escapes."

Oliver looked back over his head, and I realized he had his own entourage. When Princes Jon and Dominic pushed forward into the room, they nearly squeezed me out the far door. I could only glance gratefully at Alexander for remaining in the corridor. Someone had some sense, at least.

The poor guards finally managed to decipher the conflicting orders being called over each other, and one of them led us all through a locked door and down a plain corridor lined with barred doors. He stopped in front of one, gesturing toward it, his eyes on Oliver.

When Oliver stepped forward, choking, his eyes widening, the guard looked quickly into the cell and then fell back with a startled exclamation.

"But…he was here…I swear it!" He looked desperately toward the other guard, bringing up the rear. But the second man looked just as shocked and horrified.

Dominic shouldered his way forward to peer through into the empty cell.

"I think he was our man, right enough," he said, his voice grim.

"Don't worry," said Jon, clapping a hand on the shoulder of one of the guards. "No one's going to blame you. We've seen this before."

Dominic looked up and nodded once. "And my guards were the same. They thought the prisoner still in position until someone else called their attention to the escape. It must be part of the enchantment, somehow, although I don't understand how it works."

"So we don't even know how long he's been gone," I cried,

aghast. My eyes flew to Oliver. "And that might not be the only object he smuggled out of that palace. As long as they were small enough..."

"You'll send out a search for him, I'm sure," said Dominic, also looking at Oliver. "But he won't have lingered in Eldon." He rubbed his chin. "I'd put my money on his having headed straight for the southern border."

Alexander, still trailing us, sucked in a breath. "Eliam. And who knows what trouble he'll wreak there?"

"I'm so sorry, Alexander," I said. "This is my fault. I should have thought to put on an extra guard. To have him searched..." I bit my lip.

Oliver's strong arm came around my shoulders. "If he used an enchanted object, then it's unlikely more guards would have stopped him. I won't have you blaming yourself. You aren't responsible for security in the Eldonian palace." He sighed. "And we've had a few other things on our mind."

We all traipsed back up to the higher levels of the palace in silence, each of the couples walking together, with Alexander trailing behind, clearly unhappy and wishing himself gone from Eldon. When we reached the entry hall, we encountered a group of new arrivals milling around. I tried to remember who else was due to arrive today.

"Snow," I exclaimed at last. "This must be Snow."

An older man turned around at my words and hurried forward to bow to me. "I'm afraid I bring sad tidings, Your Highness. Princess Blanche does not accompany me. Her father, our esteemed king, has succumbed to his illness. He passed away mere hours before we left."

"Oh no." I pressed a hand to my heart. It had been coming for months, if not years, but I still felt for my friend. She loved her father. "How awful. Of course we understand that she could not tear herself away in such a circumstance. We shall have to settle for welcoming her when the actual wedding arrives."

The man shifted uncomfortably. "I'm afraid Her Highness will not be able to attend the wedding at all. Grieving customs, you understand..." His voice trailed away, and he looked so awkward that I rushed to assure him that no offense had been taken.

But when the whole delegation had been led off to their rooms by a stream of palace servants, I turned thoughtfully to Alexander.

"Grieving customs? Do you do things so differently in Eliam, then?"

He shook his head, still frowning at the place where the delegation head had stood, his face looking gray. "I do not know what customs he refers to, Your Highness."

"Hmmm..." I tapped my lips thoughtfully. "You have been so kind as to grace us with your presence all these weeks, Alexander. But I understand that you knew King George personally. No doubt you will wish to return and pay your respects. Perhaps you would be willing to carry a message from us with you? We will send our condolences, of course, but also a warning about Sterling."

Alexander looked at me, relief in his eyes. "I would be honored to carry a message, Princess Celine."

I smiled a sad smile. "I suspected as much. I shall have it drawn up immediately."

Alexander bowed. "Then I shall leave you so that I may prepare for my departure."

As he strode away, almost running in his haste, I looked up at Oliver. "Something is going on over there. I just hope it doesn't have anything to do with Sterling."

He pulled me into a tight hug. "No, I'm sure it does not. But even if it does, we can trust Alexander to sort things out. I've spent some time with him these last weeks while all of you ladies were busy with planning. He's the type you can rely on. And his loyalty to King George was absolute."

I breathed a sigh of relief, sinking against him. "I hope you're right." I stiffened at a sudden thought. "Wedding planning! The betrothal banquet! I had forgotten all about it."

"I hadn't," he said. "Not with you wearing that dress."

I smiled, relaxing a little. "It is rather magnificent, isn't it?" I surveyed his plain clothes and wrinkled my nose. "You, on the other hand, are far from ready."

"My apologies, my lady," he said, laughing down at me, "I would never want to disappoint you."

I shook my head. "Enough of that. You go and get ready. If you're going to marry me, then you'll need to learn how to make a good entrance at my side."

"With you at my side, no one will be looking at me," he said.

And I could hardly send him away without a kiss after that. Which I somehow suspected had been his intention all along.

NOTE FROM THE AUTHOR

To discover the full adventures of the Lanoverian royal siblings, read the Four Kingdoms series, starting with *The Princess Companion: A Retelling of The Princess and the Pea.*

For Celine's earlier adventures in Marin, read the first book in the Beyond the Four Kingdoms series, *A Dance of Silver and Shadow: A Retelling of The Twelve Dancing Princesses.*

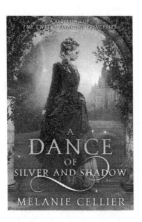

To be kept informed of my new releases, please sign up to my mailing list at www.melaniecellier.com. At my website, you'll also find an array of free extra content, including a bonus epilogue to *A Tale of Beauty and Beast* that includes Celine and leads into the story of Eldon.

Thank you for taking the time to read my book. I hope you enjoyed it. If you did, please spread the word! You could start by leaving a review on Amazon (or Goodreads or Facebook or any other social media site). Your review would be very much appreciated and would make a big difference!

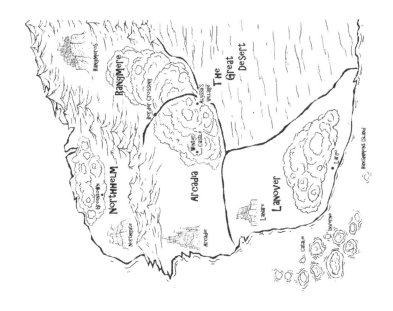

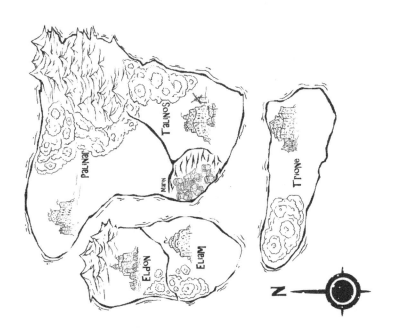

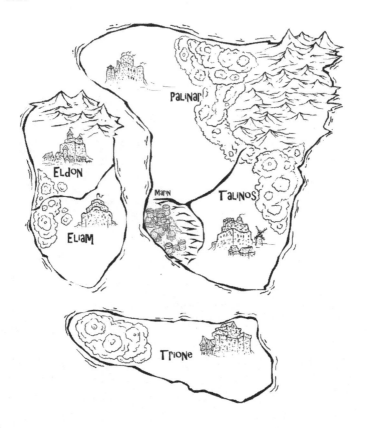

ACKNOWLEDGMENTS

It's been a long time building to Celine getting her own adventure, and that doesn't come without some measure of pressure. I've had all sorts of emotions about this book, and I'm so grateful to the many people who have borne with me through them all. Add to that the fact that A Crown of Snow and Ice was written during some major life transitions, including a house move, and I feel like my team have been required to show extra patience with me this time around! And as always, I appreciate them more than I can say.

Particularly my husband, Marc, who bears with every up and down, and keeps me fed, clothed, and sane in the midst of it all. You are an amazing partner in this writing journey. And to both our families, thank you for housing and supporting us despite our irregular schedule! We value your support enormously.

A big thanks to my beta readers—an even longer list than usual due to my uncertainty over this story. Rachel, Greg, Katie, Priya, and Ber, your faithfulness through over ten books now continues to astound me. And Shari and Cheri, your willingness to jump on at the last minute was so gratefully appreciated!

For my writing community—I love taking this rollercoaster

journey with you all. Kitty, Kenley, Shari, Aya, Brittany, and Diana, it's such an amazing gift to have you only a tap of the keyboard away, despite living on different continents. You're the best! But it's equally amazing to have an Australian author friend —same time zone for the win, yay—who is available for daily writing sprints, chats, and mental downloads. I'm not sure I would have finished this book on schedule without you, Marina, so thank you!

Thank you also to my three editors who do so much to help me bring each of my books through to completion. Mary, Dad, and Deborah, your input and expertise is greatly appreciated!

And another thanks to the amazing Karri, who has made so many beautiful covers for me now. It's almost impossible to pick a favorite, but this one would be a contender for top of my list.

Which leaves God—the only one who sees each of us as we truly are and loves us unflinchingly and unendingly. No thanks could be enough.

ABOUT THE AUTHOR

 Melanie Cellier grew up on a staple diet of books, books and more books. And although she got older, she never stopped loving children's and young adult novels.

She always wanted to write one herself, but it took three careers and three different continents before she actually managed it.

She now feels incredibly fortunate to spend her time writing from her home in Adelaide, Australia where she keeps an eye out for koalas in her backyard. Her staple diet hasn't changed much, although she's added choc mint Rooibos tea and Chicken Crimpies to the list.

Her young adult *Four Kingdoms* and *Beyond the Four Kingdoms* series are made up of linked stand-alone stories that retell classic fairy tales.

35055829R00200

Made in the USA
San Bernardino, CA
06 May 2019